The Soldier's Burden

The Soldier's Burden

Pete Biehl

This is a work of fiction. Names, characters, places, and incidents either are the product of the author's imagination or are used fictitiously. Any resemblance to actual persons, living or dead, events, or locales is entirely coincidental.

Copyright © 2024 by Pete Biehl

All rights reserved. No part of this book may be reproduced, replicated, or used in any manner without written permission of the copyright owner except for the use of quotations in a book review.

The Soldier's Burden – First hardcover edition June 2024

Cover Art by Joseph Gruber

Map made with Inkarnate

www.petebiehl.com

*For Diamond, Paris, Dahlia, Klemm, and Dozer
My four-legged friends who are missed every day.*

Books by Pete Biehl

The Rawl Wielder Trilogy
The Path of the Rawl Wielder
The Throne of Thornata
The Hoyt War

The Imperial Soldier Trilogy
The Soldier's Burden

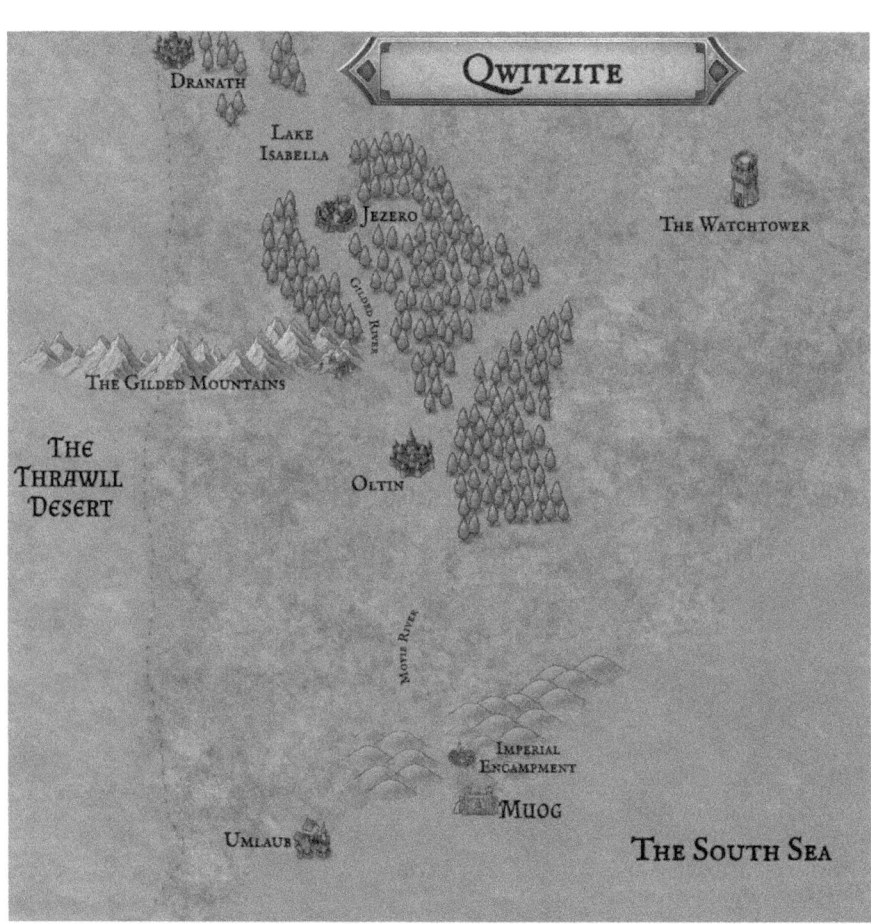

Chapter One

The blast rattled every bone in Darian Tor's body, lifting him from his feet and tossing him to the ground like a rag doll. The armor issued to him by the Imperial Army did little to blunt the pain of the impact as the air was forced from his chest. The fireball was rising about twenty yards to the left of him, and the small company had already scattered in a full-blown panic.

Where was Preston? He was meant to be leading this ridiculous assault, but he was nowhere to be found.

Darian tried to listen for orders as he scrambled back to his feet, but the blast had rendered his ears all but useless; a sharp high-pitched ringing was all that greeted his attempts to listen through the chaos.

Gripping his spear tightly in hand, Darian pressed onward toward the objective. Were any of his fellow soldiers still alive? There was no way to know the answer, but orders were orders. They had a job to do, and even if he was the last man standing, those orders didn't change.

Darian had advanced perhaps another thirty feet when enemy combatants came into view ahead of him. Counting five foes, Darian dropped into a defensive crouch, assessing the weakest point that he could attack. These men were warriors of the Order of the Scar, a mercenary group known to every Imperial soldier for their ferocious skill and lack of mercy.

This assault had all gone wrong from the start. The first ambush had occurred only two minutes into the offensive. Ever since, there had been a constant stream of enemy fighters and archer fire directed toward them.

Cursing under his breath, the young private prepared himself for yet another fight in close quarters.

The foremost attacker came toward him with his spear leveled straight at Darian's head. Darian brought up his shield, deflecting the blow with a mighty crash that managed to break through the ringing in his ears. He struck back, sliding his own spear under the guard of his opponent and driving it straight into the man's midsection. He was not fast enough, though; as he tried to pull his spear back, another of the attackers brought his shield down on the wooden shaft, snapping the weapon cleanly in half.

Flinging the worthless handle to the mud, Darian Tor backpedaled desperately, trying to put distance between himself and his attackers. He raised his shield high in front of him, his fingers scrabbling for the sword hanging at his belt, slipping over the rain-soaked pommel as he struggled draw it.

He thought he was all but done for until there was a flash of movement to his left. To Darian's relief, Berj Jenson appeared as if from nowhere, sword in hand. Berj charged right into the enemy ranks, his sword slashing and his deep voice bellowing out like a wild man, as it usually did in a fight. A second later, Darnold Dans appeared, his entrance far less bombastic than Berj's, but every bit as welcome. Darnold, it seemed, had managed to hold on to his spear and held it in front of him as he slammed into the attackers as well.

Breathing a sigh of relief, Darian finally pulled his sword free from its sheath and rushed forward to fight alongside the friends who had finally come to his aid.

The fight was fast but furious, and the three young Imperial privates overcame their four opponents in short order. One sword slash came dangerously close to Darian's face, but he got his shield up in time to deflect it. The Scar fighter tried to launch another attack but was caught from behind by Berj before he could, the latter's sword splitting his skull, killing him before he struck the ground.

"I was starting to think I was all alone on this mission," Darian said, looking from one to the other. "I'm glad you found your way over here eventually."

"Oh, don't be so dramatic, Darian. We were on the left flank when that blast went off. We both got sent flying, and it's a good thing we weren't knocked out cold, or you would have been all alone. We caught up as fast as we could. They've been all over us every step of the way. Where is that useless prat Preston?" Berj asked.

"Haven't seen him since we ran into that first group of defenders. He probably got himself killed right out of the gate. Big surprise," Darian said. "We should have known it would go this way."

"So, what do we do? Preston was the squad leader—not that he was very good at it. I don't know what they were thinking, putting him in charge," Darnold said, his nervous eyes continually sweeping their surroundings for signs of more enemies.

"We have our orders. We're supposed to take the hill. Preston or no Preston, squad leader or no squad leader, we have to take the hill. The Order of the Scar doesn't scare me as much as Sergeant Arsch. I don't know about you boys, but I for one don't want to go back to base having not obeyed orders. Remember what happened to the last squad who gave up on a mission?" Berj replied, and Darian thought he spotted an involuntary shudder at those last words. "I'd rather die with a dozen arrows in my gut than face that."

He's right, Darian thought. They had to proceed with the mission, no matter what. There was no commanding officer to tell them otherwise.

They were Imperial soldiers, and Imperial soldiers followed their orders until their last breath left their lungs. It had been driven into their heads from their first day of basic training. They would take the hill or die trying. Given how many Order of the Scar fighters they had already encountered, the latter seemed the more likely outcome.

"Berj is right; we have to keep going. But I think we should try to keep a low profile for as long as possible. This frontal assault that Preston had us on is sheer madness. They're countering us at every turn. We should stay low, go wide to the north, and approach the hill from the other side. They may not see that coming," Darian suggested.

His two fellow privates nodded their agreement, and they were off once more. They kept their heads low, Darian silently hoping their black Imperial Army uniforms would keep them concealed in the darkness of the night. It had not been the case thus far, but their luck could always turn for the better.

Sure it could. Keep telling yourself that, Darian thought to himself. They could not have gone more than a few hundred feet when yet another cry split the night. This time, Darian cursed out loud. It seemed as though this mission was doomed to fail no matter what they tried to do.

They spun toward the cry to find six men advancing on them from the east. Drawing their weapons, they charged into the fight, not giving their foes an opportunity to encircle them. Darian took one down with a thrust to the chest, then hurriedly ducked under the blow that another man had sent racing toward his skull. Darnold cut the man's legs out from under him, allowing Darian to regain his form and engage another opponent. He sidestepped the spear thrust the man aimed toward him, attacking with his sword. The man caught the first blow on his shield, but the second slipped past his guard and found a home deep in his gut.

Darian spun, searching for more enemies, just in time to see Berj finish off the last of them with a beautifully timed counterattack.

So much for sneaking our way up to the top of the hill, Darian Tor thought sarcastically.

This assault was feeling more like a doomed operation with each passing second. Nobody had even told them why taking this hill was so important; they knew nothing about the strategic value it held for the army. Of course, there was nothing unusual about that. Why should anything be explained to the likes of them? It was not the job of an Imperial soldier to ask questions. It was the job of an Imperial soldier to do as he was told until he was told to do otherwise.

"How do they keep finding us?" Darnold sounded every bit as frustrated as Darian felt.

Before Darian could think of an answer, another explosion rang out. This time, the fireball was not as close, perhaps a hundred yards off to their west. But as the flames rose into the night sky, the three of them were very clearly illuminated for a moment to anybody who might've been watching from higher ground.

"That's probably not going to help us stay hidden. We should double back south and then come at the hill from the east. They won't be expecting it now that they think we're going north. It's the best shot we're going to get at reaching the top," Berj said.

None of them had a more practical solution, so back south they trekked. Berj led them, bringing them south for almost a mile before turning west. They were well south of their last two encounters with the Order of the Scar, so Darian's hopes were high that they could avoid another confrontation. Such hopes were doomed to be short-lived. They had been traveling west for only a few minutes when they heard a sudden horn blast off to their right. How was this possible? Nobody should've been able to find them so easily in the blackness of night.

Their enemy did not engage in close quarters this time but instead opened fire on them with longbows from a distance. The trio scrambled once more to defend themselves, shuffling sideways while trying to cover themselves and one another as thoroughly as possible with their shields.

The occasional clang told Darian that he had successfully deflected one of the enemy's arrows. Their training had taught them that most people couldn't shoot at a stationary target worth a damn, let alone one who was in constant motion. Still, while the movement kept them alive, they couldn't advance their position under such heavy fire.

"Any ideas on how to get out of this one?" he asked, hoping one of his companions was thinking more clearly.

Darnold Dans never had a chance to respond. One of the arrows found its way over the top of his shield, striking him in the neck. His legs went limp, and he collapsed to the ground, the wound bleeding profusely, before Darian could even register what had happened. The sharp clang of yet another arrow glancing off his shield snapped him quickly back to reality. There was nothing they could do for Darnold; he was dead, or would be in the next few seconds. They needed to get themselves free of this archer fire if they were going to survive the next few minutes themselves.

"Darian, we have to lower our shields and just make a break for it," Berj said.

"Are you mad? The second we lower the shields, they'll cut us to shreds!" Darian protested, shocked that a young man as savvy as Berj Jenson would even suggest such a thing.

"We don't have a choice! We can't move fast enough like this. We'll never escape them by standing still. Eventually, we'll end up like Darnold. I know it's not ideal, but it's the best chance we have. Make a break and hope they can't hit a fast-moving target. On the count of three?"

Darian Tor did not like it, but he had no choice but to acknowledge that Berj was right. They could make a break for it and probably die, or they could keep doing what they were doing and end up dead for sure. Swearing out loud, as much to himself as he was to Berj, he agreed.

"One!"

What had he just agreed to do?

"Two!"

His grip on his shield tightened in anticipation.

"Three!"

Letting his shield drop to his side, Darian bolted as fast as his legs would carry him. Berj was a few feet in front of him, leading the way. His fellow private had drawn his sword once more, obviously anticipating further troubles ahead. It was probably an accurate assessment, given how well their assault on the hill had gone thus far, so Darian drew his as well. Arrows fell around them, but by some miracle, not a single one found its mark.

To Darian's surprise, it took longer than expected for trouble to find them again. He had expected the archers to immediately give chase once they were beyond range, but there was no sign of such a pursuit. He was briefly foolish enough to believe that they just might make it to the hill without encountering any additional Scar forces. No sooner had the thought flashed through his mind than four of them appeared again, blocking their path, spears at the ready.

Berj never slowed down, slamming into their midst with the ferocity of a wild animal, his sword hacking and hammering at them in pure desperation. Darian charged in behind him, never hesitating. An Imperial soldier never hesitated when there was an enemy to fight, no matter how greatly the odds were stacked against him. If another man stood in the way of carrying out his orders, that man must die.

He blocked a spear thrust with his shield and brought his sword down onto the shaft, snapping it in two just as an opponent had done to his own weapon earlier that night. He thrust his sword through his foe's chest before the man could reach for another weapon.

Never pausing, he drove forward, right into another enemy fighter. He slashed out repeatedly with his sword, desperately trying to breach his opponent's defenses. If he could have seen his attack from a distance, he would have been reminded more of Berj's reckless fighting style than his own. It wasn't a technique the Imperial Army instructors would've approved of, but there was no denying its effectiveness in such dire circumstances.

At last, he broke through his enemy's guard, his sword finding its way down through the man's shoulder and into his chest. He spun to assist Berj only to find that his comrade did not need his assistance, having just finished off his second foe.

"I don't know how many more fights like that we can survive," Darian said, gasping. He reached for the small waterskin on his belt and drank deeply. There wasn't much left, but he didn't let that deter him. After all, he wasn't likely to live long enough to need to refill.

"I don't understand how there can be any more of them left. They told us this hill would have minimal defenses. At most, we were told to expect a dozen Order of the Scar fighters. So much for the fabled Imperial Intelligence Unit, eh?"

"We've tried coming at this hill from every possible direction, and they meet us at every turn. I'm out of ideas. What have you got?" Darian asked.

"Damned if I know. Thinking was supposed to be your specialty, you and Darnold. I'm just supposed to be the dumb brute who kills anyone who gets in our way. You think we should keep pushing west and hope we can eventually get around their perimeter?"

"I don't think we have any other options. Let's get moving before they come upon us again," Darian said, trying to sound as upbeat as possible.

The pair pressed on westward, Darian trying hard not to think of the fact that there had been four of them at the onset of this mission. Even if they were fortunate enough to survive and take the hill as ordered, they could expect a severe reprimand for their failures. It would not matter that their squad leader had gotten himself killed minutes into the operation; Imperial soldiers were always accountable under all circumstances. They were supposed to have been in control of this hill over an hour ago. None of their excuses would make a difference to Sergeant Arsch.

To Darian's surprise, no enemies came upon them, and the night grew relatively silent.

"I think we've gone far enough. What do you think? Much farther and we'll hit the river. If they have boats out on the water, they could spot us. I don't think we're going to get a better chance at this than we have right now," Berj whispered.

He was right. They had come far enough west that the hill would now be to the northeast of their location. It must have been close to thirty minutes since their last skirmish with enemy forces, and their odds were not going to improve. There was no point in delaying the inevitable any longer. They needed to make for the hilltop one last time and hope for the best.

With Berj still in the lead, they began to make their way northeast, slower now, listening carefully for any hints of an ambush. They sheathed their swords, knowing that even the briefest reflection of starlight off of their blades could betray them to the enemy.

"We have to be getting close now," Darian whispered. Berj did not reply, and Darian was uncertain if his totally focused companion had heard him at all.

Within minutes, the ground seemed to begin sloping steadily upward. A rush of excitement flooded through Darian; they were going to pull this off. They were going to successfully take the hilltop, just as they had been instructed to do. Everything had gone wrong, and virtually nothing had gone according to plan, but they were going to succeed nonetheless. He wondered if Berj was feeling the same sense of tense anticipation. They may still be able to snatch victory from the jaws of defeat.

"Halt right there, Imperial scum!"

The cry split the night out of nowhere, causing Darian Tor's feet to leave the ground in shock.

He pulled his sword free of the sheath once more, and Berj did the same in front of him. It had been too good to be true, as they should have known. They would need to fight one more time if they were going to take the hilltop.

He turned in all directions, searching for the source of the shout. To his horror, he found Order of the Scar fighters approaching from all four sides. Somehow, the enemy had converged on the hill from behind and surrounded them. They would fight, but a quick scan told him this was a fight they could not hope to win. Berj Jenson turned to him and gave him a final nod. No words needed to be spoken; they both knew that there was only one option left.

Darian followed Berj into the midst of the enemy combatants in front of them. They might as well make one last valiant effort to reach the top of the hill. Maybe one of them would even manage to break through the enemy ranks before he fell, though Darian doubted it. This was where their mission would end. Fear and disappointment flooded through him as he crashed into the enemy forces; they had come so close to victory, only to have it snatched away from them.

He saw Berj cut down two foes with ferocious swings of his sword, but he could not turn in time to defend against the spear thrust that was coming for him. It plunged deep into his gut, and another enemy fighter shoved a sword into his back for good measure as he slumped to the ground. Furious, Darian charged the two men who had cut Berj down. He killed the one with the spear, his sword slashing through the man's neck before he could raise his defenses. The swordsman parried his first attack, and he never got a chance to try a second. A sharp pain washed over him, and he looked down just in time to see the blade of a spear being wrenched from his side, just under his ribs. His legs were going numb, suddenly no longer able to support his weight. The ground raced up to greet him as he sunk to his knees.

Darian Tor looked up to the night sky and accepted his failure. They had given it their best effort, but their valiant attempt had fallen short. The pain in his side seemed to vanish at once, and the night sky above his head shimmered. He closed his eyes, knowing what was coming next.

When he opened them again, a bright light burned into them, drawing immediate tears. He blinked furiously, trying to fight back the tears. He was no longer on a war-torn hillside in the dark of night; he was kneeling in the middle of the Imperial Army Training Grounds in broad daylight. Sergeant Harter Arsch was striding toward him, and just as Darian had expected, he did not appear pleased.

Chapter Two

Darian Tor took a deep breath, trying to steady himself for what was to come. His heart was still racing; the stress of the life-and-death battle he had just been engaged in was slow to dissipate. He understood from experience that this was not likely to improve anytime soon, and the conversation to come wouldn't help.

Sergeant Harter Arsch was already bearing down on him, never one to give his men a moment of respite, even under the most trying of circumstances. Facing Arsch was frequently more stressful than a fight for your life; almost every soldier who came through his training program agreed. It was said that if a veteran soldier were given a choice between fighting on the front line of a bloody conflict or going through Sergeant Harter Arsch's boot camp again, almost all of them would choose the former.

Darian glanced to his left to see Berj Jenson rising to his feet, shaking his head to clear the disorientation. Darian knew they had gotten off relatively easily. The longer you had to lie dead in the combat simulation, the harder it was to compose yourself afterward. He looked around, searching for any sign of Darnold Dans or Max Preston, but they were still nowhere to be found. He silently prayed they would hurry it up. The only thing worse than a Harter Arsch tirade was one you made him wait to deliver to you. Like a fine wine, they only improved with age.

The drill sergeant was within feet of them now, but he continued to approach until he could have reached out and touched them. Any man who valued his personal space was a man who would not care much for Harter Arsch's teaching style. Darian could see that Arsch was red in the face and identified several familiar veins bulging in the drill sergeant's forehead. The sergeant was well into his fifties, and many men wondered why Harter Arsch had not yet retired. The prevailing theory among the recruits was that he took a considerable amount of pleasure in tormenting the young men who were unfortunate enough to come through his program. Considering that Arsch moved with the energy of a much younger man, Darian was inclined to concur with the theory.

"Well, well, well. That was quite a display you imbeciles put on in there. I'm almost impressed. I had shockingly low expectations, yet somehow you managed to sink beneath them. I should have known not to expect anything resembling competence from you morons. I can't recall them ever burdening me with such a dull-witted assortment of incompetent fools. But we shouldn't get started too early, should we? Let's stand here and wait for your boneheaded friends together, shall we?"

He was not yelling, at least not entirely. Harter Arsch never did. He was not a man who needed to shout to get his point across. His orders, his criticisms, and even his rare praise all came in the form of a curt bark. Darian suspected this was by design, intended to force the recruits to listen carefully to each word to determine his true feelings.

"Yes, sir," Darian and Berj replied as one, their backs straight and their eyes forward. Arsch had not requested any other response, and they knew better by now than to try to offer one. Anything they said now would only make things worse for them.

They waited for several minutes, Darian Tor making every effort not to make eye contact with the fuming drill sergeant as he paced back and forth before them. He would have loved nothing more than to retire to his bunk and sleep off the soreness that was beginning to set into every part of his body. Mages from the Order of Mages conjured up the battle simulations to the specifications requested by Harter Arsch. The wounds suffered in them were not real, and they would leave no lasting damage, despite the genuine pain they caused the men suffering them in the moment.

Still, the effort expended by the soldiers within the simulations was all too real, leaving the young recruits physically and mentally exhausted each time. Each recruit in the camp had faced the infamous Order of the Scar more times than they cared to remember. The Scar was, of course, nothing more than a faceless enemy fabricated to give the Imperial recruits an enemy with a name. But, as Harter Arsch loved to remind them, if they could not defeat a simulated enemy, how could they hope to prevail against a real one?

Five minutes passed before Darnold Dans finally arrived. The sandy-haired young man took his place in line beside Darian. Sergeant Arsch did not speak to him or acknowledge his arrival in any way, and Darnold knew better than to open his mouth unprompted. They waited in agonizing silence for another ten minutes until Max Preston finally arrived as well, sweat pouring down his heavily freckled face. Of the four of them, Preston was the most intimidated by Harter Arsch, and his nervous eyes betrayed him. He knew as well as the rest of them that they were in store for a lengthy diatribe.

"So, we are finally all together again. What a happy family of nitwits I have gathered before me. I trust you all had time to rest comfortably. I don't see any other reason why you would keep me waiting for this long," Arsch said.

None of them had rested for even a second, and Arsch knew this as well as they did. Darian had been foolish enough to say something to this effect the first time he had been on the receiving end of one of these lectures. A month of scrubbing out the latrines later, he had learned his lesson. He continued to stare straight ahead, desperately trying to keep his face as stoic as possible. Any hint of emotion was a weapon Sergeant Arsch would be all too happy to turn against him. The drill sergeant could read the face of a nervous private as easily as one might read a book.

"Let's go over what happened, shall we? Your orders were simple enough, or so I thought. Perhaps I had too much faith in your ability to understand them. Maybe the fault is mine. Maybe I need to search for newer, more innovative ways of drilling orders into your overly thick skulls. Preston!"

"Yes, sir!" Max Preston cried out, his voice quivering noticeably. Darian had to fight down a groan. Preston being asked to speak for the group did not bode well for them. He looked the part of a soldier, tall and thickset, his red hair cut close to his head even before they had been required to do so. He was a capable fighter, but he had proven time and again that his mental aptitude fell well short of his physical ability. He was nearly always the first to fall in the simulation due to his nervous tendencies and inability to see the big picture.

"You were tasked with commanding this squad, were you not, Private Preston?" Arsch asked.

"Yes, sir, you placed me in command. I thank you for the honor," Preston said, almost causing Darian's eyes to roll clear into the back of his head. All of these months in this training program, and he was still foolish enough to think flattery would work on the likes of Harter Arsch? Max Preston was a good man, but he was naive to a fault.

"It was not meant as an honor, you boneheaded moron. It was meant as a means of assessing your leadership capabilities. I thought you might even show evidence of possessing something inside that skull of yours. I should have known better. Refresh my memory, Private Preston. What was the objective the four of you were given to complete?"

"Sir, our objective was to seize control of the hilltop from the Order of the Scar," Preston replied, this time at least having the good sense not to try buttering Arsch up.

"Take control of the hilltop; right you are, Private Preston. However, I must admit, I'm a bit surprised you answered correctly. After witnessing the display you four put on, I was worried perhaps you had not heard me correctly. It was a rather simple command, I would say. Was there some aspect of this command you found confusing? Perhaps the fault lies with me. Was your goal not made perfectly clear?"

"Sir, the objective was clear. The methods we were expected to use were not."

Darian dared not look left or right, but he knew instinctively that Berj and Darnold were fighting back the same look of exasperation as him. Preston's nerves were going to land all of them in deep water. Harter Arsch was no doubt already scheming the most fitting punishment for this asinine remark. Any comment that levied even the slightest touch of the blame on Sergeant Arsch would be met with unpleasant consequences. How could Preston not realize this by now?

"Forgive me, Private Preston. I must be growing old and senile. I was under the impression that an Imperial squad leader should be capable of determining such things as simple as a method of assault. Can you please explain to me what happened after the first explosion?"

"Sir, I-I don't know," Preston stammered. Were it not for the horrendous punishment that he was likely making worse for them with each word that came out of his mouth, Darian might have felt sorry for him.

"You don't know? Would you care to explain to me why that is, Private Preston? Is there a problem with your eyes? Do you need to see a healer?"

"Sir, we were attacked by an enemy force shortly after the simulation began. I was killed in the struggle. I don't know anything that happened after that."

"Oh, so you were killed, yet I still have to stand here, listening to you spew your ineptitude. If only I were so fortunate, Private Preston. No dead man is capable of displaying this level of incompetence. So, you managed to get yourself killed within minutes, leaving your squad without a squad leader. Who was your appointed second-in-command?"

This is getting worse by the second, Darian thought. *Preston has stunk things up plenty of times before, but Arsch is really letting him have it this time.* He knew before the answer left Preston's lips that it would only serve to infuriate Arsch even further. Still, he dared not speak up to come to his fellow recruit's aid. The first rule of Imperial Army training was that you never interrupted Sergeant Harter Arsch while he was teaching. *If that is indeed what this is meant to be.*

"Sir, there was no designated chain of command."

Arsch did not reply right away. He resumed his pacing, walking back and forth before them as though daring one of them to break the silence first. Four months into their training, they all knew better, even Preston. Darian suspected that these moments were meant to be as much of a test as the battle simulations. A soldier's ability to keep his mouth shut was one the Imperial Army valued greatly.

It was a full minute that felt like an eternity before Arsch finally spoke once more.

"Don't try to deflect responsibility for your blunders by using cleverly crafted statements with me. There was no designated chain of command because you did not appoint one. You will speak more clearly in the future, and you will not attempt to soften the impact of your own incompetence by being clever. You have no talent for it anyway. Can you please explain to me, Private Preston, why you did not appoint a second-in-command?"

"Sir, I didn't deem it necessary for such a simple objective."

It was the wrong answer, of course, but Darian had to acknowledge there was no answer that would have satisfied Arsch.

"I will admit, Private Preston, that I doubted even a fool as dimwitted as you could manage to get yourself killed as fast as you did. But you proved me wrong, and in doing so, you left your squad leaderless in the process. You have brought shame to the Imperial Army with the depths of your incompetence. Now, shut your mouth, Private Preston. I do not want to hear another word out of you. Understood?"

Darian held his breath in anticipation, waiting to see if Preston would make one final mistake. To his surprise, the naive young man did not. He had fully expected his squad leader to acknowledge the order out loud, as they were trained to do. But Preston apparently fought down the instinct, contenting himself with a curt nod and allowing Darian a slight sigh of relief. That was bad, but it could have been worse. With Harter Arsch, it could always be worse.

"Now, let's get to those of you who managed to live long enough to see the explosion, which was meant as your first true test," Arsch said, casting Preston a final withering look. "After the blast, you abandoned your direct assault on the hill. Jenson, explain why."

"Sir, we met several strong bands of resistance during our direct approach. We were met multiple times by Order of the Scar fighters. We agreed we should take a more circuitous route to the objective in the hope that we could reach the hill unseen," Berj said. Out of all of them, Berj was the best at maintaining his composure under Arsch's questioning, and Darian was grateful he had not been asked the same question.

"So, you believed, after you had been spotted and engaged by your enemy, that they would decide to leave vast swaths of ground unguarded? Your theory was that they would simply forget you were trying to reach the hill, all because you took a different route?" Arsch asked.

Darian did not envy Berj having to come up with an answer to that question. The simple truth of the matter was that none of them had thought their tactics out thoroughly. They had merely chosen what had seemed the best of a myriad of imperfect options. Standing here, listening to Harter Arsch poke holes in their strategy—or lack thereof—at every turn made him see the truth of just how poorly they had thought things out. An Imperial soldier needed to be fast to react to any situation in an intelligent manner. They had been quick to react, but their decisions had been far from brilliant.

"Sir, there was no clear path to the hilltop. There were more enemy fighters than we were expecting. We elected to choose the path we felt would have the least resistance," Berj replied, and Darian couldn't help but admire him. His voice projected a confidence Darian knew full well he did not actually possess in his answer.

"So, you felt that running to and fro like headless chickens would be the path of least resistance? I will make sure to pass the suggestion along to Imperial High Command, Private Jenson. They are always on the lookout for brilliant new tactics. Maybe you will all receive commendations for your innovation. Congratulations, men. You have disappointed me more thoroughly than I ever could have imagined, even a few seconds ago. Now, I have a question for you, Private Tor."

Darian's heart immediately began to race at a pace that nearly matched its rhythm during the simulated battle. He had never done an adequate job of answering Arsch's riddles, and he had often paid the price for it. The last time he had failed to acceptably reply to one of the drill sergeant's questions, he had been forced to run a full ten laps around the entire training complex.

"What do you think was the objective of this simulation?" Arsch asked.

What was the objective of any of these simulations that Arsch put them through? Each time, it seemed as though the drill sergeant took great pleasure in setting them up for failure. It was as though the drill sergeant received some sort of vindictive satisfaction from witnessing their struggles and then berating them for it. He could not say this, of course, no matter how badly he wished that he could. Fortunately, he thought he had an inkling of what Arsch had intended with this exercise.

"Sir, I believe you wanted to test our willingness to undertake a mission against impossible odds. Once we saw that our plan of slipping around the enemy forces was not working, we should have resumed our direct assault. You wanted to see how we would react to being forced to make an unpleasant decision. You wanted us to face our objective head-on even in the face of impossible odds. We failed you," he replied, hoping that Arsch would find his answer at least somewhat acceptable.

"Well, Private Tor here might not be quite as stupid as he looks, not that it's much of a compliment. You four were told to take control of the hilltop. Did you think it would not be a violent affair? Why did you feel the need to make me waste hours of my time watching you all try your best to avoid a fight? I don't recall telling you this was meant to be a stealthy operation. Why did you do everything possible to avoid getting your hands dirty? Except for Private Preston here, of course. I'll give credit where it's due. He is always quick to rush into a fight, which would be far more impressive if he ever managed to win one."

The point of the lesson was simple enough that Darian kicked himself for not realizing it sooner. Arsch had not expected them to be successful in taking control of the hill. He wanted them to demonstrate that they would follow orders at all costs, just as an Imperial soldier was sworn to do. They were not meant to succeed; they were being tested on how they would confront inevitable failure. It was a test they had failed spectacularly.

"I want all of you out of my sight before I heave out my lunch in disgust. I was appalled at the display of combat prowess you put on in there, so I think it would do the four of you some good to drill for a few hours. You will train from now until bunk time, and I feel a great deal of pity for the man I catch slacking. Understood?"

"Yes, sir!"

Harter Arsch stormed off across the field without another word, no doubt searching for another poor recruit to torment. The foursome stole nervous glances at one another as he walked away, each of them breathing a small sigh of relief. Drilling until bunk time would be brutal. There were still several hours of daylight left, and they were already exhausted from the simulation. But they understood they were fortunate to have received no worse punishment for their failure. Darian had suspected they would be cleaning the latrines or the kitchens for a week, so he allowed a small smile onto his face as they made their way across the simulation field and back toward the main camp.

The Imperial Army's main training facility was situated in the very southern reaches of the province of Salvamoan. The area was scarcely populated, and the duke of Salvamoan had been all too happy to allow the Imperials to train on his land. The use of the land was given in exchange for a generous tax cut, of course. It was a miserable place, one Darian could not wait to bid farewell to for the last time.

Lying on the far eastern coast of the Empire, Salvamoan was perhaps the poorest of the ten provinces. There was little to speak of in terms of natural resources in this region. Almost all of the province's wealth came from the fish they pulled from the sea. Little of that wealth found its way to this desolate windswept part of the province, far from the coast or any of the larger cities, so the training facility had been welcomed by all.

As they came into the main encampment, Darian saw with a pang in his stomach that most of their fellow recruits were heading into the chow hall for supper. Arsch's orders had been clear, and none of them dared defy them. They were to drill until the sun went down. There had been no mention of supper, so they would be hungry until breakfast the following morning. There was no use in complaining about it, so none of them did. It was a lesson they had all learned early on. Complaining only made matters worse.

They entered the fenced paddock designated for close combat training and retrieved four sparring swords from the weapons rack. They were the only recruits in the paddock, everyone else having already left for supper. A few passing recruits shot them sympathetic looks while others openly laughed at their misfortune. Only privates who had drawn the ire of Sergeant Harter Arsch would be in the paddock at this time of day.

The four split into pairs for sparring, Darian squaring off against Darnold and Berj against Preston.

Darian launched into a complex sequence of attacks against Darnold only to see each strike swatted away or dodged. Darian was a skilled swordsman, one of the higher-ranked recruits in that regard, but Darnold had excellent defensive techniques that were nearly impossible to breach. Had it not been for a fluke arrow, Darnold would most likely have been the last recruit standing during the simulation; he usually was. Darnold countered the attacks, sending Darian into a hasty backward retreat. For as good as his defense was, Darnold's attacks lacked aggression, and though they forced Darian to backpedal, he was never in genuine danger of being struck.

There was a sharp squeal off to their left, and neither of them had to look to know what had happened. Berj had broken past Preston's defenses and put a new welt on him. Over the next few minutes, several more cries of pain sounded out until the four switched pairings. Now Darian was paired off against Berj, a prospect none of them were ever happy to face.

What Berj lacked in refined skill he made up for in reckless aggression. In the battle simulations, he had by far the highest kill count of any recruit in the camp, but he also had a habit of being struck down by well-placed counterattacks. A few minutes into their spar, Darian successfully landed a counterstrike on him, taking advantage of a powerful but wild swing that had put Berj off-balance. His sparring sword slashed out before Berj could recover, tapping him sharply on the shoulder.

"Arsch is a miserable old bastard, isn't he?" Berj asked, shaking his arm to relieve the pain of Darian's strike, already searching for an opening to attack again.

"What did you think was going to happen? He was going to greet us with a bouquet of flowers and send us off to a feast in our honor?" Darnold quipped while effortlessly parrying every assault Preston launched against him.

"You would think the fact that we all went down fighting to our last breath would at least earn us the slightest bit of praise, or even the right to have supper tonight. Is that too much to ask? Wasn't that the point of the exercise anyway? For all of us to die fighting?"

"Dead men don't hear praise, so what would be the point of it? Dead men have no need for supper," Darian pointed out. "Arsch is an ass, but there's a logic in everything he says and does. That logic may be sick and twisted, but it does exist."

"Darian's right. I hate Arsch as much as you do, but he doesn't want to praise us for getting ourselves killed," Max Preston said, all while still trying in vain to hack his way through Darnold's defenses. "The Imperial Army needs its soldiers alive, no matter how hard they try to make us feel like our lives are meaningless and we are all nothing more than expendable assets."

"Three months in and you still haven't learned that lesson, though, have you, Preston?" Berj shot back while launching into a fresh assault against Darian.

"Shut up, Berj. You've been just as reckless as I have, if not more, and you know it."

"Yes, but how many times have I died in the first five minutes of a simulation? You've lasted to the end how many times? Two? Don't you start with me, Maxwell."

"I've told you not to call me that!" Preston broke off his attack on Darnold and spun on Berj, raising his sparring sword.

Darian and Darnold quickly stepped between them, not wanting things to escalate. If Harter Arsch had been displeased with them before, walking up and finding them engaged in an all-out brawl would not improve his feelings. Their first week in the camp, two recruits had gotten into a dispute in the chow hall. Arsch had broken them up personally, none too gently, and had put both of them to work scrubbing the fencing around the entire camp until it was spotless. The task had held seemingly no purpose other than to punish the brash young recruits. It had taken them over a month to finish, working every spare minute.

"Look, let's just agree you're both boneheaded idiots and move on, shall we?" Darnold asked, one hand still firmly on Preston's shoulder.

"Truer words have never been spoken," Darian added, his arm wrapped tightly around Berj's waist.

The two young men glared daggers at each other for a few more seconds before finally relaxing. The four switched one last time, with Darian facing off against Max Preston this time.

Preston was an eager fighter, always happy to rush headfirst into a battle. Unfortunately, his martial prowess had not yet caught up to his bravery, and Darian landed a few solid strikes against him before the sun fell out of sight to the west at last.

After putting their sparring swords away, the four young recruits made their way out of the paddock and back toward the barracks.

As they walked in silence, it seemed surreal to Darian that they were already three months into the four-month training regimen of the Imperial Army. A month later, most of them would receive their assignments and be deployed to the front lines of the Dwarven Rebellion in the province of Qwitzite. Four months earlier, just two days after his eighteenth birthday, he had said his goodbyes to his family and set off to join the Imperial Army, not knowing when he would see them again.

He was the fourth consecutive male in his family to serve in the Imperial Army. His father had served as well, though he had been fortunate enough to serve his term in peacetime. Darian's grandfather and great-grandfather had been less fortunate, both serving in bloody conflicts that had raged on for years. The Dwarven Rebellion was not likely to be such a lengthy war, and there was even speculation that the dwarves were on the verge of surrender. If that happened, Darian and the rest of his fellow recruits would probably end up pulling patrol duty in one of the fortresses that policed the borders between provinces. While Darian would not much mind such an assignment, many of these young men were spoiling for a fight, just itching to get a piece of the dwarven rebels. An early end to the war would be a bitter disappointment for men like that.

"Look, I'm sorry, Preston."

Darian's head snapped up; Berj had broken his train of thought.

"You may be a poor excuse for a squad leader, but you have guts, and no man can deny that. As much crap as I give you for dying in those simulations, you know it's only because I don't want it to happen for real on the front. I've grown used to your face, ugly as it is."

"Don't worry about it. You're a dumb brute, but those dwarves will surrender within an hour of seeing you in action," Preston said, extending a hand to Berj, who shook it.

Darian and Darnold exchanged exasperated glances. They had been a foursome since being grouped together on the first day of training. They had become fast friends, but the bickering between Berj and Preston was nearly nonstop. Darian suspected it was because neither of them was used to being around a man with such a similar personality. While Preston was more cautious and calculating than Berj with his words, the similarities were still striking.

"Darian, have you heard from your friend on the front lately?" Darnold asked, clearly wanting to change the subject.

Darian's childhood friend Axel Stark had joined the Imperial Army a year prior and had spent the better part of the last six months on the front lines in Qwitzite. They had been friends since before they could walk, growing up together in the distant province of Verizia. Darian had received several letters from Axel during training, but it had been weeks since he had last heard from his friend. The long silence was beginning to worry him, though he had not shared his worries with his fellow recruits.

"No, it's been a few weeks. He said the fighting was fierce in his last letters. Apparently, the dwarven separatists are passionate about their cause."

"Damn fools. Why would they want out of the Empire? Do they realize how many enemies would come after their precious gold and ores if they weren't under Imperial protection? The pirates who run the South Sea would attack them relentlessly, among others," Berj said.

"According to Axel, they do a pretty sufficient job of defending themselves. We have the numbers, but you have to admit, they've inflicted serious losses on us from everything we've heard," Darian pointed out.

"Yes, but just wait until our fabulous foursome arrives! They won't know what hit them." Berj laughed, though his friends knew he was only half joking; Berj was nothing if not sure of himself.

Darian stole a sideways glance at him, searching for hints that his words were bluster. A broad smirk stretched across Berj's face, and as usual, there were no such hints to be found. If there was any man who looked like he was born to be a soldier, it was Berj Jenson, his broad shoulders and confident gait radiating self-belief.

"We better get some sleep. With our luck, Arsch will have us up at the crack of dawn for another simulation," Darnold said, ever the voice of reason.

He was right, and they all knew it. If Harter Arsch could be trusted for one thing, it was to take every opportunity to deny them their opportunity to rest. They could only hope he would give them the chance to have breakfast after denying them their supper. They slipped into the barracks as quietly as possible, not wanting to draw the wrath of their fellow recruits, many of whom were already falling asleep.

Darian slipped into his bunk, every muscle in his body aching from exhaustion. As much as his body longed for sleep, his mind resisted it, his thoughts now firmly on Axel's silence.

Why had his friend not written for so long? Had he been killed or wounded in battle? When Axel had left for training, they had promised to keep in touch, and this was the first time either of them had failed to do so.

The questions swirled in his head until the moment his body won the fight against his mind and he drifted off to sleep at last.

Chapter Three

It turned out Darnold was wrong. Harter Arsch did not wake them at the crack of dawn as he had predicted. He woke them long before that. It felt to Darian that his eyes had only closed a few seconds before when he was shaken violently from his sleep by the sound of the drill sergeant's frantic voice ringing out through the barracks. He scrambled to rise in his bunk, disorientated in the total darkness.

"I said get up, you lousy, no-good slouches! I swear I will flog the last recruit out of his bunk. That's if he manages to survive this, of course. We're under attack, you bunch of numbskulls. Get your feet on the ground and your armor on right this second!"

This has to be another simulation, right? Nobody would come all the way out to this wasteland to attack a camp of new recruits, Darian thought as he tried to shake himself awake. Still, he threw his legs out of bed, reaching in the dark for his armor. Simulation or not, he wasn't about to defy a direct order. They had drilled this exercise enough times that he was on his feet and fully armed and armored within a minute, just as was expected of every Imperial soldier. He hurried toward the exit, falling in line behind his fellow recruits. He was nearly to the door when Max Preston fell in line behind him.

"This has to be another simulation, right? Nobody would bother attacking the likes of us, right?" Preston asked.

"I don't know why anyone would. Leaving us here with Arsch would be a fate worse than death anyway," Darian mumbled, still disgruntled to have been woken so suddenly.

"Would you shut up, you moron? If he hears you say that, he'll do this to us every night for the rest of the program," a recruit in front of him hissed back at him.

Forced to concede the young man was right, Darian bit back his retort.

As soon as Darian stepped out of the barracks and into the chilly yet humid night air, the sounds of battle were there to greet him. Men were screaming off in the distance, their cries accompanied by the familiar sound of metal striking metal. Even at this distance, Darian could make out the faint smell of blood and death in the air.

The mages have outdone themselves with this simulation, he thought.

"They came in through the front gates. It's a bunch of bandit scum from Gryttar, here to raid our foodstuffs and weapons no doubt." Harter Arsch was coming up the line. "I don't know how they managed to muster so many men to attack us, but they have already advanced nearly to the chow hall, several dozen of them at least. The other officers tried to drive them back, but it looks like most of them have been killed in the attempt. It's up to us, recruits. I know this is sooner than you expected your first taste of a real battle, but remember your training, and you will make the Empire proud. Follow me; we have to drive them out of our camp!"

This caught Darian off guard. In all of their training simulations, Harter Arsch had never accompanied them into battle before, preferring to stay back and observe from a distance. Was it possible this was real? Or was it all part of the act, just another ruse in the elaborate games that Arsch liked to play with their minds? He stole a quick glance back at Preston only to find that the other man looked just as confused as he felt. There was no time to ponder; the line was advancing, Harter Arsch at its head, and Darian scrambled to keep up.

As they approached the chow hall, the pungent stench of smoke filled the air. The source of the aroma became clear within seconds: the bandits had set fire to the structure.

Bandits were milling around in front of the blaze, dressed in black leathers and furs. They lacked the chain mail typically seen on Order of the Scar fighters, again leading Darian to wonder if this could be a real attack. In the dark, it was hard to be sure how many, but Darian estimated their number to be approximately twenty. It was shocking to see so many, but not overly concerning. There were forty recruits in this camp, all now bearing down on the bandit scum. He tightened his grip on the shaft of his spear as they drew closer. Simulation or real life, he wanted to make a better impression this time around.

"Form a line, and let's wipe these bastards out, lads!" Harter Arsch cried, raising his sword above his head.

They immediately moved into formation, another exercise Arsch had drilled them on over and over again. Any grouping of Imperial soldiers should be able to form ranks in seconds, even if they had never fought together before. Darian ended up in the frontmost of their four rows, Preston on his right. This meant he was counting on the unreliable young man to protect his right side, a prospect that did not fill him with overly high hopes. Hopefully Preston would choose this moment to finally approach a battle in a steady, forward-thinking manner.

The bandits did not wait on the recruits to reach them, opting instead to take the offensive. They charged as one into the ranks of the young army privates. One came straight for Darian, but he managed to get his spear into position, catching the man in the chest as he drew close. The bandit stumbled back, blood gushing from his wound, and the axe he was wielding fell to the dirt.

Another bandit was lunging for the recruit on his left, a young man Darian did not know by name. Darian got his shield up in time, protecting his comrade from the bandit's attack and allowing the private to land a killing strike with his spear. There was a sudden clang by his right ear, and Darian spun, finding that Max Preston had successfully defended him from the swing of a bandit's sword. Once again, Darian struck with his spear, this time hitting the man in his shoulder and sending him reeling backward. The bandit fell to the ground, wounded, where Preston finished him off a split second later with another thrust. Their phalanx maneuver was working to perfection.

"More of them are pouring through the front gates, men. We have to get up there. If they get too many men inside, they'll surround us," Harter Arsch said, shouting so all could hear him. Darian spotted blood on the drill sergeant's blade, once again leading him to wonder if this was no simulation. He had never seen Harter Arsch engage in combat in any battle simulation.

There was no time to stand about contemplating the reality of the situation. The platoon was already on the move once more. Darian scrambled to keep up again, hurrying toward the front gates of the complex. Max Preston was still to his right. He cast glances over each shoulder, spotting Darnold Dans behind him and to the left. There was no sign of Berj Jenson until he spoke.

"You think this is real, Darian? Or is this another one of Arsch's cruel jokes?"

Darian turned toward the voice to find that the strongheaded young man was in the front row as well, several men to his left. Darian had no time to respond to his friend; the front gates were already coming into view. What he saw was not encouraging.

Close to a hundred bandits had already gathered inside the fences, and more were still pouring through the gates. If this was a simulation, it was a cruel one; they could never hope to defeat so many men, no matter how well they executed their formation. If this was a real battle, at least it would be over quickly.

"What are you waiting for? Attack! Get this bandit scum out of our camp, now. Fight to kill, men, because they sure will," Harter Arsch ordered, once again charging forward to take the lead himself.

They charged as one, forty Imperial Army recruits formed into one cohesive unit. The bandits spun to meet them as they approached, and the two groups collided with splintering force. Darian killed one with his spear and then another before an axe came down on the shaft, breaking it in half. He didn't slow down for a second, his hand releasing the broken weapon and immediately drawing his sword.

The next few minutes were almost an out-of-body experience for the young private. He was surrounded by chaos and bloodshed. The bandits hacked away, desperately trying to kill him. But time seemed to slow down for Darian, the opposite of what he would have expected to happen. He was happy to see that Max Preston still fought beside him, alive and well. Perhaps the reckless man had learned a valuable lesson from their last simulation. He shielded the soldier to his left with his shield, but it was not enough to save the young man from the arrows that came flying into their ranks. No sooner had the soldier fallen than Berj Jenson appeared to take his place.

Berj was fighting like a man possessed, desperately trying to hack apart any foe within reach. He had lost his spear and shield in the fighting, and he swung his sword with both hands. In his frenzy, he was apparently able to ignore the pain from the numerous wounds he had sustained. Darian only caught a brief glimpse of him—he was somewhat preoccupied fighting off his own foes—and he could not help but admire Berj's skill and courage.

In the flurry of combat, he saw Darnold Dans, now fighting on Preston's right side. Somehow, the four of them had ended up in the center of the front row. He didn't know how many of their comrades had fallen, and he could not tear his eyes away from their enemies long enough to find out.

"The gates are wide-open! If we can secure them, we can stop more bandits from flooding into the camp," Darnold said, straining to make himself heard over the sounds of the battle.

Darian chanced a glance and saw that Darnold was right. Why were the gates open? Had somebody within the camp betrayed them, opened them so that the bandits could walk in unchallenged? He had never heard of such a thing happening inside of an Imperial camp. Imperial soldiers were loyal to the very end, and they would rather die than betray the oaths they had taken. Did this mean that this was, in fact, a simulation? He cast about for a sign of Harter Arsch and found the drill sergeant covered with blood, fighting off three bandits single-handedly, his sweat-drenched face contorted with rage. The uncertainty of the situation was maddening, but there was nothing to be done about it. Darnold was right; they needed to close the gates.

"The four of us could make a run for the gates," he said. The plan was still coming together in his head. He was not confident in it, but it was the best they had. "If we can get there, we can close and bar them, then hold them so that the bandits already inside can't open them again."

"Let's do it, then. We can't win this battle like this. They'll kill us all," Berj replied, ducking just in time to avoid an arrow flying for his head.

So, the four of them broke off from the rest of the recruits and made for the gates. Berj took the lead, with Darian and Preston right behind and Darnold bringing up the rear. Berj went into a frenzy, hacking his way through a group of bandits that fought to block their path. Once free of the opposition, they broke into a run, racing for the gates as fast as their legs could carry them. Darian felt an arrow glance off his shield, a stroke of pure luck, for he had not even seen it coming toward him. He thought he could hear Harter Arsch screaming something but could not make out the words. If this was a simulation, they could likely expect another angry rant for acting without orders.

The bandits seemed to realize what they were trying to do. Close to a dozen of them surged in front of the gates, blocking their path. Berj never slowed down, so neither did the rest of them. Darian got his shield up in time to deflect the sword racing toward his neck. He struck back, his sword taking his foe's arm clean off. Intense pain washed over him, and he looked down to find a knife buried in his leg. One of the bandits dying on the ground had launched one last attack against him with his dying breath. Fighting through the agony, he continued to push forward, his leg screaming in protest with each step.

Just when it seemed they would never fight their way through to the gates, they broke past the last of the defenders. Berj turned to look at them, and Darian was forced to bite back a scream. Berj had suffered a horrific wound to his face in the fighting. In the dim early-morning light, it appeared his left eye might be missing altogether.

"Don't worry about it now, just help me get these gates closed," Berj said, his voice astoundingly calm for a man bearing such a grievous injury.

Berj and Preston pressed their shoulders against the left-hand gates while Darnold and Darian did the same on the right. Slowly but surely, the heavy iron gates closed, preventing any more attackers from spilling into the encampment. Once the gates were pressed tightly together, Darian fumbled for the sturdy iron latches, pushing them into place. The gates secured at last, he allowed himself to breathe a quick sigh of relief. The moment of rest was doomed to be short-lived, however. It was Preston who broke the silence, drawing their attention to the bandits still within the camp.

"Look sharp, here they come. They're going to try to open them again."

Sure enough, nearly two dozen bandits had turned their attention away from the bulk of the platoon and toward the gates. Looking out across the camp, Darian was dismayed to find that most of their fellow recruits were dead on the ground. No more than ten were still fighting, along with Harter Arsch. He doubted the four of them could hold the gates against so many attackers, but they had no choice but to try. Resigning himself to the fact that this was the end, he tightened his grip on his sword and readied himself to take as many bandits with him as he could.

The bandits advanced on them quickly. He wished he had been able to grab a bow after being woken; he could have at least picked a few of them off from long range before they killed him.

Oh well, at least I rid the world of a few of them, he thought to himself. He closed his eyes for a moment, thinking of his family back in Verizia, of his friend Axel on the front lines, of all the days he would never get a chance to live. Making his peace with that fact, he opened his eyes to find that the bandits had stopped advancing. They were simply standing there, perfectly still, staring at the four young men.

"All right, that's enough. End the simulation," Harter Arsch shouted, looking down at his bloodstained sword.

Darian couldn't stop the groan of relief from escaping his lips as the bandits simply vanished into thin air. He looked over at Berj, watching as the young man's grievous facial wound disappeared before his eyes, leaving an exhausted but otherwise unharmed Imperial Army private standing before him. He realized the pain in his leg had dissipated. He looked down to find that the knife that had been lodged there was gone, and the wound healed. He moved the leg gingerly, trying to shake out the phantom pain that always lingered from the simulated injuries. The soldiers who had fallen in the battle were beginning to stir, the wounds that had ended their simulated lives disappearing. They rose one by one, reforming into lines, reminding the four young men who had retaken the gates that they ought to be doing the same.

As Darian took his place in line, he could not help but feel proud of himself and his friends. It was they, and nobody else, who had realized the gates were open and could be closed. Preston had even survived the entire battle, which was nearly unheard of for the overly courageous young private. He doubted even the eternally irritated Sergeant Harter Arsch would find much to complain about on this night. The drill sergeant was pacing back and forth, waiting for all of his men to get into line. Once they had all formed up, Arsch came to a halt. He stared in silence for nearly a minute before he finally began.

"Gentlemen, a more pathetic display I can scarcely recall. For three months, you men have trained in this camp to be Imperial soldiers. You are meant to serve the Empire with courage, honor, and skill in any conflict. I will not mince my words tonight. During this simulation, I saw a gaggle of confused children who are unworthy of the uniforms they are wearing. I am grateful the citizens of the Empire did not witness this. I have rarely been more disappointed in men under my command. Shame on the parents who brought your sorry lives into this world."

Darian did his best to keep the shock from revealing itself on his face. He had assumed Arsch would still have some criticisms—after all, it was his job—but the drill sergeant's entirely negative reaction still caught him off guard. At the least, he had expected a word of praise for their quick thinking in closing the gates. Such approval was not forthcoming, however, as Arsch continued on his rant.

"Let's start at the beginning, shall we? I timed you all getting out of your bunks and into your gear. As you all know, gentlemen, Imperial soldiers are expected to be able to complete this task in a minute or less, yet some of you took a full three minutes. Any man who took more than a minute will take twenty laps around the encampment after we finish here, and no breakfast until you are done. You know who you are. If you try to avoid this punishment, I'll make it fifty laps every morning for a week!"

Nobody responded; no response was necessary.

At least I don't have to do laps, Darian thought. He dared not look at his friends, but he assumed all of them had met the one-minute time requirement. He knew that Preston had because they had left the barracks together. Preston was usually the slowest among them, so they should all be in the clear in that regard, at least.

"Next, when we engaged with the bandits at the chow hall, all of you acted like you were out for a pleasant afternoon stroll. Not one man showed any urgency in trying to salvage our foodstuffs. If we were out in an active war zone, it could take us weeks or even months to receive food shipments. You all seemed quite content to sit back and let ours be destroyed in the fire. Private Kans, can you please tell me the point of surviving a battle only to starve to death afterward?"

"Sir, I have no suitable answer," the unfortunate private answered, his voice quivering as he did.

"That is the wrong answer, Private Kans, and you can join the stragglers on their twenty laps."

Darian could scarcely recall seeing the always-angry Harter Arsch in such a foul mood. The unfortunate private had been singled out for no apparent reason, and any other recruit would have had the same reply. By the luck of Arsch's random pick, Private Kans would now have to run laps as well. Darian's hope that there may be at least a small amount of praise coming his way had all but evaporated. All there was left to hope for was not being picked at random to provide a reply to a rhetorical question.

"Shall we continue, gentlemen? After you were all happy enough to let our entire food supply burn to ashes, we hurried to the main gates. The bandits were pouring into gates; they outnumbered us. I found it odd that not one of you thought to question why the gates were wide-open or whether we should try to close them. An Imperial soldier needs to be aware of his surroundings at all times."

This is it, Darian thought. The moment was fast approaching, where he and his friends would be recognized or disregarded for their quick thinking. He had a bad feeling he knew which it would be.

"Privates Tor, Jenson, Darnold, and Preston finally figured it out.

Of course, they waited until most of you were bloody corpses on the ground before they did. The rest of you just sat back, letting the bandits flood into the camp, letting them slaughter us one by one. Congratulations, Privates Tor, Jenson, Darnold, and Preston, on showing a very slightly increased level of intelligence over your dimwitted fellows. At least you performed better than yesterday. Next time, maybe you will see fit to act before the battle is hopelessly out of reach. Now, get out of my sight, all of you. There is no need to return to your bunks, gentlemen. Breakfast will be waiting in the chow hall, not that a single one of you deserves it. After breakfast, it's physical conditioning all day, gentlemen, so eat your fill. Those of you who have to run better get a move on, and don't you dare let me see you slacking. Dismissed, you sorry excuses for soldiers."

The privates broke ranks, heading toward the chow hall. They walked in silence until they were out of earshot of Harter Arsch, and then the entire company broke into furious diatribes. Darian walked in silence, not joining in with his comrades. He was bitter about Arsch completely glossing over their accomplishments, of course. Overall, though, he felt fortunate. He was one of the lucky ones to avoid punishment. With Harter Arsch, it could always be worse, a fact he kept repeating to himself all the way to the chow hall.

He took his usual seat in the chow hall, along with Berj, Darnold, and Max. Their breakfast consisted of the usual: one egg, two slices of bread, and a few thin slices of smoked sausage. The rations were lean, which they had learned to expect by now. Many of the Imperial Army's resources were being diverted to the front lines in Qwitzite, and there was not much left for the likes of them.

The four of them ate quietly, allowing Darian to listen carefully to the ranting coming from nearly every other table. At last, Berj broke the silence.

"Arsch really is a miserable old bastard. Would it have killed him to give us a tiny bit more acknowledgment for fighting our way to the gates?

Real or not, that knife I took to the eye hurt a lot. It still feels like there's a shard of steel in there," he said, his eye blinking furiously.

"What have you seen or heard from Arsch in the last three months that made you think praise was even a slight possibility?" Darnold asked. "If anything, just be glad that we don't have to do laps. I figured he would have us all run, just out of spite."

"Darnold's right, but still, it gets old, doesn't it?" Max Preston asked. "If nothing else, they could feed us a little more after dragging us out of our bunks at that hour."

"Hey, you just reminded me of something, Preston," Berj said. "You didn't die in the first five minutes this time. You made it all the way to the end and helped us get that gate closed. There's a first time for everything, isn't there?"

"Oh, shut up, you prick," Preston said, flicking a piece of his egg at Berj's face and sending the small group into fits of laughter. Privates at neighboring tables shot them glares, obviously still disgruntled with the morning's events, but none of the four paid them any mind.

Darian wolfed down the last of his breakfast, not wanting to be late to physical conditioning. He did not know what the rest of this training program had in store for him, but he felt fortunate to have made these three friends. He was confident that together they could survive anything the vindictive Harter Arsch threw their way. Hopefully they could stay together, even after training. If he had to go to the front lines, there were no three men he would rather have by his side.

Chapter Four

Darian Tor squinted against the midmorning sun, focusing on the target. Harter Arsch had undoubtedly staged this archery practice facing into the morning sun on purpose, and there was no denying the challenge it presented. The mark he was aiming for was only thirty yards away, though he knew the shots would get more challenging as the exercise progressed. He stood at the line along with nine other privates, Darnold Dans among them, waiting for Arsch's orders.

"All right, privates, I hope for your sakes this goes better than the last time I tested you all on archery. I told you all to put in more practice at the range. We are about to find out who didn't follow orders. Ready!"

Darian set his orange-feathered arrow to the string of his bow.

"Aim!"

He raised the bow in front of him and slowly drew back on the string, lining up his shot. Arsch kept them waiting for a few seconds, no doubt hoping that the strain of holding the bowstring in place would disrupt some of their shots. There was a purpose to everything the drill sergeant put them through.

"Fire!"

Darian released the arrow, keeping his eye on the distinct orange hue as it raced toward the target. To his relief, the arrow found its mark, sinking deep into the straw target that Arsch had set for them. Every time they ran this exercise, he was terrified he would miss on the first shot. The thought of what Harter Arsch would put him through for such an unforgivable offense was one he did not care to consider. He took a quick count and found that ten different arrows with different-colored feathers had found their way to the mark.

"I'm somewhat surprised you all managed that. Hopefully you can keep surprising me. Move the target!" Arsch called out. Two unlucky privates who must have done something to draw the drill sergeant's ire rushed to move the straw target to a longer distance. They pulled the arrows free of the straw and scrambled back to the line, handing each recruit his designated color.

The target was now set fifty yards away. It was a more challenging shot, no doubt, but one Darian was reasonably confident in his ability to make. Back in Verizia, his father had taught him how to shoot a bow from a young age, and he had been quite proficient before arriving for Imperial Army training. Of their group of four friends, he was by far the best shot, though Darnold Dans could usually give him a run for his money. Both Berj and Preston struggled with archery; they lacked the patience required to be a skilled shot. Their brash personalities tended to lead to compounding struggles when it came time to shoot.

"Ready!"

Once again, Darian set his orange-feathered arrow to the string of his bow, taking a deep breath as he did.

"Aim!"

He slowly drew back on the string, lining up his shot. He gave a silent thanks that there was no wind to speak of that morning, which could seriously complicate longer shots. He slightly adjusted his aim from his previous shot, aiming marginally higher to compensate for the longer distance.

"Fire!"

Darian released his arrow and followed its flight to the target. Once again, he breathed a sigh of relief as it sunk deep into the hay, leaving only a hint of orange visible. This time, however, only eight of the arrows had found their mark. Searching the ground around the target, Darian found the two errant arrows at last. The feathers were red and white, respectively, meaning that two recruits were about to receive unpleasant feedback from Harter Arsch.

"Tomson and Mayne, it seems the two of you were unable to hit the target. An Imperial soldier who cannot hit a stationary target a mere fifty yards away is a liability to his fellow soldiers. Both of you will take five laps around the camp, and then you will go to the practice range and shoot until supper time. Get out of my sight!"

Darian watched the two recruits speed off, feeling almost envious. While the laps were no fun, at least the midday heat had not yet set in, and there were worse ways to spend a day than archery practice. At least they would not have to bear any more of Harter Arsch's relentless criticism. But there was no time to dwell on his jealousy. Arsch was already calling for the two privates assisting him to move the target back to seventy-five yards.

Darian glanced down the line to Darnold, who was standing at the end. Darnold shot him a quick grin and mouthed, "Good luck."

Seventy-five yards was no easy shot, though both of them had hit from such a distance before. Adding to the challenge was the pressure of knowing you would face Harter Arsch if you missed, and the sergeant would accept no excuses, no matter how great the distance.

The privates had returned and were moving down the line handing back the arrows. Darian accepted his and took a deep breath to steady himself.

"Okay, privates, let's see what you can do from this range. Ready!"

Darian nocked the orange-feathered arrow, his heart racing.

"Aim!"

Darian sighted his shot, praying for no sudden wind gusts. A shot of such a distance would be difficult enough in perfect conditions.

"Fire!"

Once more, Darian followed the orange-feathered arrow as best he could along its flight path. To his relief, he saw it strike the target for a third time, along with three others. Darnold's green feathers were clearly visible embedded in the straw target, as were the colors of purple and yellow. The other four privates had missed the mark, and, scanning the surrounding area, Darian saw no sign of their arrows anywhere near the target. The pity he felt for them almost matched the elation he felt at his own success.

"I must admit, that was almost impressive. I've rarely seen four men miss the target by such a wide berth all at once. Do you men not understand the importance of precision? In a battle, missing by such a great distance could mean the difference between killing a friend or a foe." Harter Arsch was livid, his face a dark shade of scarlet. "The four of you will take ten laps around the encampment. You will then practice shooting at a target seventy-five yards away, and you will not stop until all four of you have succeeded. Oh, and I don't see any need for you to have any more than one arrow for this exercise. Every time you miss, you can run and retrieve it. Maybe that will help you boneheaded twats learn to shoot properly. I don't care if it takes you a week. Now move!"

The four rushed away, probably trying to get out of there before Harter Arsch could think of any additional punishment to throw at them. The drill sergeant was red in the face, the familiar vein throbbing in his forehead. He called for his two helpers to move the target once more, and Darian tried to relax his muscles. One hundred yards was the farthest shot he had ever made in these sessions. If he could repeat the feat and possibly be the only one to do so, he might avoid discipline for once.

He accepted his arrow back from the private who scrambled to bring it to him and stared downrange at the target, already trying to determine the correct angle for the shot.

"Ready!"

Darian was rarely so tense, and he strained to loosen his muscles as he nocked his arrow.

"Aim!"

He raised the bow to the height he had decided best; there was little to be gained by second-guessing himself at this point.

"Fire!"

There was no hope in following the flight of his arrow this time; the distance was simply too great. He'd felt good about the shot as he released it, but the moment it was away, the doubt began to creep in. How would Arsch punish him if he had missed?

"Get out there and move the target back. Bring me back only the arrows that struck the target. And hurry it up; I don't have all morning," Arsch instructed his assistants.

The wait could not have been more than five minutes, but they were five minutes that felt like an eternity. Harter Arsch did not say a word as they waited, and none of the privates dared to break the silence. They understood that even the most innocent of comments could be turned against them if the assistants returned without their arrow.

At last, the two privates came into view, jogging back to Harter Arsch. Darian held his breath, hoping for the best but expecting the worst. They held no arrows, and he surmised that they must be keeping them in the burlap sack that one of them carried to add to the suspense. It was just the type of thing Arsch would order them to do.

"Well, how many arrows do you have for me?" Arsch asked as they approached.

"None, Sergeant Arsch. All four arrows were in the dirt at the feet of the target, but none of them actually struck the mark," one of the privates said, while the other looked at them apologetically.

Darian felt as though someone had punched him in the stomach. All of them had missed? He could not imagine how furious Harter Arsch would be with them for this failure. Would it have killed the privates to lie and say that one of them had at least made the shot? But he knew that was not fair, that he himself would never dare to tell such a lie to the volatile drill sergeant. He shuddered at the thought of the punishment such an offense would bring.

"Not a single one of them? If you had told me this would be the case before we began this exercise, I would not have been surprised. But after that last round, I was foolish enough to get my hopes up. I should have realized that it is my curse in life to be eternally disappointed by the sorry excuses for men they send me to train. It would be best if you gentlemen realized that final evaluations are not far off. I hope you will keep that in mind when you reflect on your performance today. Not a single one of you should walk away from here feeling good about yourself. It will be five laps for all of you. Now get out of my sight before I make it twenty," Arsch said in his normal barking tone of voice.

The four of them headed out at once on their laps. Five was not all that bad. Darian had expected much worse. Arsch must have felt at least a small measure of satisfaction with the four of them, even if he would never acknowledge as much out loud. He waited until they were well beyond the drill sergeant's earshot before turning to Darnold.

"Five laps isn't too bad. He must be in a better mood than usual."

"He's probably looking forward to putting us through the torture of final evaluations," Darnold said.

Once they completed their laps, the pair headed to the chow hall to find Berj and Max already seated at their usual table. The two were wolfing down as much food as they could get their hands on, reminding Darian that their own archery drill would be later in the day. Clearly, they were anticipating that they may not get supper that night. Remembering that neither of them was that great of a shot, Darian immediately sympathized with them. It was unlikely either of them would hit the target beyond the first round.

"Not to make your day any worse, but Arsch hinted this morning that final evaluations would be happening soon," Darnold told them.

"Make my day worse? Are you kidding me, Darnold? I can't wait to be rid of this camp," Berj said through a mouthful of bread while Preston nodded his agreement, his mouth too full to speak. "The day I wake up without the prospect of listening to that bitter old man piss and moan over every little mistake I make will be the happiest day of my life."

"Do you think they will ship us off to the front lines? Assuming we all pass evaluations, of course," Darian said, not wanting to acknowledge the possibility that he could fail and be sent home to Verizia in shame. What would his father have to say about that?

"I suppose it all depends on if the dwarves really do surrender soon, doesn't it?" Darnold replied, watching Berj and Preston eat, an expression of mild disgust etched across his face.

"Wherever we get sent, I hope the four of us end up together. The three of you may be as ugly as sin, but at least you make me look better by comparison," Berj said, eliciting a chuckle from all of them.

It may have been meant as a joke, but Darian did sincerely hope that the four of them would end up together. Having three close friends by his side had made the experience of training far less intimidating. He had arrived in a state of apprehension that bordered on terror and considered himself blessed to have made three such good friends so quickly. He did not know everything that the future held in store, but he would rather face it with his three friends by his side.

His train of thought was interrupted by Harter Arsch storming into the chow hall and clearing his throat loudly to draw their attention. The room went instantly silent; the tension was palpable. Harter Arsch appearing suddenly never meant anything good.

"Attention, recruits! I have an announcement you will all want to hear. Your final evaluations will commence three days from today. I suggest you all use the time to drill harder than you have ever drilled in your lives, because I doubt more than half of you are capable of passing at your current skill level. I will be quite displeased with any man who brings shame to my program by failing his evaluation. As you were, recruits."

The hall remained silent for a few seconds after Arsch's departure and then erupted into excited chatter all at once. Darian was not sure if he was excited, nervous, or both. Final evaluations were spoken of in many terms, all of them horrifying. Nobody knew exactly what they entailed. It was considered a rite of passage for an Imperial soldier, one which he had to face on his own. All they were told was to expect the most grueling test of their entire lives.

"Well, it looks like you're going to get your wish, Berj," Preston said. "Only a few more days of Harter Arsch."

"Did I say that? Why would I say that? I'm a fool!"

Darian had never seen Berj so pale in the face.

"Any ideas on what they are going to put us through? Do you think it will be another battle simulation?" Darian asked, trying to sound as casual as possible.

"I would expect everything they have already thrown at us and more," Darnold said. "Simulations, archery drills, close-quarters combat evaluations, tests of our physical conditioning, you name it. If it's awful, they will probably put us through it."

It was not the answer Darian wanted to hear, but it was the same one he would have given if posed the same question. It was a daunting prospect, facing the unknown. At that moment, he wondered if the final evaluations were kept so secretive as another means of testing them. Even Axel Stark had been evasive in his letters when Darian had asked about them. An Imperial soldier needed to be ready to face the unknown at any time, after all. They would be sent on perilous assignments with orders, but they needed to be able to adjust to meet any situation that arose.

"I almost wish he hadn't warned us in advance," Darian said. "I feel like we are more likely to make a mental mistake after worrying about the evaluations for three days."

"That's probably the point. He wants to see how well we can overcome our fears," Berj said. "Speaking of my fears, if I'm late to this archery drill, Arsch will probably have me flogged and then make me run laps. Can't imagine that will help me pass. We had better get moving, Preston."

Darian and Darnold bid their friends farewell and good luck in their drill. There were no additional required drills for them to complete that day. Their original plan had been to join a few other recruits for a game of dice in the barracks, but the looming specter of final evaluations had caused them to rethink those plans. Instead, after a hurried lunch, they headed for the sparring paddock, deciding that the free time would be more productively spent honing their close-combat skills.

"How do you think Berj and Preston will do in their archery drill?" Darnold asked as they retrieved a pair of training spears.

"Well, maybe Arsch will be in a better mood than he was this morning," Darian said, drawing a laugh from his friend. Their working theory was that it was better to draw a drill early in the morning before other recruits had the opportunity to enrage Arsch.

"I just hope they get to have supper tonight. I can't believe final evaluations are upon us already. How do you think we will do?"

"One minute I'm confident, sure that my skills have developed exactly as expected. I mean, all of the lectures and rants have to be teaching us something, right? As much as Arsch rants about us, there's no way we are as bad as he says, right? He is like this with every group of recruits, isn't he? The next minute I think I'm doomed to fail and be sent home in disgrace. Maybe we really are as bad as he says we are. I can't imagine what my father would have to say."

"I suppose I'm lucky I'm the first soldier in my family. At least if I fail, they aren't as likely to judge me too harshly," Darnold said. "But to be honest with you, I doubt we will fail. I watch some of our fellow recruits in these drills, and I honestly think all four of us are better than them. Even Preston is better than we give him credit for. I just hope he doesn't lose his head like he is prone to do. Maybe that's arrogant on my part, but it's truly how I feel."

It was true. Darian had thought similarly while observing many of the recruits in camp. Maybe he was better than he was giving himself credit for being. While he lacked confidence, he could acknowledge that he had relatively few weaknesses, especially compared to most of his peers. He was not the best at close combat, but he would probably rank himself in the top ten out of the forty recruits. It was the same with archery; he regularly outshot most of the others. When they ran the battle simulations, he had never been among the first to fall, and more often than not, he had survived to the end. Darnold was right; he was in an excellent position to pass the final evaluation.

Hoping this newfound confidence would last for a few more days, he followed Darnold out into the paddock for practice.

Chapter Five

Darian stared down at his tray, trying to force himself to work up the will to eat. The kitchens had actually produced a decent breakfast for a change, even including a few strips of bacon, which he had not tasted since leaving home. But it was as though his body knew what was coming after the meal was over, and it was rejecting the idea of eating in the hopes of delaying the inevitable. He took a few bites of bread, knowing he would need all the strength he could get. He had barely forced himself to swallow them when he felt like he might throw them right back up.

It didn't seem possible that final evaluations had already arrived. Sitting in the chow hall, it felt like just yesterday that he had entered this training camp for the first time. He had been full of nervous energy as they had sheared his hair short, taken his measurements, and handed him his freshly carved identification tags. He had been full of optimism, knowing he had made the right choice by joining the Imperial Army. Sitting there almost four months later, unable to keep his food down, Darian felt like a fool. Who had he been kidding, thinking he was equal to this challenge? He was no soldier. He was a scared child of Verizia, nothing more. How could he have been so arrogant as to assume he was worthy of carrying on his family's proud military tradition?

His friends were not doing much better. None of them had said a word since taking their seats, each seemingly off in a world of their own. Berj Jenson was the only one eating, wolfing down his food with reckless abandon, as though he might never see another meal. Darnold Dans was drinking cup after cup of water, which Darian could not imagine was doing much to help calm him down. Max Preston was not even looking at his food. His eyes were constantly darting around the room, his skin paler than Darian had ever seen it, contrasting sharply with his bright red hair. Looking around the room, Darian saw similar scenes playing out at every table. Most eyes shot to the door every few seconds. Harter Arsch would be coming shortly to explain how the final evaluation would work, and everybody was on the edge of their seat waiting.

The drill sergeant kept them waiting, as they should have known he would. Darian suspected it was one final test of their patience and ability to stay calm under duress. Giving up on eating, he contented himself with merely trying to control his breathing. Every few seconds he would discover his hand or foot tapping rapidly and force it to stop for a few seconds. He could feel his heart thumping against the inside of his chest, and he wished something would come along to distract him.

When Harter Arsch finally arrived, nearly twenty minutes past the expected time, he was smiling from ear to ear, a sight that his trainees had never seen before.

He must genuinely relish this one last chance to make us all miserable, Darian thought.

"Listen up, recruits, because I won't be repeating myself. Congratulations are in order for all of you for making it to final evaluations. You have one final test before you. If you succeed, you may call yourself a soldier of the Imperial Army. If you fail now, you can still walk away with your head held high, knowing you served your Empire with honor and courage. I will now explain to you what exactly the final evaluations entail."

The entire chow hall was as silent as a crypt; you could have heard a pin fall to the ground. Each and every recruit stared at Harter Arsch intently, not wanting to miss a single word.

"You will be split into four groups of ten. The first group will begin immediately, and the following groups will take their evaluations in one-hour intervals after that. You will line up in front of this building. On my mark, you will run to the far eastern end of the encampment, and you will be timed. Once you reach the far eastern edge of the camp, you will find an obstacle course has been assembled. You will complete the course as quickly as possible and then continue, following the red flags we have planted to guide your path. If you fail any section of the course, you will return to the beginning and try again."

Not bad so far, Darian thought. A run and an obstacle course were reasonably straightforward, and hopefully the rest of the evaluation would be in the same mold. Knowing Harter Arsch, he dared not dream that would be the case. *You know he's going to have some sort of unpleasant surprise for you.*

"The red flags will lead you to an archery range. You will need to hit four targets successfully. Three are at a distance of fifty yards, and the fourth is at a distance of seventy-five. You will have seven arrows at your disposal. If you spend all of your arrows and have not successfully made all four shots, you must retrieve and try again. To be clear, if you do not hit all four targets in seven shots, you will have to repeat all shots, even if you hit three of them."

With each word spoken, Darian grew more optimistic. With seven tries, he was confident he could hit all four shots without issue. He just hoped all of his friends would be able to hit the targets on their first try. Berj and Preston struggled mightily with archery. They had spent several hours practicing the day before, but it had done little to bolster their confidence.

"Once you have successfully hit all four targets, you will continue to follow the red flags. You will find an enclosure outfitted with armor, as well as swords and shields. You will fully equip. Once more, you are being timed for efficiency. You are expected to wear all of this gear for the remainder of the evaluation. We have mages from the Order waiting to generate an opponent for you to fight. Their weapons will not hurt you but will leave a mark where they strike. Your armor will be inspected upon completion of the evaluation."

This made Darian slightly nervous. He was good with a sword, probably better than most of the recruits, but fighting in such a pressurized situation was nerve-racking. Knowing that Harter Arsch's eyes would be carefully checking for any signs of failure after the fact made it so much worse. He wished for a moment that he had some of Berj's aggression. His fellow recruit would likely make short work of the simulated warrior.

"Once you have defeated your opponent, you will continue to follow the red flags until you reach your final test. You will come to heavy sacks filled with sand. These are meant to simulate the weight of a wounded comrade. You will pick up one of the bags and carry it back to the starting point as quickly as possible. I remind you that you are expected to be fully armed and armored upon your arrival. If you return without even a single piece of your equipment, you will be sent back to retrieve it, and yes, you will be expected to carry the sandbag all the while."

So, that was it. All things considered, it was not as daunting as Darian had expected. He was sure the simulated warrior would put up a real fight. Running a long distance with a heavy weight while fully armored would undoubtedly be a challenge as well. But no task had been listed that he felt he was not capable of performing. Looking at his friends, he saw their expressions seemed more at ease as well, though Preston still seemed quite nervous.

"I will now read the first group assignments. If you are in the first group, step outside as soon as I read your name. If I do not read your name in this group, you must remain here in the chow hall until your time has come. You are welcome to have second helpings if you so wish."

Arsch unfolded a piece of parchment and began to read names.

Just as all four friends thought they were in the clear, the drill sergeant read the name of Darnold Dans as he reached the end of his list. Darnold's face turned from tan to ghostly pale in the blink of an eye. He rose wordlessly, seemingly unable to respond as his friends whispered words of encouragement. Darian shot him a grin as he walked away, hoping his own relief at not being chosen first wasn't too apparent.

Once Darnold and the others had gone, the waiting began again. Somewhat relieved after learning what the evaluation consisted of, Darian was finally able to slowly eat some of his breakfast. It was cold, but he hardly noticed. He found the simple process of chewing and swallowing to be oddly relaxing. It was a few minutes before several recruits at neighboring tables finally started to murmur. Seemingly buoyed, Berj finally broke the silence at their table.

"It's not so bad after all, is it? Even I should be able to hit the targets with seven tries. I'm sure you won't have any trouble with that one, Darian."

"At least you will make short work of the simulated enemy fighter. I'll be holding my breath while Arsch is inspecting my armor," Darian replied.

"You're telling me," Preston said. "He'll probably throw me out after one look at my armor, assuming I get that far. I might never make the long shot. I'll just be out there trying until the sun goes down, and they'll come tell me it's time to leave."

"You just need to control your breathing and keep calm while you shoot. You get in your own head," Darian said. "If you miss, don't dwell on it; just move on to the next shot."

"You're great with a sword, Preston; you just get too aggressive for your own good. You attack with rage, which is good, but it needs to be a controlled rage. You get into such a frenzied attack that you don't see the enemy attacks coming back at you. It's the same as Darian just said with archery: control your breathing, and keep yourself calm. Focus on the moment you are in," Berj said.

Their conversation helped all of them relax further, and it also helped to pass the time. An hour had passed in what had felt like minutes, and before they knew it, Harter Arsch had come for the next group. Max Preston was the first name on the list, and Berj Jenson was the last. Darian did his best to shoot each of them an encouraging smile as they left, though his nerves were increasing once more. Now he was alone with his thoughts. The simple act of making small talk with his friends had been comforting.

Darian sat in silence, as did most of the men in the chow hall now that half of their comrades were gone. He had hoped Darnold Dans would rejoin him after completing his evaluation, but none of the men who had left the hall with the first group returned. He hoped he would be in the next grouping. Waiting until the very end was an unappealing prospect. He wondered how Darnold had done and how Berj and Preston were doing at that very moment. He hoped both of them were able to keep calm under pressure, particularly on the archery range. He hoped the same for himself, but he could hardly bear the waiting.

When Harter Arsch returned with his third list of names an hour later, Darian was ready to spring to his feet in anticipation. Unfortunately, it was not to be, as once again, his name was not called. It would be well into the afternoon before he was called, meaning he would be running his evaluation during the hottest part of the day. *You should have known this would be the case.*

Around him, some of the remaining recruits had risen from their seats and were restlessly pacing the room, but he felt he might pass out if he did the same.

It was almost a surreal experience when Harter Arsch returned for the last time and Darian's name was finally called. He stepped out of the chow hall, his eyes squinting against the bright midday sun. He began to sweat almost immediately, though he was not entirely sure if it was from the heat or his own nervousness. Harter Arsch was moving down the line, making sure that they were all lined up evenly. Darian took several deep breaths to steady himself. When the start came, it came without preamble.

"Go!" Harter Arsch cried, sending the recruits scrambling away from the chow hall.

Darian assumed a rapid jog, even though several of the other recruits had begun at a dead sprint. The far end of the encampment was over a mile away, and he knew he would burn himself out by going too fast in this intense heat. Sure enough, a few minutes later, he passed several of the faster starters, who were struggling to maintain even a quick walk, drenched in sweat and already breathing heavily. In the distance, near the camp's perimeter fence, he could see several wooden objects and realized he was already drawing close to the obstacle course. He was making good time; he just had to complete the obstacles efficiently.

Darian was the second recruit to reach the course, which filled him with more confidence. The first obstacle was a series of elevated bars extended over a roughly dug pond. He leaped for the first bar, which was several feet over the water. He caught it with both hands and quickly went to work, swinging from one to the next with ease.

As he reached the last bar, he realized he would have to throw himself several feet to the far side of the pond. After swinging back and forth a few times to build momentum, he launched himself through the air, landing on the far side of the pond. He struck the ground hard, knocking the wind out of himself, but there was no time to delay.

The next obstacle was a high wall, roughly forty feet, and a single rope with which to climb it. Darian saw the recruit ahead of him near the top, struggling to pull himself up the last few feet. The young man was making a beginner's mistake, primarily using his arms to bear his entire weight. This would cause your arm muscles to burn out quickly, which would be a problem for him in the upcoming archery and combat tests. Darian took the rope in both hands and quickly made his way up the wall, using his legs to do most of the work and his hands to keep himself steady.

He reached the top of the wall in less than a minute and repelled down the other side in only a few seconds.

The third obstacle was netting hung so low that his only option was to crawl through the mud underneath. Never hesitating, Darian flung himself under the net, trying to propel himself as far as possible with his initial surge. Mud flooded his mouth as he dragged himself along, but he paid it no mind. Halfway through the obstacle, he passed by the recruit ahead of him and moved into the lead. As he drew toward the end, he was forced to close his eyes against the mud and pull himself forward on touch alone. At last, the ground beneath him began to feel firmer, and he brought up his hand to wipe away the mud that had caked in front of his eyes. Realizing he was free of the net, he climbed back to his feet.

The next obstacle was a short one: a massive log on a rope swinging back and forth across a narrow stream. He would have to jump the stream while avoiding the long. A senior officer saw him coming and gave the log a shove, causing it to swing more rapidly. Knowing if he failed this task he would have to start over with the hand bars, Darian paused for a moment, observing the log as it swung. When he thought he had its timing figured out, he sped forward. As soon as the officer saw him speed up, he gave the log another shove, throwing Darian's timing off completely. It was too late to slow down now. Darian charged on, leaping with all his might and bracing himself for the impact of the log. To his relief, it did not come, and he landed safely on the far side of the stream.

There was only one more obstacle to face on the course: a rope bridge. A far wider creek had been dug, and over it spanned a bridge made only of two ropes. Leaping up the wooden stairs to the bridge, Darian took one last deep breath, urging himself not to fail here. One rope hung slightly higher than the other, allowing him to use it as a handle of sorts as his feet traversed the other. He moved far more slowly than he had with the other obstacles, knowing how close he was to completing the course.

He did not know how close behind him the other recruits were, and he dared not break his focus long enough to look and see. Though the evaluations were not a race, he couldn't help but feel the overwhelming need to finish first.

Inch by inch, he made his way across the bridge. Twice he nearly lost his grip on the handhold, and once his feet were dangerously close to slipping, but he persevered. He reached the end and sped down the stairs.

It took him only a moment to spot the red flags marking the path to the next test. Darian set off at the same rapid jog as before. He limped slightly at first, his legs tired from straining on the rope bridge, but there would be time to rest later. The final evaluations were making more sense by the second. Each test on its own was no difficult feat, but combined, they were designed to push a man to the utmost limits of his endurance. Each obstacle was meant to make the next one more difficult. By the time he finished all of the tests, he would probably hardly be able to stand.

It was a longer distance than he had expected, but at last, he could see the archery range come into view. The four targets were visible in the distance as Darian stepped toward the firing line. There were ten bows and ten sets of arrows, each with different-colored feathers, just like those they used in their training. Selecting the green-feathered arrows, he stepped up to the line, examining the targets.

Three targets were stationed in a line at fifty yards out, each about ten feet from the next. Behind them, at seventy-five yards, was one last target. A small breeze was blowing from the west, a wind that would be unnoticeable to anybody who was not about to attempt four difficult shots with a bow. Nocking his first arrow, Darian brought up the bow and sighted for the center target at fifty yards. Not wanting to overthink the shot, he let the arrow fly, watching it carefully in its flight. The breeze moved it slightly to the left, but not enough to miss the target, and it found its mark, sinking in and bringing a smile to Darian's face.

Knowing now that the breeze would not significantly impact the fifty-yard shots, Darian quickly nocked his second arrow. Aiming at the target on the left, he let fly once more, and again, his shot found its mark. His confidence growing by the second, he nocked the third arrow and let fly for the target on the right. To his dismay, the slight breeze picked up just enough to drive his arrow off course, and it landed mere inches to the left of his target. Cursing and reminding himself that he had only four arrows left, he sighted again. This time his shot was true, and there was only one more target to hit.

Glancing behind him for the first time, he saw several other recruits running along the red flags, only a minute or so from reaching the range. He had a good lead, and now was not the time to blow it. This may not have been a race, but his pride wanted more than anything to finish first.

Nocking what he hoped would be his last arrow, he took aim for the farthest target. The breeze was now gusting unpredictably, complicating matters. Darian decided at that moment to aim his shot slightly to the right of his intended target and let it fly. Just as he had suspected, the wind gusted once more while the arrow was in flight, driving it just far enough to the left to sink into the edge of the distant target.

Dropping the bow and remaining arrows, Darian tore out of the archery range just as two other recruits were entering it. *I might actually be the first to finish*, he thought, scarcely believing it could be true.

He followed the red flags once more, trying to keep from overexerting himself in his excitement. There was still a fight ahead, and another long run while fully armored and carrying a heavy weight. He needed to leave himself the strength for those challenges, and he must not get too far ahead of himself. Being in the lead at this point was irrelevant, but putting himself in a position to finish first could be a big deal.

It did not take as long as he had anticipated to reach the combat paddock. Lined up against the fence were ten sets of full Imperial armor, along with swords and shields. Darian wasted no time getting outfitted. He had practiced armoring himself many times, and that practice paid off, as he was able to be ready within a minute. Picking up a sword and shield and bracing himself for the fight of his life, he stepped into the paddock.

The mages were not in the paddock. To his knowledge, none of the recruits had even seen one of them in the flesh over the past four months. They took great care to keep themselves hidden for reasons that were a mystery to the young army recruits. Still, they must've been keeping a close eye on the paddock, because as soon as Darian entered, his opponent appeared from thin air in front of him.

His foe took the form of a man slightly larger than him. The fighter was wearing a steel breastplate and leg plates, though there were several weak points near the man's gut, under his arms, and around his neck. He carried a pair of swords, eliciting a small groan from Darian. Opponents who could effectively wield two weapons at once were exceptionally rare but exceedingly challenging to fight. Of course, Arsch would have wanted to test them against such a foe. Darian tightened his grip on his sword, scrutinizing his simulated opponent. Now more than ever, it was essential to take a measured approach. Harter Arsch would be inspecting his armor for even the slightest hint that he had been struck, and he wanted to be spotless.

The simulated fighter was not moving, seemingly content to allow Darian to make the first move. He advanced on it slowly, cautiously, knowing that its tactics could shift in the blink of an eye. His caution paid off; he had just drawn within ten paces when it sprung into action without warning, leaping forward and slashing at him with one of its swords. Darian planted his feet and brought up his shield, blocking the attack effectively. To his surprise, the fighter did not attack again right away, instead backing off and beginning to circle him like a predator stalking its prey.

Darian held his position, his shield raised in a defensive position, slowly turning to match his opponent's circling. After a minute, he concluded that the simulation wanted him to mount an attack of his own. He stepped forward, feinting high, as though he meant to swing for the fighter's neck. As soon as the swords snapped up to deflect his attack, he reversed course, thrusting instead toward the simulation's exposed gut. It sprung backward, avoiding his attack and swinging one of its swords toward him in a downward strike. Darian brought up his shield, deflecting the attack once again, and then scrambled back, putting distance between them.

Darian tried to attack his foe twice more, taking a careful, measured approach each time, not wanting to leave himself vulnerable. Both times, the fighter avoided his attacks with ease.

This is pointless, he thought. *This isn't what a real battle is like at all. A real battle is chaos, frenzied fighting in all directions, not a one-on-one duel.* No sooner had the thought passed through his head than he realized he had found the answer to Harter Arsch's riddle.

The simulation was meant as a test not only of his physical skills but of his mental preparedness to face the chaos of battle. He could continue with this cautious approach for days and never land a blow to the enemy fighter. Arsch wanted them to show a willingness to take part in the type of fight they would undoubtedly encounter if sent to the front lines of a war zone. He needed to fight like Berj or Preston would, wading into a chaotic maelstrom with no regard for his own well-being.

I might as well get on with it, Darian thought. Taking one last deep breath, he launched himself at his foe, shield raised high in front of him. He swung his sword with all of his might, but the simulated warrior caught the blow with one of its own swords. It launched a counterattack, but Darian had already moved his shield into position to deflect it. This time, instead of just deflecting the attack and retreating to a safe distance, he continued moving forward, driving the shield into his opponent's body and knocking it backward.

Darian attacked again just as the enemy fighter was regaining its balance. It managed to deflect the attack, but the force of Darian's swing tore the sword from its grip, leaving it with a single weapon. Darian did not let up his attack, slashing out at his opponent over and over. It parried a few strikes and avoided a few more, but he now had it in a steady backward retreat, suppressing its ability to counter. At last, he found his mark, his sword slipping underneath the fighter's guard and sliding deep into its gut. The simulation vanished instantly as soon as the blow had landed, and he knew he had passed the test. *As long as they don't find any marks on your armor,* he reminded himself.

For the first time since the test had begun, Darian took a look around the paddock. There were three other recruits there now, each still battling a simulated warrior with varying degrees of success. He did not know if any others had already come and gone, but he was still ahead of at least three. Sheathing his sword and attaching his shield to the back of his armor, he tore out of the enclosure. He was so close to the end now that he could feel it.

The red flags led him only a short distance to a spot where a large collection of heavy sacks was waiting. Wrapping his arms around one, he hoisted it up onto his shoulders. He had known it would be heavy, but its weight still caught him somewhat off guard. The sand that stuffed the sack shifted continuously, making the task of carrying it all the more challenging. He had to get back to the chow hall, which was at least half a mile away. He set off at a slow jog, the quickest pace he felt he would be able to maintain with such a heavy weight on his shoulders.

The minutes passed slowly for Darian as he trudged along in his armor with the heavy sack on his back, the heat of the midday sun beating down on him. If there was an inch of his body that was not coated in sweat and grime, he didn't know what it was. Every one of his limbs ached from the strain of carrying the weight, but he forced the pain to the back of his mind. He pressed on, focusing solely on the act of putting one foot in front of the other.

As the chow hall finally came into view, Darian felt his stomach soar. Four months of intense physical, mental, and emotional training were finally coming to an end. The days of dealing with the volatile Harter Arsch were about to be behind him. So many emotions ran through his mind as he finally came to a halt in front of the chow hall, dropping his sack of sand at the drill instructor's feet.

"Welcome back, Private Tor. How do you think you performed in your final evaluation?" Arsch asked, his expression unreadable.

"Thank you, Sergeant Arsch, sir. I completed every assigned task fully and to the best of my ability," Darian responded, trying his utmost to give the impression that he was not breathing heavily and utterly failing.

"Very well, Private Tor. You are the first member of your group to complete the evaluation. An impressive feat, assuming, of course, that you have passed. Lay your sword and shield on the ground and step to the right for inspection."

Darian did as he was asked, unstrapping his sword and shield and laying them on the ground alongside his sack. He took a few steps to the right to find a mage waiting for him. It was the first time he had seen one in person. The man was dressed from head to toe in robes of bright blue, and he carried a long staff made of what appeared to be oak.

"Raise your arms to shoulder height, out to your sides," the mage said, not bothering with pleasantries.

Darian did as he was asked, and the mage began to examine him. A faint light emanated from the tip of the mage's staff, and the man held it out as he examined Darian's armor, shining the light on every inch of him. Darian held his breath, reflecting on his battle with the simulated warrior. He did not think that he had been struck at all, but he was replaying the entire fight in his head, trying to remember even the slightest mistake. The examination lasted only a minute, though for Darian, it might as well have been several weeks.

"No signs of damage," the mage abruptly announced, the light fading from his staff.

"Very well, Private Tor. Congratulations are in order. You have passed your final evaluation, and you may now officially call yourself a soldier of the Imperial Army. You may return to the barracks while the rest of the recruits finish their evaluations. There are tubs of warmed water you can use to clean yourself up. There will be a feast tonight in the chow hall to honor those who have passed the evaluation. You will receive your next assignment tomorrow. Dismissed, Private Tor," Harter Arsch said, turning away to greet the next approaching recruit.

"Yes, sir. Thank you, sir," Darian said. He managed to keep his smile under wraps until the drill sergeant could no longer see his face. Restraining the urge the skip, he made his way back toward the barracks, feeling as though the weight of the world had been lifted from his shoulders.

Chapter Six

Darian had barely set foot inside the barracks when Berj, Darnold, and Preston were gathered around him. It was a relief to see all of them; he assumed any man who had not passed the evaluations would have been sent elsewhere. The four immediately headed for a quiet corner of the building to discuss their evaluations.

"You're the first one back from your group. I figured you would be," Berj said, clapping him on the back. "You're really well-rounded."

"You all passed, though?" Darian asked, wanting to make his assumptions official.

"We sure did. It only took Preston and me two tries at the archery range, so it wasn't as bad as it could have been. Darnold here hit all of his targets on the first try, of course."

"Yeah, but it took me a long time to figure out that simulated fighter. You must have done pretty well against it to have made it back so fast, Darian. It sounds like that's the test that gave most of the recruits a lot of trouble. Everybody sat back and fought it cautiously, not wanting to get hit," Darnold said. "Should've seen that coming. I was kicking myself the whole way back with that stupid sack of sand on my back."

"I started the same way, but it just didn't feel right to me. The more

I thought about it, the more it made sense. We're infantry soldiers, and it's not like our typical battle is going to play out like that," Darian said. "I guess something from one of Arsch's countless rants came to me at the right moment."

"You're right, and I still can't believe I didn't figure it out sooner. I could have been the first of my group to get back, but two others passed me during that test. Brilliant move on Arsch's part, though. Putting emphasis on the fact that we would be evaluated was meant to make us fight afraid, I'm sure of it," Darnold said.

Darian took a seat on the ground and allowed himself to truly absorb the moment for the first time. He had passed his final evaluations, and he was officially an Imperial Army soldier. He had not failed to live up to the legacies of his father and grandfather. There would be no return to Verizia with his head hung in shame. He had spent so much of the past few months living in constant fear of failure. It was surreal to think those days were finally over. No matter what happened from this day forward, he could call himself an Imperial soldier, and nobody could ever take that away from him.

"How many men didn't pass from the first three groups?" Darian asked, a sense of guilt at his own jubilation suddenly washing over him.

"There has been no official word, but two men haven't come back—that we know of. We assumed Arsch sent them someplace else so they wouldn't have to tell everybody what happened," Preston said. "He may be an ass, but at least he isn't that nasty; I'll give him that."

Darian could not imagine having come so far only to fail at the final evaluation. The thought of having endured four months of brutal training under the vindictive Harter Arsch for nothing was horrific. Only a few hours ago, he had feared that exact thing. The fact that it was a reality for at least two men gave him a greater appreciation for what he had accomplished. The idea of walking into his family home in failure had been a recurring nightmare for him for months.

"So, what do you all think comes next?" Preston asked.

"I'd bet my left hand most of us are going to be sent to Qwitzite. All the talk of a dwarven surrender aside, they'll want as many men there as possible," Berj replied. "The more men they have on hand to keep the peace, the better. Truce or not, I'm willing to bet there will be a lengthy occupation. The Empire won't forget a secession attempt anytime soon."

That reminded Darian once again that he had still not heard from Axel. His friend had written to him at least every two weeks since he had arrived at the training camp, but it had now been over a month since the last letter.

Excusing himself from his friends, he made his way to his bunk and riffled through his possessions, searching for Axel's last letter. He unfolded it, hoping he would spot a previously overlooked clue that would explain the lack of correspondence.

Darian,

I hope all is going well with your training. Sorry to hear that Arsch is being a pain in the neck, but it's not that surprising. He was the same way with my group, and probably with every other one he teaches. He gets the job done, though, there's no doubt about it. He isn't there to coddle you, he's there to shape you into an Imperial soldier, and he's the best the army has at doing just that. It doesn't earn him any love from the recruits, but I guarantee you senior command loves him. It's good to hear you're making friends there; it makes training a heck of a lot easier to face.

I'm still at the front in Qwitzite. You have to give the dwarves credit where it's due; they are ferocious warriors. I've never seen anything like it. I've heard the same rumors you mentioned in your last letter, that they are on the verge of surrender. To be honest, I don't see it happening, but let's hope I'm wrong about that. Their capital city of Muog is the most impenetrable fortress I've ever seen, and I don't know why they would quit now. We lost one of our sergeants a few days ago, and there have been rumblings that I'm going to be promoted to replace him. It doesn't seem like the type of move that Imperial High Command would make if we were going to be leaving shortly.

The fighting here is intense, mostly guerilla-style attacks by the dwarves against our forces. I know a lot of men want to get a taste of battle; they all change their minds once they see it firsthand. I hope for your sake that you end up in a boring guard duty in one of the peaceful provinces. The dwarves' guerilla tactics aren't something most men are prepared to deal with. But if you do get sent here, it will be good to see you again. What's it been, almost two years now? Time has a way of slipping away for a soldier, but you'll learn that for yourself soon enough. It's so strange to think I've been away from home that long. I still have two years left on my commitment, and they are already in my ear about recommitting for another four.

That's all I've got to say for now, Darian. Good luck with your training, and don't let Arsch get you down too much. It's really for your own good, I promise. I'll write again in a couple of weeks.

~Axel

Darian read the letter word by word and then reread it several more times. Axel had even made a point to say he would write again soon, but that letter had never come. Darian had responded to this letter. Had Axel received that? He had no way of knowing. Axel had mentioned that the fighting on the front was still intense and that he did not believe the rumors of a dwarven surrender. Had he been killed in the fighting? No, that wasn't possible. Axel was the toughest person Darian had ever met. He was sure his friend was fine; the fighting probably just made it difficult to get letters out of Qwitzite. It was far more likely the message had just been lost along the way. At least that was what he told himself as he folded the letter and tucked it away again.

***

When they arrived in the chow hall that night, they found the most extensive array of food they had enjoyed since arriving in the encampment.

The tables were laden with plates of chicken, pork, and fish, as well as fruits, vegetables, and breads of every kind. To their surprise, they even found flagons of ale waiting for them, a treat they had not had in four months. Darian and his friends took their usual table and loaded their plates enthusiastically.

"I didn't realize how hungry I was until I walked in and saw all of this food. I don't think I had a single bite at breakfast," Preston said through a mouthful of chicken.

"Wherever they send us, I doubt we'll ever eat this well again," Berj said after downing a cup of ale in a single gulp.

"My friends, I just want to say one thing," Darnold cut in, raising a glass of ale. "I don't know where we are going to end up after this. I hope we all end up together, wherever that is. But I will say that I am grateful to have suffered through this training alongside the three of you. If we are separated and never see one another again, I'm grateful to all of you for your friendship. I want you all to know it."

The four of them touched their cups and drank. It was a sentiment Darian shared. He did not know how he would have survived training without having three friends like these. The idea of making his way through the gauntlet of Imperial Army training on his own was unthinkable.

"Well said, Darnold. I think we all feel the same way. You've all become like brothers to me these past four months. Even you, Preston," Berj said, giving Preston a shove.

It was the best night they had ever shared. For those few hours, the looming specter of possibly being sent to war and the trials they had been through seemed to vanish. The future did not matter to them at that moment; all that mattered was enjoying what could've been their last few hours together. They ate and drank well into the night, only stumbling back to their bunks when their bodies could hold no more. As Darian lay in his bunk, waiting for sleep to overcome him, he had the feeling that he may have just lived the best night of his life.

***

Morning came sooner than Darian would have thought possible. He was shaken from the deepest slumber he had enjoyed in months by the jarring sound of Harter Arsch moving through the barracks, banging two steel shields together. *We really should have known he wouldn't pass up one last chance to do this to us.* His eyes forcefully resisted his attempts to open them, refusing to do so until Arsch started yelling as well.

"On your feet, privates! Don't tell me your feast sapped you of all your strength. It would be a darned shame if I had to run you back and forth across the camp to work off the meal from last night. Wake up, wake up. An Imperial soldier is always on duty, and you are now Imperial soldiers. Move it, move it, move it! Don't think I won't discipline you on your first full day as an Imperial soldier. How did you sorry sacks of dung pass the evaluation? Maybe we should run them again just to make sure there wasn't a mistake."

Darian's legs groaned in protest as soon as his feet hit the cold floor, but he forced himself to stand nonetheless. He was among the first to find his feet. Many of his fellows were holding their pillows to their ears, trying to drown out the sound of Harter Arsch. One by one, they slowly came to, murmuring in protest all the while. A few stragglers were compelled from their bunks by forceful kicks from Harter Arsch. Once they were all finally on their feet, Harter Arsch walked straight down the line between them, a broad smile on his face.

"I'm sure you didn't think that your feast last night relieved you of your obligations to the Imperial Army," he said.

"Sir, no, sir!" the newly minted privates replied as one.

"That is a relief, because there is work to be done, gentlemen. This camp needs to be cleaned and brought up to order so it is ready for the next bunch of recruits who come through. I do hope they prove themselves more competent than the lot of you. Who better to complete such a task than the Imperial Army's newest privates? Breakfast is waiting in the chow hall. I will assign you your chores once you have eaten. Do take care not to dawdle, gentlemen. You will be receiving your next assignments this afternoon, and if I see any man slacking in his duties, it may just change my mind about where he should go next. I hear there are caravans of cow dung that need to be guarded on their journeys between provinces. Crops aren't going to feed themselves. Sounds like a fun assignment. Now move!"

The young men hurried to dress and get to the chow hall. They weren't eager to work on cleaning the training encampment, but no one wanted to receive an undesirable assignment either. The breakfast that was waiting for them was quite underwhelming compared to their feast the previous night, but Darian still devoured everything in sight. His body still ached from the strain of his final evaluation the day before, but he knew he would find no sympathy from Harter Arsch.

When he had finished eating, Darian approached Harter Arsch outside the chow hall and was assigned to collect arrows that had gone astray on the archery range. In all, it was not that bad of an assignment; Max Preston had been charged with filling in the old latrines, and Berj Jenson drew the honor of helping to dig new ones.

Darian stalked the archery range slowly, taking great care not to miss a single arrow. His time with Harter Arsch was drawing to a close, and he would rather not infuriate the volatile man now. Before long, he had collected several dozen arrows, shots gone awry that recruits had been too lazy to chase down.

Darian returned to the chow hall at midday for lunch, finding the room overcome with a buzz of nervous energy. They would receive their assignments after lunch, and everyone was eager to get on with it. Darian and his friends wolfed down their food, hardly tasting it on the way down. Once they had finished eating, they sat nervously, waiting for the drill sergeant to call them outside to receive their assignment.

"He's going to keep us waiting awhile. It's his last chance to make us suffer, and he knows it," Berj said. "He's probably sad to see us go."

"I don't know about that. I'm sure he'll be delighted to have fresh recruits to torment soon enough," Darian said. "He probably gets bored with each group after a while. He can finally start reusing some of his better insults on the poor saps."

There was a bit more idle talk, but nobody was able to keep a conversation going. They were all ready to receive their assignments and be done with it. The mystery of where they were going next was eating away at every single soldier in the hall.

When Harter Arsch finally entered the room, every head spun to look at him as if they were on a swivel. Reveling in the moment, Arsch walked to the nearest table, where he poured himself a cup of water and drank it slowly. After gently setting it back down on the table, he slowly walked back toward the hall entrance.

"Well, gentlemen, the time has come. Your training is complete, and I have assigned each of you to your next duty in your service to the Imperial Army. It's a monumental moment indeed. Step outside and line up, gentlemen, to receive your assignments," he said at last.

The privates filed out of the chow hall, their ranks buzzing with nervous energy. As Darian emerged from the building, he saw there were four Imperial captains lined up behind Harter Arsch.

These must be our new commanding officers, he thought, examining each man's face, trying to get a measure of them.

"All right, everybody, listen up and listen well, because I won't repeat myself, as you should all be aware of by now. One of these four men standing behind me is your next commanding officer. I wish them the best of luck. I have four lists; I will read the assignment, the captain's name, and then the names of the men who are meant to report to him. Your new commanding officer will then take you aside and give you your next orders. Once your name is read, you are no longer my problem. I wish these captains all the best in the task of keeping you alive without allowing you to get them killed. Am I clear?"

"Sir, yes, sir!" the privates said as one.

"Good. First, we have Captain Gustav Balke. The men reporting to him will be stationed in a fortress on the border of Thornata and Verizia. I hope you brought your mittens; it can get quite nippy up there in the winter. Reporting to Captain Balke are Privates Tomson, Dastillo, Jugson, and Polson."

The first four privates stepped out of line and over to Captain Balke. Their captain motioned for them to follow him away from the chow hall, leaving their comrades eagerly awaiting their assignment.

Though it would have been nice to be stationed so close to home, Darian was grateful not to be stuck in a border security assignment; they were known to be notoriously dull.

"Next, we have Captain Rohin Vestra. The men reporting to him will be chasing down crop thieves in Kardia. They've been stealing food meant for our troops across the Empire, so do try to do an adequate job, gentlemen. Our stomachs will thank you. Reporting to Captain Vestra are Privates McCroy, Donaldson, and Ians. Good luck, gentlemen. Give those thieves hell for us."

Three more men left the line and followed Captain Vestra away.

That wouldn't have been such a bad assignment. At least I would be making a difference, Darian thought. The anticipation was beginning to eat away at him. He wished Arsch would hurry up and get on with it, but if anything, the drill sergeant seemed to be relishing making them wait.

"Next, we have Captain Gerald Saffron. The men reporting to him will be joining the reserve force stationed in Valdovas. You are the Emperor's strike force, always on call in the event of a sudden threat to Imperial interests. Reporting to Captain Saffron are Privates Carlson, Stahl, Brown, Grundee, Brunson, and Jacobs. Make us proud, gentlemen."

The six men named filed off to join Captain Saffron, leaving two dozen men standing in line and one last captain waiting behind Harter Arsch. Darian's heart was racing; there was only one assignment that would require so many men. He didn't dare glance to the side—he had no wish to incur the wrath of Harter Arsch one last time—but he could feel Preston tensed up beside him.

"As I am sure you can guess, gentlemen, the rest of you have been placed together. This is Captain Thaddeus Dunstan, and he will be your commanding officer. I'm sure you have figured out that you are being sent to bolster our forces in Qwitzite. I selected you for this assignment because I felt you were the best men we have here to fulfill it. It won't be a pleasant time, but you all have what it takes to survive it. I wish you all nothing but the best. Go serve the Empire with honor and courage."

Darian could hardly register that training was actually done. He fell into line with the remaining privates, following Captain Thaddeus Dunstan as he beckoned them away from the chow hall.

The captain was older than most of the officers Darian had encountered since joining the Imperial Army. His face was covered with faded battle scars, and his head was wholly overcome by gray hair; only a few small flecks of his younger color remained. Dunstan did not say a word as he led them to a quiet area near the perimeter fence. Darian looked to his friends; they all appeared nervous but excited.

"Congratulations on passing your final evaluations, soldiers. The Imperial Army is made stronger by your presence. As Sergeant Arsch told you, my name is Captain Thaddeus Dunstan, and I am now your commanding officer. I have served in the Imperial Army for decades, and I have fought in conflicts in six provinces in that time. Qwitzite will be the seventh. I hope to see the end of this conflict with all of you by my side, alive and well. We will depart this camp tomorrow at dawn. You may return to your bunks for tonight. Be warned: we have a long, hard march ahead of us. The navy had no ships to spare for the likes of us. We will be moving at an intense pace. We are badly needed in Qwitzite. Please report to the main gates just before dawn. You are expected to be fully outfitted and have all of your belongings in hand. We will be escorting a wagon train of supplies to the front on our way. I look forward to serving with all of you. Enjoy your last night in this camp; it will be a long time before you have a comfortable bunk to sleep in again. Dismissed."

The two dozen soldiers broke apart into smaller groups. Darian and his friends slowly made their way back toward the barracks. He walked in silence, still processing everything Harter Arsch and Captain Dunstan had said. The reality that they were about to leave for an active war zone was truly sinking in. It was a prospect that many of them had looked forward to during their training. Now the truth of what that meant was swimming through his mind, and likely those of his friends as well.

"Well, we got our wish. We're all together," Darnold Dans said, breaking the silence.

"I won't lie, the idea of going to the front lines scares the living hell out of me," Max Preston said. "But if that's what it has to be, I'm glad it's with the three of you. Better to stay together, no matter where we go."

"We'll be able to watch one another's backs, at least," Berj said. "And we're in good company. You all know I will watch out for you, and I know that each of you will do the same for me. I still wish they could have gotten us on a ship, though. Marching there will take weeks. And it's been so blazing hot lately. A nice welcome to the Imperial Army, I suppose."

"It's true. I do like my chances of survival a lot more having the three of you around. Except maybe you, Preston. Please don't get me killed," Darian said, giving Preston a playful shove and drawing a laugh from all of them.

Darian spent the afternoon packing his few belongings into his rucksack and checking his weapons and armor for damage. The rest of the day was spent leisurely talking with his friends. They didn't want to overly exert themselves. Their bodies were still recovering from the intensity of final evaluations, and Qwitzite was a long march away.

Darian wondered if he would see Axel when they arrived at the front lines. His worry for his childhood friend had been temporarily forgotten in his anxiety, but now it was at the forefront of his mind once more.

When I get there, I will find him. I know I will, he thought, not wanting to share his concerns with the others.

As he lay in his bunk that evening, Darian struggled to sleep. He knew he needed to, that it was his last chance to sleep in a bunk for the foreseeable future, but so many thoughts were racing through his head. Worries about war, Axel, his friends, and how he would respond to the challenges ahead of him danced through his mind one by one.

When he finally drifted off to sleep, the dreams that greeted him were no better.

Chapter Seven

General Alexander Sylvester made his way through the Imperial Army camp, paying no mind to the stares following him with every step he took. Word of his mission would have leaked by now; it was inevitable in a camp like this one. While deemed highly classified, there were far too many senior officers with loose lips for such a thing to stay quiet for long. Many of these men were likely wondering if they would ever see their general alive again. Such a lack of confidence was why most of them could never aspire to be more than the infantry grunts they were. Alexander Sylvester had never found himself overly concerned about anything. Every situation could be turned to your advantage if only you were intelligent enough to see how. Challenges were nothing more than puzzles just waiting for him to solve them. The more complex they were, the more satisfying their resolution.

Captain Terrence Garrison followed close behind, always his most faithful officer. Garrison had provided Sylvester with close to twenty years of loyal, reliable service, and Sylvester had rewarded him richly for it. A man with a mind as simple as Garrison's could never have aspired to reach the rank of captain under any other commanding officer. Unlike the vast majority of his peers, Alexander Sylvester saw the value in all men, even those who appeared to lack it on the surface. Servants of Garrison's loyalty were hard to come by, regardless of his other shortcomings. If anything, those shortcomings made him even more valuable. Sylvester didn't need subordinates who were prolific thinkers; he was more than capable of handling those responsibilities himself.

"Sir, are you sure you don't want me to arrange a protection detail to accompany us?" Garrison asked as they walked. It was at least the third time he had posed the question, much to Sylvester's irritation, but he took it in stride.

"I see no point, Captain Garrison. The dwarves will insist we hand over our weapons immediately upon arrival anyway. If these negotiations go badly, we would just be leading more men to their demise unnecessarily. Besides, with just the two of us, it will be more convincing that we are truly seeking a peaceful agreement. The Imperial Army would never send only two officers if they had ill intent. The lack of a security detail will aid us in earning their trust. Do not concern yourself too deeply, Captain Garrison. I foresee these negotiations going very well for us."

"Yes, sir, as you wish. When do you wish to depart?"

"We will leave camp just after dawn. I dare not approach their walls in the black of night. They might mistake our intentions and feather us with arrows before we can say a word. Will you please make the necessary preparations? We will require no provisions, as we will return to camp within hours, but we will need a white flag to convey our message of peace to their sentries," General Sylvester said, understanding such a task would make a man like Terrence Garrison feel important.

"Yes, sir, General Sylvester. I will have everything ready before dawn. Shall I bring you breakfast as well?"

"That would be much appreciated, Captain Garrison, and bring some for yourself too. We have a big day ahead of us tomorrow, and we will need our strength. Sleep well."

Captain Garrison saluted and hurried off to work on his assignments, leaving General Sylvester to duck into his tent alone. It was the first moment of peace and quiet he had gotten all day, and he intended to enjoy it. He had spent the day in a war council, an endeavor which seemed to become increasingly fruitless by the day. They were not winning the war against the dwarves, no matter how often his peers attempted to otherwise bloviate to one another. At best, they had forced a stalemate, which could go on for years, only for the Imperials to lose in the end. Not that he would allow that to happen, of course. The time had come for him to bring matters under control.

He was the second-highest-ranking soldier stationed at the front in Qwitzite, behind only Imperial Supreme General Cadmus Twilcox, who commanded all Imperial forces across the Empire. Twilcox was a fool, a fossil of a bygone era, and he was quickly dragging the Imperial Army down into obscurity with him. The man was fast approaching his seventieth year, yet still he refused to yield his command to new blood. His tactics were archaic, and his mind was withering away more with each passing day. Sylvester could not allow such a travesty to continue. He had devoted the entirety of his adult life to the Imperial Army, and he would not see its reputation tarnished.

He had been surprised at the lack of strenuous objection to his suggestion in the war council that afternoon. He supposed even a man as foolish as Cadmus Twilcox must realize this siege was getting them nowhere. Of course, only a man as foolish as Cadmus Twilcox would consent to his second-in-command going into the enemy fortress to treat with them directly. Often, the foolishness of others could be turned to your advantage, as Sylvester had learned over the past twenty years.

He and Captain Garrison would approach the gates of the dwarven capital city of Muog shortly after dawn. The Imperial Army had been entrenched outside of the city's walls for months, never coming any closer to ending this conflict. The dwarves were demanding the right to secede from the Empire, something the Emperor could not allow to happen.

Qwitzite was perhaps the most prosperous of the Empire's provinces, and the taxes the dwarves paid were sorely needed to keep things running smoothly. When the dwarves had moved to expel all Imperial forces from the province almost a year earlier, the Emperor had been forced to act.

Nobody had expected the conflict to last this long—nobody except Alexander Sylvester. The common assumption had been that the dwarves would simply negotiate a slightly lower tax rate and things would go back to normal. This assumption had proven to be false. The dwarven chieftain, a man named Odpor, was particularly stubborn. He had served the Empire, essentially as the duke of Qwitzite, for ten years before suddenly feeling the need to seize more power for himself. Thought had been given to merely assassinating him when he began having his delusions of grandeur, but the Emperor had quickly put a stop to those plans. He feared killing Odpor in such a way could militarize his followers against the Empire even further, a belief which was most likely correct.

So, the Imperial Army had been dispatched to Muog with instructions to form a blockade and force the dwarves to concede to remaining under Imperial rule. Thus far, it had not gone according to plan. The dwarves had proven to be quite skilled in the art of guerilla warfare, and they had struck back against the Imperials at every opportunity. It did not help that Muog was perhaps the most formidable fortress in the Empire outside of the Imperial capital city of Ionad. The dwarves were certainly industrious, and it showed in the construction of their cities.

Muog was surrounded by two granite walls, each rising over two hundred feet in height. Within the walls was a moat, crossable only by a series of bridges. Any of the bridges could be raised in seconds by the dwarves on the inside. There were rumors of additional defenses, but even Imperial records were uncertain of everything the dwarves had added to their capital city. The army had made no legitimate attempt to seize control of the city, understanding they were unlikely to succeed without catastrophic casualties. But the siege was not working, and they were losing men to the guerilla tactics of the dwarves at an alarming rate every week, so General Alexander Sylvester had suggested a new strategy, and to his surprise, his fellow commanders had possessed the wisdom to agree.

When he had asked to be sent to negotiate in person with Odpor, he had doubted Cadmus Twilcox would agree so quickly. Perhaps the old man was tired of the war effort already and was desperate to see an end to it. Maybe he thought the dwarves would simply kill Sylvester and remove an irritating thorn from his side. Whatever the reasoning, he had played right into Sylvester's hands. If everything went according to plan, Cadmus Twilcox would not be the Supreme General of the Imperial Forces for much longer.

***

Morning came quickly, and with it came Captain Garrison, bringing the promised breakfast along with him. General Sylvester had not needed to walk to the chow hall the entire time he had been in Qwitzite. Captain Garrison was always happy to make sure he was served in his tent, away from the common foot soldiers. Sylvester had never been one who sought to mix with the common people, and the bulk of the army was made up of commoners and peasants. There was little to be gained by wasting valuable time fraternizing with such people.

He invited Captain Garrison to take a seat at his table and join him for the morning meal. *Some of the commoners have value,* he reminded himself.

"Thank you for bringing this, Captain Garrison. I assume all relevant preparations have been made for our negotiations with the dwarves?"

"Yes, sir. I have the white flag, and I took the liberty of obtaining a rather fine pendant for you to gift to the chieftain. I am told that their people place a high value on such gestures," Captain Garrison replied.

"You have done well, Captain Garrison, as always. You have been a valued friend and advisor to me for many years, and I truly appreciate all you have done for me. I could not ask for a finer man to accompany me today. We are facing a dangerous undertaking, no doubt. But fear not, old friend. I have a feeling these negotiations will prove to be a turning point in this war. Any man who goes home alive at the end of this war will owe you a debt of gratitude."

"It has been the honor of my life to serve at your side, General Sylvester," Garrison said, his face turning red at the compliment.

Sylvester had always been careful not to heap too much praise on the man, but he had a knack for determining when such crumbs would prove most effective. There were aspects of these negotiations that were sure to make Garrison uncomfortable. It was best to make sure he knew how valuable and appreciated he was now.

They finished eating, and Captain Garrison helped Sylvester outfit himself in his armor. The pair of them carried no weapons other than a single sword on their belt. There was no point in bringing more. The dwarves would confiscate any weapon they carried as soon as they entered Muog.

Assuming we live long enough to get inside Muog, Sylvester thought darkly. He was confident in himself and his plan, as always, but only a fool would be utterly blind to the risks he was about to face. The dwarves were unpredictable, and they might very well see him as more valuable to them dead than alive. They could also take him prisoner to use as a bargaining chip. He had weighed all of these risks repeatedly in his mind. In the end, he had decided the risk was worth the potential reward. He had faith in his abilities as a negotiator, and he had to believe they would see him through this day.

"Captain Garrison, I believe we have waited long enough. Shall we get underway?" Sylvester asked, his voice giving off a soothing confidence.

Garrison scrambled to his feet, rushing to hold the tent flap open.

Upon stepping outside, Sylvester saw the white flag Garrison had procured for them lying on the ground a few feet away. Garrison hurried to retrieve it, then took his place a few steps ahead of the general. Sylvester was perfectly content to allow his man to take the lead. If the dwarves did elect to open fire on their approach, they would likely strike Garrison first and give Sylvester an opportunity to escape.

They made their way through the vast Imperial encampment, paying no mind to the stares and whispers that followed them. If the entire camp had not already known about this mission the night before, they did now. Under Twilcox's spineless leadership, gossip was permitted to spread through the encampment like wildfire.

Some of the men were undoubtedly hoping that it would go poorly, for Alexander Sylvester was not a particularly popular figure among his men. His reputation was one of arrogance, and he had always known it. It mattered not to him. He had not joined the army seeking love; he had joined seeking power and influence. His success in this mission would give him more than he had ever wielded before.

They cleared the camp within minutes and immediately slowed their pace as they made their way into the barren neutral territory that led to the gates of Muog. The Imperial Army had purposefully made their camp well away from the walls of Muog, not wanting to leave themselves open to archer attacks from above. They moved far more slowly now, not wanting to take any chance of the dwarves mistaking their intent. Garrison held the white flag high, and even the intensely confident General Sylvester caught himself tensing up more with each step. Twice Garrison turned to him for reassurance, and twice he managed to pull off a self-assured smile.

They were just over halfway across the neutral territory when Sylvester heard the faint blowing of a horn atop the walls of Muog. They had been spotted, and now they would see how receptive the dwarves were willing to be toward them. Praying they would not respond by merely sending a flurry of arrows their way, Sylvester continued without breaking stride, determined to put on the aura of supreme confidence.

To his relief, no attacks were forthcoming. He breathed slightly more comfortably as he and Garrison closed in on the main gates of Muog.

The dwarves must've been willing to hear a little of what they had to say. If not, they would have simply shot them and been done with it.

General Alexander Sylvester craned his neck to look up toward the top of the formidable walls, waiting for the occupants of Muog to address him. They waited in silence for several long minutes before the expected voice came.

"State your business, Imperials!"

"My name is General Alexander Sylvester, and this is my comrade Captain Terrence Garrison," Sylvester said, shouting to make his voice heard. "We are designated representatives of the Imperial Army, and we have been sent to negotiate with the honorable Chieftain Odpor. I have terms to offer that I believe a man of his great wisdom will find most agreeable. There are only two of us, and we are willing to surrender our weapons upon admission to your fine city."

The dwarves did not respond right away, leaving the two men in awkward silence below. Sylvester and Garrison exchanged uncertain looks. If the dwarves decided to move against them, they were too close to the city walls to escape.

No reply ever came from above; instead, the gates merely began to open after several minutes had passed, the sound of grinding gears causing both men to jump in surprise. The gates opened just far enough to allow a party of six dwarves to approach them.

Alexander Sylvester had not seen many dwarves up close before. Like most of their people, the dwarves in this group hovered around four and a half feet in height, with the very tallest being closer to five. They were all stoutly built and armed to the teeth; each carried at least two weapons, mostly the long-handled axes and maces favored by their people. Their faces were largely obscured by thick beards, and there was no hint of kindness to be found in their eyes. The foremost one spoke, his voice gruff, as though he had little time to deal with such trivial matters.

"You wish to negotiate with Chieftain Odpor?" he asked.

"Good day to you, my good man. Yes, that is correct. I have been sent to discuss terms with your wise and powerful chieftain," Sylvester replied, shooting the dwarf a broad smile, which was not returned.

"Remove your weapons and lay them on the ground at your feet. You will be searched after you do, so I would recommend you not attempt to hide anything. The penalty for any hostile action against our chieftain is death."

"Of course, we are happy to comply," Sylvester said, nodding at Garrison and unstrapping his sword from his belt. "We would never dream of acting dishonorably against Chieftain Odpor. I am here because I believe that he and I can reach an agreement that will allow for peace between our peoples and a great deal of prosperity for all."

If any of the dwarves were the slightest bit impressed by his statement, they didn't show it. Four of them stepped forward, two of them retrieving the dropped swords and the other two proceeding to frisk the two Imperial officers. Sylvester kept a smile on his face the entire time, determined not to show his displeasure at such rough treatment. Apparently satisfied, the dwarves stepped back and nodded to their leader.

"You may enter Muog. You are to follow me at all times. Any attempts to extricate yourselves from our custody will be met with force," the dwarf said, gesturing from them to follow.

Sylvester and Garrison fell into step behind the leader and one other dwarf, and their four companions brought up the rear. As soon as they had cleared the main gates, the gears began to grind once more, and the massive gates closed firmly behind them.

I hope I'm right about this, Sylvester thought.

Inside the main gates was a courtyard about fifty yards wide that led to the second equally massive wall that surrounded the interior of Muog.

We would never be able to seize this city by force, even if we had the entire Imperial Army and the armies of all the individual provinces fighting beside us, Sylvester thought as they passed through the second set of gates. Now the moat was before them, and as they climbed onto the bridge that spanned it, Sylvester noticed something odd about the water. It seemed to glisten strangely in the early-morning sunlight, and an unnatural smell seemed to emanate from it.

Of course they have the water laced with some sort of oil. Even if we got through both of the walls, they would raise their bridges. Once we tried to boat our way across, they would set the moat on fire. Clever for a bunch of savages.

Every step he took further convinced Alexander Sylvester that he was making the right move. He had never given the dwarves much thought as strategists, but the intricacy of their defenses impressed him nonetheless. Perhaps they were not quite the mindless, rock-scratching buffoons he had previously assumed.

As they walked through the streets of Muog, he spotted barricades that had been erected at every turn, enough to funnel any potential attackers into tight spots. Any invading force would have a very unpleasant time of it trying to sack this city. Despite their reputation as having minds only for gold and ores, their fortifications were quite formidable. Fortunately, his plans focused on a more diplomatic end to this war.

They walked for twenty minutes before coming to yet another high granite wall. Assuming this was the home of Odpor, Sylvester felt his fingers tingle with anticipation. He had always been a gifted diplomat—it had earned him his rank—but this would be his greatest challenge yet. Odpor was notoriously challenging to deal with, even before he had declared his intent to secede from the Empire. If Sylvester could get through to the stubborn dwarf, the Emperor would finally appoint him as the Supreme General, the role he had been born to fulfill.

As they approached the gates of the latest wall, a contingent of black-armored dwarven warriors stepped out to meet them. Surmising that they must be Odpor's personal guard, General Sylvester spread his arms wide to indicate that he came in peace.

"These are the Imperial officers who have come to treat with the chieftain?" one of the black-clad dwarves asked the leader of their company.

"Yes, we are," Sylvester interjected before their guide could answer, earning him an infuriated glare. "Please inform Chieftain Odpor that we have brought him a gift in thanks for his willingness to meet with us."

"Do not speak unless you are spoken to, Imperial," the black-clad dwarf snapped.

The guards spoke with their escorts in hushed tones now, obviously wanting their charges to be oblivious to their conversation. Sylvester remained silent and nodded for Garrison to do the same. The dwarves were a fickle people. It would not help their cause to anger these men, even if they were mere bodyguards. They may have been fools, but they were fools who could deny him the meeting he desperately needed. Finally, the guards dismissed their escorts and motioned for the two Imperials to follow them into the gate.

Odpor's home was not at all what Sylvester had imagined. He had pictured a vast complex flush with extensive fortifications to match those of the rest of the city. Instead, he found a relatively modest stone house within the walls, surrounded not by barricades but by gardens. The dwarves were known for their talents at mining and prospecting, not gardening. Flowers and shrubs of every type imaginable surrounded them as they walked the short path to the home's entry, and the general could even hear the gentle babbling of a nearby brook.

They were searched once more for weapons before the doors of the house swung open to admit them. The interior of the home continued to surprise the Imperial general. There were none of the gaudy gold and silver decorations he had expected to find, only more plants. The furnishings were simple, and the rooms they were led through were rather small.

You would think such an industrious people would have more of a taste for the finer things in life. I took these primitive fools for savages, but they surprise even me, Sylvester thought.

They entered the largest room he had seen thus far, and Sylvester assumed this must be where Odpor received visitors. There was a decorative pool set in the middle of the chamber and a large empty chair at the far end. The two Imperial officers were led around the pool and instructed to wait in front of the chair. Four of the black-clad dwarven guards stayed with them, their eyes never leaving their charges.

Odpor kept them waiting for several minutes before finally emerging from a side door. He was tall for a dwarf, standing over five feet, and his surprisingly well-groomed hair and beard were jet-black. He was dressed in black armor similar to that of his bodyguards, and his bright blue eyes were quite striking, even from a distance. From Sylvester's experience, this was uncommon among dwarves, who tended to have darker-colored eyes. Odpor took his seat and scrutinized them for a minute before speaking.

"Welcome to my home, Imperials. My men suggest you are spies and your wish to speak to me is a ruse designed to allow you to assassinate me. They urged that I should have you both killed right away, without meeting with you at all. I do not know why they are so concerned. After looking at the two of you, I cannot imagine two men less suited to an assassination mission. State your names."

"Greetings and salutations, Chieftain Odpor. It is a pleasure to make your acquaintance at last—"

"I believe I asked for your names, not a flowery speech," Odpor said, cutting him off.

"Of course, my apologies. I am General Alexander Sylvester of the Imperial Army. My companion and close friend here is Captain Terrence Garrison. We have been sent to negotiate with you on behalf of the Imperial Army."

"Is the Empire prepared to grant our secession?" Odpor asked.

He was blunt and to the point, a trait Sylvester would have admired if not for his insolence. By the time he was done with Odpor, the dwarf would know the proper way to address his superiors.

"I'm afraid that is not the case at this time," Sylvester began before Odpor cut him off once more.

"Then there is little that can be gained by negotiating with you, General Sylvester. Tell your Emperor the dwarves are not willing to compromise on this matter. We have lived under the yolk of the Empire for long enough. The days of the dwarves accepting their status as second-class citizens of the Empire are over. Fear not, for I will allow you to leave this city unharmed, which is more than an emissary of mine would be able to say in your camp—of that much I am certain."

"I understand your frustrations with Imperial policy, Chieftain Odpor, truly I do," Sylvester said, desperately trying to keep Odpor in his chair. To return to camp with such a resounding failure was a fate that he would not accept. It was probably what Cadmus Twilcox was hoping for; he would love to see Sylvester humiliated. *It would be the next best thing to seeing me dead.* "I wish to work with you toward achieving your goal. I believe I can help you obtain your secession from the Empire."

To his credit, Terrence Garrison did not show his surprise on his face, though Sylvester was sure concealing it was no easy task for him. Perhaps he should have confided more of his plan to the man beforehand, but it would have led to questions he did not care to answer. Garrison knew better than to speak up in this setting. Explanations could be provided later.

"You must understand my skepticism, General Sylvester. This is the first time that any Imperial official has shown the slightest willingness to consider our right to secede. Why should I believe anything you have to say?"

"Your skepticism is most understandable, Chieftain Odpor. I'm afraid many officials within the Empire are stuck living in the antiquities of another time. It is unfortunate, but it is a problem I believe you and I can overcome together if you are willing to hear me out."

The chieftain glanced to his guards, none of whom seemed overly impressed by Sylvester's statements thus far. Odpor examined him further, those bright blue eyes seemingly trying to pierce straight into his soul. *Hear me out, Odpor. You know you want to believe me.*

"Very well, General Sylvester, I will hear you out. But get to the point. You have already wasted enough of my time with your flowery talk. I have no time for grandiose speeches."

"Thank you, Chieftain Odpor. You will not regret it. The dwarves are a proud people, as well they should be. The beauty of this city is astounding to me, I must confess. You have done more than enough in service to the Empire over the past centuries that your people deserve their independence if they desire it. However, there is one voice in particular in the Emperor's ear, advising against this. That is the voice of Supreme General Cadmus Twilcox. A foolish old man, his time is long past, but he stubbornly holds on to his power, refusing to yield to a new generation. It's a result of old prejudices against those he sees as being beneath him, I'm sure. I believe that a new Supreme General would be able to sway the Emperor to grant the dwarves of Qwitzite their independence in thanks for their years of sacrifice in the name of the Empire. Any intelligent man can see this is not a war that will have a good ending for the Empire."

"So, you are here merely to improve your own position? You want to take your Supreme General's job, and you want me to help you do it. How much of a fool do you take me for, General Sylvester? You could not possibly have thought this would work."

Insolent little fool. Enjoy hurling insults at me while you still can, Sylvester thought, all the while fighting to maintain his composure. This was the most delicate part of the negotiation, and he had to make Odpor believe he was not there to merely serve his own interests. While he had not a care in the world for the well-being of the dwarves, it was essential that he convince Odpor he did.

"You misunderstand me, Chieftain Odpor. Yes, I do believe I would be a better fit in the role of Supreme General than Cadmus Twilcox; I do not deny it. However, I do not act out of greed or ambition. I act solely out of love for the men who serve under me. My dear man, I am sure you can sympathize with this. Do you wish to continue to see your own men continue to perish in this conflict? If we have the means to settle this matter peacefully, do we not owe it to the men under us to at least try?"

"What exactly are you proposing, General Sylvester? You have said a great many words, but very few of substance. Get to the point," Odpor said. He did not seem impressed, but at least he was still listening.

"To achieve a peaceful resolution to this conflict, we have to remove Cadmus Twilcox from command of the Imperial Army. The way to do this is simpler than you might think. We need to make him look like the incompetent fool that he is. To this point, you have struck at us occasionally, but with limited success. Your warriors are fierce, no doubt. But the limited impact of their attacks has drawn little notice. If we wish to see Twilcox removed from power, you need to hit more high-value targets successfully. I can provide you with these targets."

This time, he caught Garrison glancing in his direction. Sylvester did not expect the captain to understand, nor did he much care if he did. Garrison's job was to follow orders, not to think. He was a man of certain talents, but thinking had never been one of them.

Odpor seemed intrigued for the first time since they had met.

"You are telling me that you will provide me with Imperial targets to attack? You understand this will result in the deaths of Imperial soldiers, the same men you claim to care so deeply about. You must see, General Sylvester, why this strikes me as suspicious. How am I to know that you are not leading me into a trap?"

"A fair question, Chieftain Odpor. You may well suffer casualties. I cannot promise otherwise. The Imperial soldiers responsible for protecting these targets will fight back, I will make no promises otherwise.

However, the targets will not be heavily guarded and so will not require many of your men to attack them. This will further expose Twilcox's ineptitude, leaving such important targets insufficiently protected. The deaths of Imperial soldiers is a tragic thing, but ultimately a necessary sacrifice. They will die so that countless numbers of their brothers-in-arms can live. I can think of no more honorable death."

"Very well, General Sylvester. What targets do you have to offer me?"

"A week from today, a supply train of wagons will be arriving to replenish Imperial stores, which are running dangerously low in our encampment. Without these supplies, the army will be forced to cut rations to their troops significantly. Supreme General Twilcox has seen fit to assign fewer than thirty new recruits with protecting these supplies. Kill the soldiers if you must, but most importantly, put the wagons up in flames. It will take the Empire weeks to send replacement supplies—weeks that will be very hard on our camp's foot soldiers. Soldiers thinks with their stomachs. They will already begin to turn on their Supreme General."

"Once we have destroyed these supplies, you will give us additional targets?" Odpor asked, and Sylvester could almost see the wheels turning in the dwarf's head.

"Of course, Chieftain Odpor, all in good time. We have to plan our moves carefully to avoid suspicion. If I am unable to return to Muog myself, I will send Captain Garrison here in my stead. A few simple operations, and I will be named to replace Twilcox. Once that happens, I will immediately go to work persuading the Emperor that this war is a lost cause. Do we have an agreement?"

Odpor did not answer right away; his piercing blue eyes were still carefully examining Sylvester.

This was the moment of truth. Either the chieftain would buy what he was selling, or Sylvester would have to find a new way to get what he sought. *Assuming he lets you walk out of this room alive,* he reminded himself. He waited in silence, sensing that speaking at that moment would be the wrong move to make. Odpor was unlikely to trust him completely, but Sylvester had to believe what he was offering was too tempting for the dwarf to pass up.

"Very well, General Sylvester. I accept your offer. You provide the targets, and we will eliminate them. But be warned: if I discover you are playing games with me, you will live to regret it. But not for long."

"I would expect no less from a man of your nobility, Chieftain Odpor," Sylvester said, trying to avoid breathing an audible sigh of relief. He withdrew a piece of parchment from his belt, leaving the pendant where it was. Odpor would not be bought by such trinkets, and it would likely be seen as an insult to offer it. "This parchment details everything you need to know about the supply caravan. Once it has been destroyed, I will be in touch again once it is safe."

The chieftain's guards escorted the two Imperial officers back through the house and city. They left them safely outside the main gates and returned their weapons once they were beyond the city walls. It had gone so well that even Sylvester could scarcely believe it. He had the utmost belief in himself but never could have suspected that Odpor would be so easily swayed.

"General, you know I would never question you," Garrison said, breaking the silence as they made their way back across the neutral territory.

"And yet I sense you are about to do so in your very next breath. No worries, Captain Garrison. I would be ashamed of you if you didn't. My negotiations with Odpor were unorthodox, to say the least."

"I thought we were going to negotiate a peace treaty. I do not like Supreme General Twilcox any more than you do, but giving up Imperial targets to sully his name seems like a rather extreme measure to me."

You should know better by now than to try to use your brain, Sylvester thought. Garrison had served him long enough that he should know better than to ask these types of questions. Still, he could not risk alienating the captain. If Garrison told the wrong people what he had just heard, Sylvester would dangle from a noose by nightfall. For better or worse, they were in this business together now.

"It is an extreme measure, but one I feel is necessary, my friend. If we do not act, I fear that Supreme General Twilcox will launch an all-out assault against Muog sooner rather than later. You just saw their defenses firsthand. How many thousands of men do you think would perish in such an attack, only for it to end in failure and humiliation for the Empire?"

"You are right about that, of course you are, General Sylvester. But I have to wonder, do you honestly think you can persuade the Emperor to grant the dwarves their independence?"

"I have no intention of trying, my friend. Once we have earned the dwarves' trust, we will deceive them into allowing us into their city for the signing of a peace treaty. They will willingly give up their greatest defensive advantage: their walls. We will insist on a full company being admitted to serve as protection over the signing of the treaty, or some other guise. We can work out those details when the time comes. Once they have willingly opened their gates to welcome us, we will slaughter them like the traitors they are. We shouldn't need to kill all of them, just enough to get our point across. And the dwarves in their other cities will fall in line quickly once word reaches them. Unpleasant business, but it will send a message to any other province that might be foolish enough to suggest secession."

Chapter Eight

The steady uphill climb seemed to go on forever as far as Darian Tor could tell. Squinting ahead, he kept hoping to spot some sign that the end of their journey was close at hand, and he was continually disappointed. Nearly a month had passed since they had left the Imperial training camp, and they were finally expecting to arrive at the siege of Muog by the end of the day. The march from Salvamoan had been long and tedious, a journey Darian doubted would have been bearable if not for the presence of his three friends. For weeks they had trekked across the entire southern reaches of the province of Valdovas. It was the Empire's most enormous province and home to the Imperial government, though there had been few signs of life so far south.

To be fair, the journey had improved since reaching the western border of Valdovas. They had taken charge of a supply train bound for Muog, and now the soldiers were able to spend most of their days riding in the wagons. It was a marked improvement from the seemingly endless days of slogging along on foot. On this day, however, Darian and his friends had drawn the task of marching on foot. Captain Dunstan believed having men on foot would be an advantage in the event of a sudden assault against the caravan.

Their new commanding officer was still something of an enigma to the young privates under his command. He had been reserved throughout the journey, speaking only when orders needed to be given. It was certainly a marked improvement over the volatile and always-vocal Harter Arsch, for sure, but Darian still wanted to learn more about their new captain. Dunstan exuded confidence in all of their interactions with him, but Darian could sense there was more to the man than met the eye. He had the impression that Dunstan was a loyal, dependable soldier, but one who bore little love for the soldier's life. Given the man's age, it wasn't all that much of a surprise. Most soldiers his age would have retired long ago.

They had been traveling uphill for close to a week now, a slow, steady climb toward the rocky southern coast of Qwitzite. The bulk of the dwarven forces had taken up refuge in their capital city of Muog. It was a fortress renowned for its physical defenses and had never been breached by an invading force. As he slogged up the never-ending hill, Darian wondered what could have possibly driven the dwarves to build their capital in such a place.

"How do you think the dwarves got all of the granite for their walls up these hills?" he asked, desperate to break up the monotony of the long march. "If they are as tall as everyone says they are, it must have taken decades."

"Well, they're known as a stout people. They probably dragged the wagons up the hills themselves." Berj laughed. "They are probably better suited for the task than any pack mule."

It was true: the dwarves were known for being stout of body and dim of mind. They possessed a natural talent for mining and prospecting, but most other pursuits were over their heads, or so Darian had always been told. He allowed himself to chuckle at Berj's joke, though he still wondered what their reasoning had been.

"How much do you know about the dwarves, Private Jenson?" a voice asked from behind them, and the four friends spun to find Captain

Thaddeus Dunstan striding along behind them. Darian's face flushed; he had not known Dunstan was there. He had assumed Dunstan would be riding in one of the wagons, as any other commanding officer would.

"Not a whole lot, sir," Berj replied uncertainly, clearly wondering if he was about to be reprimanded for his joke.

"Well, perhaps you ought to take the time to learn. There is more to them than most people believe. They're an industrious people with quite a talent for building things; that's one thing everyone does know. You will see their skill for yourselves once Muog comes into view. However, it is a common misconception that they have no knowledge that does not revolve around mining or building. In fact, they are quite skilled at the art of gardening, believe it or not," Dunstan said.

"Gardening, sir? I've never heard of dwarves gardening," Max Preston said, one eyebrow raised.

"It's true, Private Preston. They also have a passion for cooking, another of those things that most people don't seem to know about them. Private Tor, you asked how they got the granite up these hills. It's a fair question, and I confess I don't know the answer. But do you know why they wanted to build their fortress here in the first place?"

"No, sir," Darian replied, wishing he hadn't started the conversation in the first place.

"Muog was built well before the Empire was formed, over two thousand years ago. In those days, men and dwarves and elves were always at war with one another. The dwarves were known for mining gems and precious metals. Men and elves always sought to take what the dwarves mined as their own, so the dwarves selected the spot up ahead and built their city. It was done out of necessity, not out of desire. The city sits on the edge of a cliff overlooking the South Sea, though the waters below are so choppy that it is virtually impossible to attack from the water. Any ship would end up splintered on the rocks below before they could hope to unload troops. Any invader would have to climb these hills, just as we are doing, to attack them. Of course, they would meet the dwarves' formidable defenses at the end of that climb. It's no wonder that this siege has lasted so long."

"Have you been to Muog before, Captain?" Darnold asked.

"No, this is my first time in the province of Qwitzite. It's one of the few places in the Empire my service hasn't brought me yet."

"How do you know so much about the dwarves? I've never met any man who knew much about them. They are so reclusive, almost as much as the ogres, that most people go their whole lives without even seeing one," Preston said.

"A word of advice for you, men. You are young and naive, but this is not your fault. You haven't seen much of life yet; it is natural for men as young as you. I was not so different when I was your age. If you are going to go to war, you should take the time to learn about the people you will be fighting. Not only might it save your life on the battlefield, but you also owe your enemy the courtesy of knowing something about them and their way of life before you kill them. The dwarves are not so very different from us, gentlemen. For that matter, neither are the ogres, now that you mention them. I actually do have firsthand experience to draw from on that account. But I'm afraid that's a story for another time," Dunstan said before picking up his pace, moving past them and up toward the front of the caravan.

Darian reflected on what Dunstan had said. Everything he had been told indicated that the dwarves were simpleminded savages, barely more civilized than animals. They knew how to mine, build, and fight, and that was the extent of their knowledge. Dunstan's description seemed to suggest otherwise; could he be right? He thought back to Axel's letters and how his friend described the dwarves as having battle tactics well beyond what he had expected. Perhaps Dunstan was right. Maybe he should have taken the time to learn more about the dwarves before joining the Imperial Army.

"So, now that he's gone, I've been wanting to tell you all something," Berj said once the captain was well out of earshot. "I actually heard a few rumors about Captain Dunstan."

"Like what?" Preston asked.

"Apparently, he was only a few years away from retirement. He was in command of one of the fortresses along the border of Thornata and Verizia about five years ago. I assume you all know what else happened in Thornata about five years ago?"

"Wasn't that when their civil war happened? I forget all the details, but didn't some outlaw group kill their duke and take control of the province?" Darian asked, trying to remember what he had learned about the conflict. "We heard a little about it in Verizia, but not too much. Our cities are far from their borders, and the Thornatans tend to keep to themselves. They always seem to believe themselves above mingling with the likes of us Verizians."

"Right you are, Darian. The rumor is, Dunstan led Imperial forces into the fray to help the Thornatans take back their capital. He did it without getting approval from Imperial High Command, and a lot of those men ended up dead. High Command was not pleased with him afterward, as I'm sure you would suspect. He was given a choice: an additional eight-year commitment or the rest of his life in the stockade. I can't blame him for his choice; I would have made the same one. I just think it's a bit odd for a man who went against orders to lecture us about educating ourselves, don't you?"

"I don't know about that, Berj," Darnold said. "You said it yourself—it's just a rumor. And even if it's true, it's easy to judge when you don't know what his reasons were. You can't deny, he has seen a lot more than we have, and there have to be things we can learn from him."

"You may be right, Darnold, but ogres? Seriously? Dwarves are one thing, but I've never heard a good thing about an ogre. Have you?"

"No, but I've also never met one," Darnold shot back. "Have you?"

Berj paid the question no mind as he plowed on. "You wouldn't be so quick to embrace Dunstan if you heard some of the cockamamie stories he came back with from Thornata. They say he was on some tirade about some boy younger than us who was able to conjure lightning strikes from thin air. Have you ever heard such nonsense? I can't believe they are letting him command men in a war zone after that. They must have been truly desperate for commanders. I'm glad we're all here together because I don't think we can count on him."

"I doubt they would have him in a command position if they thought there was any danger in it," Darian said, though the rumors made him a bit uneasy about their commanding officer.

"I'm sure those men who were stationed with him in that fortress thought there was no danger before he involved them in Thornata's civil war," Berj snapped back, catching Darian by surprise. He couldn't recall seeing Berj so passionate about anything. The typically lighthearted soldier seemed downright angry.

"This is a little different, though. We are heading into a war, and we know very well what we can expect," Preston pointed out.

Berj opened his mouth to retort once more, but Darian raised a hand, calling for silence.

Something didn't feel right, though he could not quite identify what it was. Something had changed about their surroundings, but what was it?

Looking around, he could see no change to the terrain, but still, he could not shake the feeling that something was horribly wrong. *Something is off here. What is it?*

It was Max Preston who figured it out first.

"What is that smell?" he asked, and Darian knew at once what was wrong.

Without another word, he bolted toward the front of the caravan, hoping he would not be too late. He found Captain Dunstan walking alongside the frontmost wagon.

"Captain Dunstan, sir, we have a problem."

"What is it, Private Tor?"

"Sir, do you smell pitch?"

Dunstan came to a stop beside him, his nose working the air like a bloodhound. The color left the captain's face, and he sprung into action at once.

"Move away from the wagons right now, men! Move, move, move!" Dunstan screamed, projecting his voice so the entire caravan could hear him while also shoving Darian away from the wagons.

Dunstan had drawn his sword and used it to cut the mules free from the first wagon, sending them bolting with a shout. He was already moving toward the second. Darian spun to see several men leaping from their wagons, but for most of them, it was already too late. The flaming arrows came down without warning, striking the grass around the wagons—dry grass that somebody had doused with pitch. Darian broke into a sprint, desperate to put as much distance between himself and the wagons as possible.

He felt the heat rise up impossibly fast behind him. He spun to see the dwarves had doused the ground thoroughly enough that the entire caravan had gone up in flames within seconds. Looking around desperately, he saw that many of his fellow soldiers had gotten far enough away before the arrows struck, but at least a few were not so fortunate. He couldn't see them, but he could hear them, trapped inside the blazing inferno, the flame rising too fast for them to escape. Darian forced himself to turn away from the sight, tears flooding his eyes. He knew there was nothing he could do to save them.

A panicked mule raced by him, and Darian was reminded of Captain Dunstan. He had been making his way down the line, trying to free the loyal beasts, but now there was no sign of him. It was the first mistake Harter Arsch had warned them not to make in the early days of their training. In his search, he got distracted from his surroundings. He was staring so intently into the blaze, searching for a way to help, that he did not hear the armored footsteps behind him until it was almost too late.

Darian spun at the sound, his shield coming up on reflex alone. The instinctive maneuver saved his life. The dwarf's mace crashed into the shield with shocking force. If he had not turned in time, the blow would have crushed his skull. The dwarf swung again, this time aiming for his legs, but Darian managed to backpedal quickly enough to avoid the swing. The move also bought him enough time to rip his sword from its sheath. The mace came for him once again, and again he managed to get his shield up in time, but this time, that was not enough. The dwarf was incredibly strong, and the force of the impact knocked Darian from his feet, leaving him fully exposed on the ground. The dwarf advanced once more, his mace coming up for a final killing blow.

Darian braced himself, trying to get his shield up to his defense once again, though he knew he was not strong enough to stop the dwarf's attack from this position. But the attack would never come, as Captain Thaddeus Dunstan appeared as if from nowhere. The captain was covered in soot from head to toe, sword in hand. His first strike took the dwarf's hand off, taking the mace along with it. The second strike struck the dwarf clean through the neck. Dunstan extended a hand, which Darian gladly accepted. *I never thought I would come so close to ending up dead before even reaching my first assignment.*

"Not many of them bothered to attack us on foot; the supplies must have been their primary target. Let's regroup with the others. We need to know what this attack just cost us," the captain said.

It had cost them even more than Darian had feared. Every single wagon full of supplies for the front lines had been reduced to smoldering piles of charred wood and ash. Seven men had been unable to get clear of them in time, leaving only seventeen of them under Dunstan's command. Most of the mules had died in the attack as well. The few Dunstan had managed to free in time had fled in a panic when the wagons went up in flames. The men who remained could hardly believe what had happened; none of them had expected this to happen before they had even reached the front lines.

Scanning the ground, Darian spotted only three fallen dwarves, in addition to the one Captain Dunstan had killed to save him. Such a small attack, but it had done grievous damage to them. Berj Jenson was wiping blood from his sword. He must have killed one or more of the attackers. Four attackers had just destroyed countless supplies, which could have kept the Imperial encampment fed for several weeks. The attack had come so suddenly; how could they have been better prepared?

"Well, gentlemen, you've had your first taste of war. I hope you don't have too many more. The wagons will be too hot for us to recover our fallen comrades for hours, and we can't wait here that long; we are too exposed for another attack. Without the wagons for cover, we would be lambs for the slaughter. We will proceed to the encampment; we should arrive within the hour. I will return with a larger company and see that our dead receive the proper burial they deserve. Let's move," Dunstan instructed.

The remaining men marched on in stunned silence. It was a surreal experience; they were still trying to come to terms with what had just happened. How had the dwarves known when they would be arriving? They could not have just been lying in wait for days; the Imperials had regular patrols through these areas to guard against such attacks. This attack must have been coordinated with precise timing. Axel had been right in his letters: the dwarves were more intelligent than the Imperials were giving them credit for being.

The remainder of the journey was filled with tension, everybody expecting another attack to happen at any moment.

Just when it seemed the hill would never stop climbing, they reached the top at last, and the Imperial Army encampment was sprawled out before them. Hundreds upon hundreds of black Imperial tents fluttered in the breeze, and thousands of soldiers milled about the camp, blissfully unaware of what had just happened to their newest recruits. Darian breathed a sigh of relief. After the last few hours, it was reassuring to see so many friendly forces stretched out in front of him.

Beyond the Imperial encampment, he could see the dwarven city of Muog off in the distance. He had assumed Axel had been exaggerating in his letters when describing the city, but now that he could see it with his own eyes, he was a believer. The walls must've been at least two hundred feet high, just like Axel had said. *How would we ever get past those?*

Beyond the dwarven city, just barely within sight, was the faint blue of the South Sea far below. It occurred to Darian at that moment that this was the farthest he had ever been from Verizia in his entire life, and a powerful feeling of homesickness washed over him.

Qwitzite was desolate, a far cry from the beautiful lakes and waterways of his homeland. He had spent most of his childhood swimming through Verizia's numerous lakes and rivers; he was not accustomed to seeing so much rock and sand. Everything here was dried out, as though there had been no rain in months. *And they used it to their advantage. Look how easily they were able to make those wagons go up in flames in all of that dry grass.* He couldn't imagine a more inhospitable environment.

"Let's get down there, men. You will be living in tent forty-six. The rest of the day is yours to familiarize yourselves with the camp. I will check in on you once I have your assignments. I need to report the attack to command. Excuse me," Dunstan said before moving away toward the camp.

Darian and the other recruits made their way through the maze of tents until they found the one marked with the number forty-six. Darian stepped inside to find that the shelter was built to hold around sixty soldiers. Bunks even smaller than those they had endured during training lined the walls, though the tent was almost empty in the middle of the afternoon. Their fellow soldiers must've all been out on assignments throughout the camp.

Darian, Berj, Darnold, and Preston deposited their belongings and stepped back out, eager to explore their new home. No sooner had they stepped back outside then Darian heard a familiar voice.

"Darian? Is that you? I had heard we were getting new recruits in this tent, and I hoped you would be one of them!"

Darian spun toward the sound of the voice, hardly believing it could be true. But there he was, Darian's childhood friend Axel Stark walking toward him. He looked different than Darian remembered. His once-smooth face was partially concealed by a scraggly red beard, and a few thin scars crisscrossed his forehead. He was also much leaner than Darian remembered, reminding him of the dozen wagons' worth of foodstuffs they had just lost.

"Axel, is that really you?"

"Sure is, old friend. It's good to see you. Welcome to the front lines!"

Chapter Nine

Darian could still hardly believe it was true as he introduced Axel to Berj, Darnold, and Preston. He noted Axel's armor bore a sergeant stripe on the shoulders and remembered in his last letter that there had been rumors of a promotion. He had received the message over a month before the end of training, leading him to wonder if his friend was even alive. Yet here Axel was, alive and apparently well. Why had he not written again?

"When I didn't hear from you, I feared the worse," Darian said, trying his best to sound casual, as though he had not spent weeks imagining his friend's gruesome death.

"So that's why you never responded to my last letter—you never got it!" Axel exclaimed. "The dwarves have been hitting more and more of our outgoing communications. They must have taken out the men carrying that batch of mail. They're trying to cripple our ability to communicate with Valdovas, and the unfortunate side effect is that a lot of our letters end up lost as well. To be honest, it's getting hard to keep track of all the attacks they make against us. I'm sorry, Darian. It certainly wasn't my intent to worry you. As you can see, I'm alive and mostly well."

It was such an obvious explanation that Darian felt stupid for not giving it more consideration sooner. Of course it was a possibility the dwarves had interfered with Imperial communications. He would've been shocked if they hadn't employed such a tactic against the Imperials.

Silently kicking himself for being so stupid, he extended a hand to Axel, and his old friend clasped it before forcibly pulling him into an embrace. When they broke, Axel was beaming.

"So, you survived Harter Arsch? He didn't kill anyone?" Axel asked laughingly.

"Not for lack of trying," Berj mumbled, drawing another laugh.

"He's a tough old bastard, no doubt about it. But he's the best there is at making future soldiers; you're all lucky to have suffered through him—hopefully you never end up in a situation bad enough to make you realize just how lucky."

"I see you got the promotion you mentioned," Darian said, pointing at Axel's shoulder. "Congratulations."

"Well, I don't know how many congratulations are deserved, but thanks. The sergeants in this camp have an unfortunate habit of dying young, so there have been a lot of promotions lately. I'm hoping I can buck that particular trend. In the meantime, I'm doing my best to look like I know what I'm doing and hoping nobody realizes otherwise. Maybe by the time they figure it out, I'll actually be close to competent."

"The dwarves are hitting us quite often, I take it?" Darnold asked.

"They have a knack for it. We have men watching their gates around the clock, but somehow, they still get out of Muog unseen. The working theory is that they have constructed tunnels to get across the neutral area undetected, but nobody has been able to sniff them out just yet. They're brilliant when it comes to such things. I have to give them credit."

"We got a small taste of their talents a short time ago," Preston said darkly.

"You're kidding! I haven't heard about any attack. What happened?" Axel asked.

The four new recruits recounted the story of the attack on the supply wagon. Axel grew more agitated by the second, repeatedly cursing as they spoke. By the time they had finished, he was pacing back and forth, hardly able to control his anger. It was the first time in over a decade of friendship that Darian had seen him so angry.

"This is not good. This camp needed those supplies badly. They've already cut our rations down to the bare minimum, and even with those cuts, we only have a few weeks' worth of food left. When word gets out about this, the men are not going to be pleased. How did the dwarves even know the supplies were coming? We do our best to make their arrivals random, so there is no pattern for them to spot. It sounds like a well-planned and well-executed attack, not a spur-of-the-moment hit. It doesn't make any sense. They don't exactly announce to the entire camp when caravans are coming in. They like to keep the dwarves guessing."

"I thought the same; they put a lot of work into preparing for our arrival," Darian said. "I would be dead if Captain Dunstan hadn't gotten to me in time. You weren't lying about the dwarves being ferocious warriors. That fighter had me on my back before I knew what was happening. I'd never been bested so easily. I felt like a child trying to defend myself against him."

"A lot of the men here discredited them at first. I think their size makes it easy for some men to underestimate them. They thought this siege would last a week and then we would be heading home. The dwarves believe in what they are fighting for, that's for sure. I won't sit here and say they should be grateful for all the Empire has done for them, which is the tone that command likes to take. I understand why the Empire is so desperate to stop their secession. They pay more in taxes than a few of the other provinces combined. But in my opinion, the Emperor should take a long hard look at whether or not this war is truly going to be worth the costs."

"Do you think we're going to lose?" Darnold asked.

"I'll tell you all something you're about to learn soon enough anyway. When it comes to war, there are no winners. There are only losers and those who still lose a lot in the name of claiming victory. Which one will we be? I can't say, but thus far, things aren't looking promising, at least not in my eyes. But I have to get going. I have a war council to attend. I'm sure the tone will not be especially pleasant after what happened to your caravan. I'll look for you in the chow hall later. Speaking of which, expect to be disappointed with your portion sizes. Don't say I didn't warn you."

With that, Axel was gone, leaving the four friends to head back to their assigned bunks, no longer in any mood to explore. Darian gladly removed his armor, noticing for the first time how much ash had landed on it during the caravan attack. He would need to clean it; an Imperial soldier was always expected to maintain his equipment. He'd better get right to it. If the commanders here were similar in any way to Harter Arsch, he could expect to be reprimanded if it was not done promptly. Retrieving a brush and polish from his rucksack, he went to work, reflecting as he did on everything Axel had said.

His friend seemed quite different from the eager young man who had left Verizia the year prior. Axel had wanted to be an Imperial soldier for as long as Darian could remember. Half of their childhood had been spent sparring with tree branches, pretending they were spears and swords. They had talked often about the adventures they would go on together one day, when they were both Imperial soldiers. Now it seemed to Darian as though Axel might be regretting his decision to join the Imperial Army. Had Darian made a mistake by following in the footsteps of his father and grandfather? War was no child's game; he had seen that for himself only hours before. Real men—no older and not so different from him—had lost their lives, seemingly in the blink of an eye.

Was Axel right? Should the Empire simply grant the dwarves their independence and abandon this war effort? It was an approach Darian was certain the Empire would never take, no matter how badly the war was going. If they allowed Qwitzite its independence, how long until the Thornatans or the elves or the Kardians demanded theirs? To acquiesce to the dwarven demands at this point would show weakness, a trait the Emperor could not allow himself to be seen as possessing. For better or worse, this fight was likely to continue until one side handed the other a resounding defeat. No matter what, countless more young lives would be snuffed out before it was over.

How long would that take? Axel had made it sound as though the Imperials had made little to no progress toward defeating the dwarves. The army had been entrenched here for close to a year. If they had made no progress in that time, what hope did they have of ever achieving victory? Just looking at Muog from a distance, Darian couldn't imagine any method of toppling such a fortress. Seeing Axel had shaken him. If the last year could have so thoroughly beaten down the most carefree person Darian had ever met, what would this war do to him?

"It sounds like things aren't going so well here," Darnold Dans said, breaking Darian out of his thoughts.

"Axel said as much in his letters, but it's a different thing to see it in person," Darian replied. "I suppose it's just not quite what I expected to find here on the first day."

"I know what you mean. I joined the army because it was my only choice if I didn't want to become a farmer like everyone else in my family. After all, what man our age wants to spend the rest of his life bringing in the beet harvest? I felt like I could do some good here. I hope I made the right choice."

"You did, Darnold. We all did," Berj said, walking over to join them. "Things may not be going well, but if the dwarves secede, the Empire will suffer for generations to come. The taxes they pay help to keep thousands of people in other provinces fed and clothed. What we're doing here is important, even if it's not particularly pleasant."

He made a good point. Qwitzite may have seemed like a barren wasteland to him, but a large chunk of the Empire's wealth came from this province. Almost all of the gold and precious metals and gems came from the dwarven mines. The dwarves becoming independent would have a trickle-down effect that would plunge many citizens of the Empire into poverty. While granting the dwarves their freedom may have seemed like an easy solution, it was far from a perfect one.

"Well, I don't pretend to be an expert on all of these complicated political matters, but I do know one thing: I am starving. What do you say we hunt down the chow hall and find out just how small of portions we have to enjoy? Preston! Are you done unpacking yet?" Berj called.

The four made their way out of tent forty-six and into the encampment. On their initial journey to the tent, they had not appreciated just how chaotic the army camp was. Men rushed back and forth in every direction, not paying the slightest mind to the four new recruits. Agreeing they should take time to familiarize themselves with their new home, they walked in every direction, taking in everything they saw. They spotted what looked to be the early construction of large siege towers in the distance and agreed they would go and take a closer look after eating.

They found the chow hall to be every bit as depressing as Axel had hinted. Their supper consisted of a bread roll, a small scoop of rice, and two small pieces of dried meat. From the resigned expressions on the faces of the men around them, they gathered this was nothing new. They had just found a table when Axel himself walked in, retrieving a supper of his own and moving over to join them. He noted their disappointed expressions and chuckled.

"I did warn you. At lunch we usually get a small serving of vegetables, so enjoy that while it lasts. We lost two wagons full of them this afternoon, though you may have already known that. Word is being sent to Valdovas to request more supplies. Hopefully our message gets through, though I'm certain the dwarves will try to ensure it doesn't. Even if it does, it will take weeks for them to get here, and hopefully they can get here without being burned to ash. Things are only going to get leaner around here."

"Axel, are those siege towers they are building? We were going to go take a closer look after eating, which won't take long," Darnold said, obviously wanting to turn the conversation away from their meager rations.

"They are. It's going to be months before they are ready, at best. I'm less optimistic about that time frame. Muog's walls are every bit of two hundred feet tall. In case you didn't notice on your journey here, there are not many trees in this part of the province, so also not a lot of lumber. Those wagons you were escorting were meant to be disassembled and added to the towers once they had served their purpose. Apart from that, we have an entire company tasked with bringing lumber from the forests in the northern regions of Qwitzite, but progress is slow on that front. As you can imagine, hauling large amounts of wood over a hundred miles uphill while under constant threat of attack is no easy feat. If you're all done eating, let's go take a look at them."

Axel led the four friends out of the chow hall and through the encampment toward the siege towers. He pointed out various landmarks as they walked, showing them the well nearest to their tent where they could fetch water and the armorer where they could replace broken weapons or armor.

As they drew closer to the siege towers, Darian grew more impressed. The three wooden structures were already nearly fifty feet tall, and the bases were close to a hundred feet in diameter.

"They have to be so wide to support their height, or at least that's what they tell me. I've never had a mind for such things. If they aren't wide enough, they could tip over, especially if a good wind gust hits. Today hasn't been bad, but the winds up here can be downright brutal," Axel said.

"How on earth can such things even move? Wheels or no wheels, they have to be so heavy," Berj said.

"Again, I don't have a mind for these things. From what I understand, they will build some sort of rails along the ground that will make them easier to move. But that's for men much smarter than me to figure out. At this rate, they won't be ready for another year or two anyway. Hopefully we can end this war long before we have to use them."

Darian stared up at the structures in awe. *It's incredible what we can accomplish when our goal is to kill other people*, he thought darkly to himself.

He was still staring up at the nearest tower when the first flaming arrow hit it. Over a dozen more followed in short order, sending the entire upper half of the tower up in flames. Another volley came a split second later, this time striking the next tower and drawing cries and screams from the men below.

"Over there!" Axel cried, drawing his sword.

Sure enough, there were the dwarves, over a dozen of them, right there in the heart of the Imperial camp. Armed with longbows, they were now firing on the third and final tower. Darian drew his own sword, cursing himself for not having put his armor back on before leaving their tent. It was a mistake Harter Arsch would have had him running laps all night for.

The dwarves had dropped the longbows and drawn maces, swords, and axes. Apparently, they were not there to burn the towers and retreat. They planned to die here, taking as many Imperial soldiers with them as they could in the process.

Darian watched in shock as one of the dwarves hacked an Imperial soldier's legs out from under him, leaving him to bleed out as he moved to another foe.

The dwarf took his next victim through the gut, his axe cleaving the unfortunate man open. A third man met a similar fate, and then Darian saw the dwarf's eyes lock on to him. He brought his sword up into a defensive position, once again wishing he had thought to put his armor back on or at least carry his shield. The dwarf was within five feet of him when Axel stepped between them. The dwarf swung his axe with reckless abandon, but Axel sidestepped the attack, swinging his sword toward the dwarf's head at the same time. He caught the dwarf with a glancing blow, opening a deep gash just below the eye.

If this wound troubled the dwarf at all, he did not show it. He simply charged forward, swinging the axe once more. Axel brought his shield up to parry the blow, though he was still rocked backward by the impact. How could men who were so small generate so much power? The dwarf brought the axe up again, hoping to strike while Axel was caught off-balance. Darian sprung forward, entirely forgotten by the dwarf in his bloodlust, his sword slashing out and taking the dwarf's arm off below the elbow. Axel sprung forward as well, shoving his sword deep into the dwarf's chest for good measure.

Darian turned in every direction, searching for more dwarves, but the threat seemed to have been neutralized. Berj Jenson was wrenching his sword from the slumped body of another dwarf, and Max Preston was nursing a cut on his arm. It appeared they had gotten off easy compared to the unfortunate men who had been closest to the initial rush. Darian counted at least seven dead soldiers, and more were wounded badly enough that they may soon join them. Axel was shouting for medics, and all the while, black smoke billowed from the still-burning siege towers into the air above them.

***

Darian sat alone outside of tent forty-six that night, several hours after the battle below the towers. He had not expected his first day on the front lines to unfold the way it had, and it had left him shaken. He could not bear to sit inside, listening to his fellow soldiers revel. How were they able to go about their evening as though nothing had happened? He had seen too much already—first the attack on the caravan, and then the brief battle at the siege towers.

None of his friends seemed as impacted by the day's events as he was, and he was ashamed of it. Preston had been to the healer's tent to have his wound treated and was expected to make a full recovery in short order. Darnold was quiet, which was far from unusual, and Berj was as animated as ever. Darian supposed everybody dealt with trauma differently, but he still could not help but feel self-conscious. He was still sitting in silence when the tent flap opened and Axel Stark stepped out to take a seat beside him.

"You had a messy first day, no doubt about it," Axel said, offering him a small metal flask. Darian accepted it and took a sip, the whiskey burning his throat on the way down.

"Was yours this bad?"

"Hell no. We arrived with no issues, and the dwarves didn't attack until we had been here for almost a fortnight. They were also more generous with the food in those days. Imperial High Command thought this conflict would be over quickly. Now I can hardly remember what it was like to not be able to see my own ribs when I take my shirt off. What a mess." Axel took the flask back, taking a sip of his own before passing it again.

"How do you deal with days like this, Axel? I just keep thinking about all those pretend battles we had as kids. Remember how we would fight with sticks and pretend they were swords? We couldn't wait for this. We were going to defend the innocent and strike down evil all over the Empire. We were so stupid."

"Well, you'll get no argument from me on that. But I like to tell myself that everyone is stupid when they're young. It makes it easier to bear. My first bit of advice would always be to make sure you wear your armor when you are out and about, even just to the chow hall. I should have told you that the second you arrived. The dwarves have a habit of attacking at the most unexpected times."

"Did they figure out how the dwarves got into the camp unseen today?"

"They have tunnels, but we just can't seem to find them. They sent a dozen search parties out into the neutral area after the attack to try to find them. They came back empty-handed, just like they always do. The dwarves know this country well, and they are crafty with how they use that knowledge against us. These men do their best, but they're out of their depth here. We all are."

Was every day going to be spent in fear of more sudden attacks like the ones he had endured today? Darian wasn't sure if he was mentally fit to face such stress. Who had he been fooling when he signed up to join the Imperial Army? He was no soldier. He didn't belong here. This was a place for hardier men than he.

"Look, Darian, I'm not going to tell you that it's going to get better. You know me well enough to know I wouldn't feed you a pile of cow dung like that. I don't know what's going to happen tomorrow, or the next day, or a year from now. I can pretty much guarantee there's going to be more days like this. But if I can survive this, you sure as hell can too. And you have one advantage that I didn't have."

"What's that?"

"You've got me watching your back. I wish you hadn't been sent here, but I'm still glad to have you around. It's good to have a real friend again. It sure isn't like the old days, but we'll make the best of it and get through this together. And when we get back to Verizia one day, we'll know better than to dream for nonsense like this. You should try to get some sleep. From experience, the earlier you turn in, the better. The snoring in these tents will amaze you. Like trying to sleep through a raging thunderstorm."

Darian took one last sip of the whiskey before handing the flask back to Axel. It was true: he did have one advantage over most of his fellow recruits. He had a lifelong friend in Axel to watch over him, as well as three more close friends he had been fortunate enough to find. He would survive whatever came his way. He didn't know what kind of man he would be after it was all over, but he would survive.

Chapter Ten

Darian Tor looked down at the most meager breakfast he had been served thus far and found he had no desire to eat it. Looking up at his friends, he found they were having similar reactions, except for Berj Jenson, who almost always had a healthy appetite. They had received word the night before that they were to report to the assignment tent that morning, where Captain Dunstan would be assigning them a mission. To make matters worse, when Darian had told Axel of this, his friend had given him the impression that he knew what this mission was but refused to say anything more. Axel merely insisted it was better to let Captain Dunstan explain things.

"You boys should really eat your breakfast. You don't have any idea what we have in store for us," Berj said, shoveling all of his fried potatoes into his mouth in one bite.

"How can you sit there and stuff your face at a time like this?" Preston asked incredulously.

"First of all, have you looked at these trays of food? You and I have very different definitions of 'stuffing my face.' Second, I am eating because I understand that if this mission starts right away, it may be the last chance I get to 'stuff my face' for a while, which is something the three of you should take into consideration. Unappetizing as this food is, we might need our strength. Embrace my wisdom, boys. I share it freely."

It was true, and Darian knew it. He reluctantly began to force the unappetizing breakfast down his throat. Whatever this mission was, it would likely be physically demanding, and they needed to fuel their bodies.

They had been at the front lines for just over a week, and thankfully, the first day had been their worst. There had been several more attacks by dwarven guerilla fighters, but none of them had been in the vicinity of the assaults, which were quickly put down. From what Axel had said, the army was no closer to finding the tunnels the dwarves were using to attack them. Until they did, the random attacks were bound to continue.

"Any of you have any thoughts on what type of mission they are going to assign us?" Darnold asked.

"Maybe we will be running lumber from the forests up north. I'm sure they would love to start rebuilding those siege towers," Preston suggested. "Doesn't that sound fun? Marching back and forth up and down these wretched hills?"

"That's possible, but I don't know if they will want to invest the time in that again. Not until they find these tunnels, at least. Why build new towers just so the dwarves can burn them down again?" Darnold said.

"Maybe that's our mission: searching for the tunnels," Berj said.

"Maybe, but Axel said they already have dozens of patrols out looking, men who are specifically trained to find those types of things. How much value could we add? Maybe we're being sent to guard another caravan of food. At least that's what I hope it is," Darian said. "We might get at least one good meal out of it if so."

"That would actually make sense. It would almost be like a punishment for allowing the last caravan to be destroyed," Darnold said. "I would be happy with that."

If that's the case, it won't be so bad, Darian thought. While the idea of marching back across the province and then all the way back to Muog was not overly appealing, it would be less stressful than being in camp and waiting for the next attack by the dwarves. It was a mission that made sense. They were not likely to send such new recruits into anything more dangerous, were they?

"I suppose we will find out soon enough. There's not much use stressing ourselves out over it," Berj said, which Darian had to admit was true, even if it didn't stop him.

Once they had finished their breakfast, the four friends made their way out of the chow hall and into the humid summer air. Gray rain clouds rolled overhead, and a few drops bounced off of their armor as they wound their way through the maze of tents and soldiers. It had rained several times over the past week, yet it had done nothing to bring any sign of life to their barren surroundings. As soon as the droplets reached the parched earth, the moisture seemed to vanish.

They had visited the assignment tent only once, the day after their arrival. They had each been assigned various menial jobs to complete around the encampment. Darian had spent the last week running messages between various officers. It was tedious work, but at least it had allowed him to become very familiar with the layout of the camp.

They entered the assignment tent to find Captain Thaddeus Dunstan awaiting their arrival, along with—to Darian's surprise—Axel Stark. Axel had hinted he knew more about their future assignment than he would say, but Darian had not suspected that his friend would be directly involved. Axel shot them a quick grin as they filed into the tent. Captain Dunstan indicated that they were welcome to sit in the nearby chairs, an offer all four of them accepted. Darian was silently grateful that Captain Dunstan was not as strict on the formalities as most of his fellow officers. Their interactions with their captain had been minimal, but Darian was still grateful to have Dunstan as his commanding officer.

"Welcome, gentlemen. Thank you for your punctuality," Dunstan began. "As you know, you have been summoned here to receive a new mission assignment. Sergeant Stark will be in command of this mission, and you will report directly to him until it has been completed. I am still your commanding officer, but several captains, including me, have been asked to loan out men for this mission. I have chosen the four of you because I feel all of you are equal to the task. Understood?"

All four nodded, Darian knowing each of them was thinking the same thing. Whatever this mission was, it did not sound like it would be as trivial as guarding supply wagons or running lumber for new siege towers. Whatever this was, they immediately received the impression that there was a significant amount of danger associated with it.

They're throwing us right into the fire, aren't they?

"I will allow Sergeant Stark to go over the minutia of the details with you. Just be aware that I will be appraised of your performance, and I expect nothing but the utmost professionalism from the men under my command at all times. I'm sure this won't be an issue for any of you; please do not make me regret this confidence. The floor is yours, Sergeant Stark."

"Thank you, Captain Dunstan. I assume all of you are aware that the supplies in this encampment, particularly foodstuffs, are running dangerously low?"

"Yes, sir," the four young privates answered in unison.

It felt strange for Darian to address his old friend in such a way, but the Imperial Army demanded decorum.

"Unfortunately, this is not an issue our adversaries inside of Muog are having. The extent of their foodstuffs is difficult to pinpoint precisely, but various reports have it at close to three years' worth of supplies. They were expecting a siege when they announced their secession and prepared accordingly. In addition to these stores, the dwarves have mastered the art of growing their own food in this harsh climate. It is an accomplishment that we have as yet been unable to replicate. If they are truly able to live for three years or more on their current stores, this siege may be doomed to fail."

Darian thought he could see where this was going, and he did not care for it one bit. It was almost a certainty that they were going to be sent into the city of Muog. Dealing with the random attacks on the Imperial camp was bad enough. How could they hope to survive in the heart of the enemy stronghold?

He could hear rainfall beating steadily against the roof of the canvas tent, though it was not loud enough to drown out his abnormally loud heartbeat. He did his best to remain stone-faced, not wanting to betray any hint of fear in front of Axel or Captain Dunstan.

"You're all intelligent men; you can see where I'm going with this," Axel continued. "We cannot bring the dwarves to the negotiating table under our current circumstances. They have all of the leverage at the moment. We have been asked to slip into Muog undetected and interfere with their foodstuffs. If possible, we are to smuggle some back here, though this is unlikely. Therefore, our orders are to destroy as much as we can and then get out before they know we are there. Once we have hurt their ability to wait us out, they may be more open to negotiating with us in good faith."

"How are we going to get inside of Muog?" Darnold asked. "They must have men watching every inch of their walls."

"You are correct. They have sentries on their walls at all hours, and even if we did get over the first wall, we would still have to get over the second, and then their interior moat. It's simply not plausible. However, we believe we have identified a path into the city.

"The Moyie River runs into the South Sea just west of the city. When the river reaches the cliffs, it becomes a waterfall that plunges down into the South Sea below. Imperial scouts believe there is a tunnel behind this waterfall that the dwarves have been using to slip out of the city on fishing trips down to the sea. Men from the Imperial Navy ships stationed in the sea below have reported seeing dwarves scaling the cliffs next to the waterfall, and this is the only explanation that makes sense. We will have to rappel down the cliffs until we find this tunnel entrance and then make our way into Muog via their underground passage."

Darian remained silent out of respect for Axel, though he could already see many flaws in this plan. If this tunnel did exist, there was no telling what type of security the dwarves would have in it. That was assuming they even got that far; the Moyie River ran very close to the walls of Muog. If the sentries on the wall spotted them, they would be killed by longbows before they could even begin climbing down the cliffs. He knew none of this was Axel's fault, that his friend was simply following orders from higher up, but what were they thinking with such a reckless plan? Were the potential rewards really worth the excessive risk?

For them, it is. It's not their necks on the line in there.

"Do we have any idea what type of resistance we might expect to find in the tunnel? If we get into a prolonged fight with dwarven warriors the second we reach the tunnel, the whole city will know we are coming," Berj pointed out.

"Unfortunately, we have virtually no intelligence on the inside of the tunnel. Our scouts' best guess is that it emerges somewhere in the southwestern sector of Muog. This is fortunate for us because this is where the dwarves are believed to keep the vast majority of their stockpiled food. At least that was the case before they declared their independence and shut the Empire out of the city. Things may have changed, and it will be up to us to improvise if necessary."

"It seems this mission depends on our ability to keep things quiet, at least if we want to survive to see the end of it," Preston said.

"You're absolutely right, Private Preston," Axel said. "If we are discovered while inside Muog, the dwarves will almost certainly move to block off any tunnel we might have used to gain entry. I don't much like our chances running around inside of a city they know far more intimately than we ever will. Every man selected for this mission was picked because we believe they can keep a cool head under pressure. If any of you feel you are unable to do this, you need to step forward right now."

He paused for a moment, though Darian knew Axel didn't honestly think any of them would speak up. His heart may have been racing in his chest, and his palms may have been sweaty, but Darian would never let his friend down. He was sure Axel had spoken up for his abilities while choosing the men for this mission, and he could not turn his back on that show of faith. Besides, the four of them had made a pact to watch after one another. He was not about to forsake his end of that bargain after only a week on the front lines. He would not be able to live with himself if he stepped down from this mission and one of his friends was killed.

"I didn't think any of you would step forward, but I needed to be sure. Obviously, there are a lot of things that can go wrong with a mission like this. The Moyie River is within sight of the city walls. We will be making this attempt on the night of the new moon, which is four nights from now. We will depart in the morning, hike north for several miles, and then turn west. We will wait upriver until we have the cover of darkness, and then we will come back south, under the city walls and over the cliffs."

The dwarves may not be able to see us in the light of the new moon, but there are other considerations, Darian thought to himself. He chanced a glance at his friends and could almost see the wheels turning in their heads, just as they were in his own. No one wanted to ask the questions; they didn't want to put off an aura of fear.

"I'm sure you can all see the greatest complication in this plan. This mission is dependent upon the darkness the new moon provides us. The dangers in this are twofold. We have to make our way around Muog in near-total darkness even though none of us have ever been inside before. We have maps, though they are two years old, so it is possible that the layout may have been altered. We have to believe the dwarves have been anticipating such an attack, and they have almost certainly taken steps to thwart us. I can give the four of you one copy. Study it, and do your best to memorize it. Your memory may be the difference between life and death for all of us. The second major risk is that this mission must be completed very quickly. We need to be out of Muog, back through the tunnel, up the cliffs, and out of sight of the walls before dawn if we don't want to be target practice for their archers."

There were so many aspects to the plan that it made Darian feel dizzy. There were so many things that had to go perfectly if they were going to survive, let alone succeed. There were a great number of things that could go wrong and very little chance of everything going right.

Darian thought he had understood the risks when signing up to join the Imperial Army. He had accepted the fact that he may be killed in a battle or asked to kill others. But this felt like a suicide mission they were being asked to undertake.

"I understand it is a lot to take in, especially all at once. It will not just be the five of us. Two other battalions are providing four men each as well. Let's hope thirteen is our lucky number," Axel said, trying to inject some optimism into the conversation, clearly sensing the young men's uncertainty. "I will be available to answer any questions the four of you have between now and the operation. We won't be able to wear our armor for this mission, as I'm sure you realize. It would slow us down and make too much noise. Black garments only, gentlemen; we need to be like shadows in the darkest of nights. Carry one sword and one dagger each, and I will also be procuring us bows and arrows that are compact enough to carry along on an operation like this."

"I said it earlier, and I will repeat it. You four were chosen because I believe in your ability to achieve what needs to be achieved and live to tell the tale. I won't lie to you; this operation is fraught with dangers, but I believe you will overcome them," Captain Dunstan said, speaking up for the first time since the beginning of their meeting. "You will all make the Empire proud."

"Yes, sir," four voices said in harmony.

"That's all I have to tell you at this time. Take this map," Axel said, handing Darian a folded sheet of parchment. "As I said, scrutinize it carefully, take in every detail. I also recommend you all spend some time in the sparring paddock with swords. It never hurts to be prepared for the worst-case scenario. Hope for the best, but always prepare for the worst."

"Thank you, gentlemen. You are relieved from all additional duties until this mission is complete. Your preparations are your sole responsibility at this time. Dismissed," Captain Dunstan added.

The four friends stepped out of the tent and into the heavy rain that was now falling. They walked back toward their tent in silence, each man lost deep in his thoughts. Darian was thinking of home, about how he had left to join the army, full of optimism, and now it felt as though he could feel his life coming to an end. Axel had spoken with confidence, but he knew his friend must've seen the truth just as well as he did. This mission was impossible. They may well destroy the foodstuffs inside Muog, but none of them would live to tell the tale.

They reached their tent, and each man set about busying himself with pointless tasks to keep himself occupied. When there was finally nothing more to pretend to do, they gathered around Darian's bunk. Darian laid out the map Axel had given him; they should heed his advice and try to memorize as much as possible. They found the streets of Muog were exceedingly complex, which did nothing to improve their spirits. How could anyone hope to memorize this, even if they had ten years to do it?

"Do you think they're sending us on this suicide mission as a way of punishing us for what happened to the caravan?" Preston asked, breaking the silence and putting the question they were all thinking into words.

"Why us, though? Why just the four of us? None of the other recruits were able to save any of the supplies either. And what about Dunstan? Shouldn't he have to come with us if that's the case?" Berj added.

"Maybe they honestly think we can succeed. Axel seems confident enough," Darnold tried to reason.

"Yes, but it's his job to sound confident," Berj countered. "He's not going to stand there and tell us we're marching to our demise."

"I think Axel thinks we can do this," Darian said, and three heads turned to look at him in disbelief. "He and I have been friends our entire lives. He would not have agreed to bring me on this operation if he thought we were marching to our deaths—I'm sure of that."

"Right you are, old friend," said a voice from behind them. They spun to find Axel Stark approaching, a bemused expression on his face. Berj's and Preston's faces had gone red with embarrassment, but Axel simply smiled at them. "Let's hear it, boys. What do you think? Don't feed me any standard Imperial word jumble either; it's just us here. I assure you, I can see the flaws in this mission just as well as you can. That doesn't mean we're doomed. Let's figure this out."

No one was quick to answer, and all were visibly ashamed that he had heard them venting their doubts. Knowing none of his friends were going to speak up, Darian took that duty upon himself.

"I think we're all just nervous. For our first mission to be something so sensitive, where every minute detail has to play out perfectly, is a bit baffling," he said. "This sounds difficult, even for the most experienced of soldiers. Why do they think we are a good choice?"

"I get it, I really do," Axel said. "When you stand in the assignment tent and list out everything we need to do, it can sound so daunting. It's a ritual I think ought to be retired. It's something the higher-ups forget; it's been so long since they've been in a real fight themselves. Hell, most of them probably don't even remember how to hold a spear anymore. They like to know their men are well-informed and give no thought to overwhelming them with details. But just know this: I'm not putting on any kind of act. I truly believe we are going to succeed, and I hope you all do as well. Now, why don't we head to the sparring paddock and get some valuable work done? Sitting around thinking about this isn't doing any of you any good right now. The rain is letting up. Getting out there and smacking one another around a bit might be good for all of us."

Buoyed by Axel's optimism, the four friends followed him out to the training paddock for sparring. Darian had not sparred with Axel since they were fighting with tree branches, and he quickly found himself amazed by his friend's exceptional skill. Axel broke through his defenses and had him in a frantic backward retreat within seconds. His friend moved so much faster than he remembered and fought with the technique of a man who had seen his fair share of real battles. They had not spoken much of what Axel had experienced over the past year, and Darian had not pushed him. He felt his friend would talk when he was ready.

The five men rotated sparring partners, and Darian was pleased to fend off a ferocious assault from Berj and slip a strike under his guard. On the other side of the paddock, Axel managed to break through Darnold's usually impenetrable defenses, drawing a cheer from Preston. When Darian squared off against Darnold, the customarily reserved young man seemed more motivated than usual, taking a more offensive approach than Darian was used to seeing from him. This proved to be a mistake, as Darnold left openings in his defenses that he would not have typically left. Darian managed to strike him twice. It was something nobody had ever managed to do to Darnold, causing the young man to hurl his sword to the ground in frustration.

"Don't get frustrated, Darnold. Better to learn your weaknesses in a sparring session than in a real fight against a dwarven warrior," Axel said, clapping Darnold on the back as the young man seethed. "Trust me, these blunt swords hurt a hell of a lot less than those gigantic maces and axes they will be swinging at you."

Axel's encouraging words seemed to help. Berj went up against Darnold next, launching a frenzied attack, as usual. This time, Darnold was back in form; he was calm and calculated and successfully deflected every single blow. To Darian's surprise, Max Preston was performing much better than usual under Axel's tutelage and rarely waded too quickly into more than he could handle.

The five of them sparred until lunchtime and then returned to the paddock and continued until dinner. The rain came and went, but they fought on nonetheless, knowing they may one day have to fight in such conditions. It never hurt to be prepared for every eventuality.

As they made their way back from dinner, they felt a renewed sense of confidence, all thanks to Axel Stark. Darian could not help but be proud of his childhood friend. He had become an effective sergeant who was able to properly inspire the men under his command. Axel brought them to a stop outside of tent forty-six for one last word.

"What I saw in that paddock today is exactly why this operation will be a success. You are all exceptional fighters, but it's more than that. Our goal on this mission is to avoid a fight, but your skills will still be useful. Each of you was quick to adapt to anything I threw at you in that paddock. You may be new recruits, but you need to give yourselves more credit. Don't forget, you are Imperial soldiers, and from what I saw today, every one of you is worthy of that title. Get some rest, and don't forget to study that map."

The four new recruits headed into the tent, Darian feeling far differently than he had only a few hours prior. They could not know for sure they would succeed in their mission, but he knew beyond any doubt that they could. For the time being, that would have to be enough.

Chapter Eleven

Captain Terrence Garrison spread his arms wide to consent to the search while the main gates of Muog closed tightly behind him. The dwarves relieved him of his sword, as well as the white flag he had carried once more to signal his peaceful intentions. General Alexander Sylvester had sent him to carry a message to Chieftain Odpor. Sylvester, not wanting to draw suspicion by visiting the dwarf stronghold too many times in person, had entrusted this task to his most loyal confidant.

It had been a week since the dwarves had successfully ambushed the supply caravan, just as General Sylvester had suggested they should. Supreme General Cadmus Twilcox had been furious at the assault, and though he had criticized Sylvester's negotiating skills, he had not suspected for a moment that there was more at play than met the eye. Sylvester was rather angry with the dwarves himself. The attacks on the siege towers the same day had not been part of their arrangement. The additional attacks had made Sylvester's negotiating ability appear more questionable in the eyes of his fellow generals.

Sylvester had needed to bide his time. He could not risk returning to Muog right away. In the eyes of the rest of the Imperial officers, his negotiations had been an utter failure. To return to the city so soon would arouse suspicions. Of course, the mind of Alexander Sylvester was never at rest, and he had plotted his next move long before the dwarves had destroyed the caravan. Captain Garrison would be sent back to Muog as his emissary, carrying a letter condemning the dwarves for refusing to negotiate in good faith. Garrison had no intention of actually giving this letter to Odpor. Of course, his true orders were to deliver quite a different message.

As the dwarves led him through the streets of Muog toward Odpor's home, Garrison could not help but wonder if he was doing the right thing. Such thoughts had crept into his head with regularity since their meeting with Odpor. He had served General Sylvester for nearly his entire career, and those years had been kind to him. He had never once doubted his general's judgment or methods. But willingly offering up Imperial targets to the enemy was a strategy Garrison still struggled to embrace, despite Sylvester's reassurances. He trusted General Sylvester was making sacrifices necessary in the name of the greater good, but how far would they have to go? Would his tactics succeed at ending the war? What if they failed? Even if they did succeed, would it be worth the cost?

They arrived at the walls surrounding Odpor's home, and once again, Garrison was searched. The black-clad guards took charge of him, leading him through the gates and gardens and into the house. As they passed through the various rooms, Terrence Garrison was once again surprised at how modestly the home was adorned. He could not imagine the duke of any other province living in such simple accommodations. It was strange. Odpor had seemed intelligent enough during their previous meeting, yet he lived in the home of an ordinary man.

As they entered the room adorned with the decorative pool, Garrison found that Odpor was already awaiting his arrival in the chair at the far end of the chamber. The dwarf scrutinized him as he made his way around the pool. Garrison felt as though the dwarf's piercing blue eyes could see straight into his soul, and it was a feeling he did not enjoy. He approached the chair, waiting for Odpor to say the first word, but after a long moment of silence, he realized the dwarf was waiting on him.

"Greetings and salutations, Chieftain Odpor. I have been sent to treat with you on behalf of General Alexander Sylvester. The general sends his regards but thought it would be for the best if the two of you did not meet in person so soon after your first meeting. He feels meeting too frequently may draw suspicion."

"Welcome, Captain Garrison. The information your general gave us was good, though I must admit I was skeptical. Perhaps this is a partnership that could prove fruitful after all. What word do you bring me from General Sylvester?"

"General Sylvester was curious why you attacked the siege towers, as they were not part of the agreement," Garrison said, suspecting this might anger the chieftain. His suspicion proved to be correct.

"I made no agreement with General Sylvester, and I suggest you remind him of that fact promptly upon your return. He offered me a gift, which I accepted. I never agreed to cease additional assaults, and if he was under that impression, he has nobody to blame but himself. If he thought we would sit by and allow the Imperials to keep building tools for breaching our walls, he is a fool. I appreciate you are following orders; however, I strongly advise you to refrain from attempting to scold me further, Captain Garrison."

Garrison did not reply right away; he knew he had to tread carefully. Odpor would not think twice about killing him if he said the wrong thing. He wished General Sylvester were there; the seasoned general always knew the right thing to say in every situation. Garrison was good at following orders—it was why his general loved him—but improvising on the spot had always been a weakness. Being entrusted with a meeting of such importance was new for him. Taking a deep breath, he tried to bring the situation back under control.

"My apologies, Chieftain Odpor. I meant not to offend you. General Sylvester is quite pleased that you took him up on his offer, and he looks forward to a fruitful relationship with you and your people. In fact, he has sent me to bring you another gift, one that he believes will rapidly accelerate matters. If this goes as well as General Sylvester believes it will, this war could be over—and your people independent from the Empire—within weeks."

"I am curious to hear what your general has to say. You may relay your message, Captain Garrison. Just be sure to mind your manners this time. Do not forget, you are a guest in my home and should conduct yourself accordingly."

Garrison paused for a moment, trying to collect his thoughts. It was an intricate plan, and he needed to communicate it to the dwarven chieftain perfectly. Any mistake that occurred from a miscommunication could set them back by months, and Garrison would bear the blame for it. General Sylvester had placed a great deal of trust in him by sending him here to negotiate, and he must not fail. He may not have liked what Sylvester had planned, but he had to have faith that it was the right thing to do. Who was he to question the plans of such a brilliant man?

"Supreme General Cadmus Twilcox is incensed over the attack on the supply caravan. He is planning retaliation against you, an assault that will take place on the night of the new moon. General Sylvester has sent me to bring you the details of this attack so you can be properly prepared."

Odpor did not respond immediately, his bright blue eyes simply staring into Garrison's. The Imperial captain knew the dwarf was trying to decide how far he should take this partnership with General Sylvester.

He's probably wondering if we offered up that caravan as a sacrifice to earn his trust only to betray him, Garrison thought. It was a suspicion he would have himself if he were in the dwarf's position.

When the chieftain finally began to speak, it was with a slower, more measured tone than Garrison had heard him use previously.

"We destroyed your siege towers to prevent any assault against us.

You do not have the capabilities to penetrate our defenses; you know this as well as I do, Captain Garrison. The entire Imperial Army could march against this fortress, and we could hold it for a year with a token force of a thousand warriors. I assure you, we have a lot more than that. We have provisions stored that could last us upwards of three years, and we can grow our own food in this climate, a skill I assume has continued to elude your army. How exactly does Supreme General Twilcox plan to attack us?"

"Your provisions are the target of the attack. He understands we cannot outlast you in this siege. But you must know we are not ignorant of your series of tunnels, Chieftain Odpor. Most of their entrances continue to elude us—this is true—but our scouts have discovered your passage behind the waterfall, and this is where the attack will begin," Garrison said, noticing a flicker in Odpor's eyes at the mention of the waterfall. "Thirteen men will enter Muog through this tunnel with the intention of destroying as many of your stockpiled provisions as possible. Twilcox believes by damaging your foodstuffs, he can force you to the negotiating table and eventually into surrender."

"Very well. We will position guards in the tunnel and kill your men as soon as they try to enter the city. I fail to see how this helps put an end to this war. The loss of thirteen men will not cripple your forces in any meaningful way."

Once again, Garrison knew he had to tread carefully. Odpor was not going to like what General Sylvester wanted him to do, but Garrison needed to make him see why it was necessary. It was a strategy he could not imagine the dwarf ever applying on his own accord. Odpor was a much more straightforward type of man.

"General Sylvester suggests that you do not kill the men who are sent to destroy your provisions," Garrison began, drawing a bark-like laugh from the chieftain.

"Any Imperial who enters this city uninvited will die. That is my policy, and I will not compromise on it," Odpor said. "If Sylvester thinks

I will tolerate such an intrusion, he is sorely mistaken."

"General Sylvester understands this. However, he recommends that instead of killing them outright, it would be a worthwhile investment to take them prisoner instead. They will prove to be valuable bargaining chips."

"I doubt Twilcox cares much about the lives of thirteen men. He seems perfectly willing to throw them away as it is." Odpor snorted with contempt. "What value could they possibly have?"

"You are right, Chieftain Odpor. Twilcox does not care a bit about the lives of his men, which is exactly what we need the rest of the men under his command to realize. Once you have these men as your prisoners, you can demand that Twilcox end the siege in exchange for their lives. He will not do this; he will make no concession to you whatsoever. You know this as well as I do. General Sylvester is counting on it. So, you start executing your hostages one at a time. He will still make no concession, but with each death, the opinion of Twilcox within the ranks of the Imperial Army will sour even further. How long until the men turn against him completely?"

Once again, Odpor went silent for several long moments.

Garrison knew the dwarf did not like to put his faith in the word of an Imperial. But he also knew this had to be an enticing offer, even for such a stubborn man. The fact that Sylvester had delivered on their first agreement had to make it even more tempting.

"So, the opinion about Twilcox shifts, and then what? I am still not seeing an end to this war, Captain Garrison. I could not possibly care less about the internal politics of the Imperial Army."

"General Sylvester will lobby the other officers to remove Twilcox from command and install him in his place. You will release whatever prisoners remain," Garrison said, drawing another laugh. "This will enhance General Sylvester's stature in the eyes of both his men and of the Emperor. He will immediately show Twilcox's incompetence for what it is by doing what Twilcox could not. He will negotiate on your behalf with the Emperor as Supreme General. He will argue that we cannot win this war and that Qwitzite should be granted its independence to prevent further bloodshed."

"And what makes Sylvester so certain he can convince the Emperor of this?" Odpor asked. "He seems to be placing a great deal of faith in his own abilities, but I have seen little evidence of them."

"With respect, what do you have to lose? You have said it yourself: we cannot defeat you in battle. If you go along with this plan, the worst that happens is that you humiliate Cadmus Twilcox publicly and gain nothing else. The best that happens is that you gain your independence without sacrificing the lives of more of your warriors. No matter how it plays out, you win," Garrison explained, surprising even himself with his confidence.

For the first time in two meetings, Odpor motioned for several of his men to confer with him. This caught Garrison off guard; he had been under the impression that Odpor made all decisions on his own. After several minutes of whispering, Odpor nodded and motioned his men away.

"Very well, Captain Garrison. We will capture these men, just as General Sylvester has requested. We will execute them one by one until our demands are met or they are all dead. But I have a message for you to take back to Sylvester."

"Thank you, Chieftain Odpor. I knew you would see the wisdom in General Sylvester's plan. I would be delighted to carry any message you desire," Garrison replied, doing his best to not show any physical sign of the relief washing through his body.

"If this plan does not unfold in the manner that General Sylvester claims it will, that will be the end of our working relationship. I am a patient man, but I have little tolerance for incompetence. Thus far, he has been true to his word, though the results have been underwhelming at best. He needs to deliver exactly what he promises this time. Understood?"

"I understand, Chieftain Odpor. I will deliver your message to General Sylvester. I thank you for your kind reception," Garrison said.

The black-clad guards escorted him back through the house and city to the main gates. Once they had closed behind him, Garrison hurried across the neutral territory, anxious to share his success with General Sylvester. He found the general in his tent, bent over a length of parchment with a quill in his hand. The general dropped the quill as he entered and motioned for him to take a seat.

"I am glad to see you have returned safely, Captain Garrison. Please report on everything that happened inside Muog. How did the negotiations go?"

Garrison recounted the entire negotiation with Odpor, including his warning at the end of their meeting. Sylvester listened intently, not interrupting, though his expression grew more gleeful by the second. Once Garrison had finished, the general stood up and retrieved a bottle of whiskey from a cupboard. He poured two glasses, then handed one to Garrison and raised his own in a toast.

"Well done, Captain Garrison. I had high expectations for you today, but somehow you have managed to exceed them. I foresee another promotion in the near future. Major Terrence Garrison has a rather pleasant ring to it, does it not?"

Garrison swelled with pride. It had been a stressful day, but it was all worth it to have the respect and gratitude of the man he most admired. When he had joined the Imperial Army at the age of eighteen, he had never imagined he would reach the ranks he had attained. He owed his career to Alexander Sylvester, and he knew it was a debt he could never repay. His general's tactics here in Qwitzite might baffle him, but Sylvester had earned his loyalty, and it would never waver.

"Sir, thank you for placing your trust in me to carry out this negotiation today. I hope I continue to serve you well for many years to come."

"There is nobody else I would rather have representing me, my old friend. You do the Empire proud with each day of your service. When they tell the story of this war generations from now, your name will be spoken with great reverence. Your contributions to putting a rapid end to this conflict will live for as long as the Empire itself."

Sylvester rose, taking Garrison's glass and pouring him another whiskey. Garrison accepted the drink with a quick word of thanks and drank it down, not wanting to intrude on his general's private time. As he prepared to take his leave, Sylvester stopped him.

"You know, Captain Garrison, I understand that my methods here are highly irregular. You are a career soldier, and I would understand if you have any questions. If you do, better they are discussed privately, between us."

I should have known he would see right through me, Garrison thought. He had served General Sylvester for too long and through too many conflicts to conceal his thoughts. But his general was right; Garrison had found himself questioning Sylvester over the past few weeks in ways that he would never have imagined.

"I have no questions for you, General Sylvester, sir. I know that you always act with the best interests of the Imperial Army in your heart. I would never presume to question your methods. Frankly, I'm not qualified to do that. I won't lie to you—I don't like the sacrifices that have to be made here, but I understand why they are necessary."

"I know what you mean, my old friend. It leaves a sour taste in the mouth, does it not? Yet as you say, we must sometimes make distasteful sacrifices in the name of the greater good. If we do not make these sacrifices, how many hundreds or thousands of our brothers-in-arms will pay the price? For how many generations to come would the Empire suffer? It's too high a price to pay for the sake of my own misgivings."

"You are right, sir. You always are. If you need nothing further from me, I think I will retire for the evening," Garrison replied.

"Of course, Captain Garrison. You are dismissed. Rest well, my friend."

THE SOLDIER'S BURDEN

Terrence Garrison left the tent without looking back, not wanting his general to see the shame in his eyes.

Chapter Twelve

Darian Tor woke in the early afternoon, heeding Axel Stark's advice to sleep as late as his body would allow. They didn't know when they would have another opportunity, so it was best to get plenty of rest now. In a few short hours, they would set out on their mission to destroy Muog's foodstuffs. Most of the past four days had been spent drilling with swords and studying the map Axel had given them. Darian had stared at the parchment until he felt it had been burned into his mind. All that was left to do was gather the small handful of items he would need to carry with him on the mission.

Darian sat up in his bunk, trying and utterly failing to keep his mind focused on anything except the day and night ahead of him. He realized he had never been so aware of every part of his body before: the way his fingers felt as he flexed them, the way the rough Imperial-issued blankets felt against his skin. He had always complained about the discomfort of the bunks, but now he would give anything to be able to stay in it all day. There were so many miniscule details in life that he had never taken time to appreciate, small details that made the experience of living so much sweeter. The taste of food, the feeling of the sun on his skin—he had never appreciated them as he should.

You will have plenty of time to enjoy these things. You are not going to die tonight, he told himself. It felt like he had given himself the same encouragement a thousand times, but it was still a difficult state of mind to change.

Realizing things were not likely to improve while just sitting in his bunk, Darian forced himself to his feet and set about getting dressed. He donned only the thick black underclothes issued to Imperial soldiers to wear under their armor. They would be more vulnerable to attacks, but the metal armor would make too much noise on an operation that demanded utter silence. He strapped his sword and dagger to his belt, leaving the rest of his weapons behind. He also clipped a small empty pack to his waist; Axel would be procuring them a small amount of rations to carry with them. Apart from his weapons, he carried only a single canteen of water.

Looking around, he saw his three friends going through a similar ritual. None of them seemed to want to make eye contact with any of the others. Darian assumed they, like him, did not want their friends to see the fear in their eyes or hear it in their voice.

After spending several minutes stalling, they knew there was nothing left for them to pretend to be doing and made their way to the chow hall for lunch.

They received extra rations in the chow line that day, just as Axel had told them they would, due to the nature of their mission. Soldiers at nearby tables were staring longingly at their full plates of food, but none of the four took any pleasure in the act of eating. If the men staring in envy were offered the opportunity to do what they were about to do in exchange for more food, Darian doubted any of them would jump to accept it. He looked around for some sign of Axel, but his friend was nowhere to be found. Assuming the sergeant was making final preparations for their mission, Darian continued to chew and swallow, knowing he would need the nourishment later that night.

"I know we can't discuss this too loudly, but I just want you to know I'll be watching out for all of you tonight," Preston said. "And I'm glad to have all of you beside me. I was relieved when we were all stationed here together, and nights like this are the reason. For better or for worse, we will face tonight together. That brings me a lot of comfort."

"I feel the same way, my friends," Berj replied between mouthfuls of food. Darian and Darnold could only manage silent nods of agreement. Darian felt if he opened his mouth, his lunch might come spilling back out.

Finishing their lunch, they rose from the table and left the chow hall, heading to their designated meeting place at the Imperial encampment's northeastern edge. It felt like an out-of-body experience for Darian, as though somebody else were moving his arms and legs and he was only along for the ride. It occurred to him as they wound their way through the maze of tents that he might be looking at the camp for the last time.

Stop that, you idiot. If you keep thinking like that, you're doomed. You need to get your head straight. Everyone is depending on you to be sharp tonight.

Axel Stark was waiting for them at the meeting point, along with four other privates and Captain Dunstan. The last four privates joined them a few moments later.

"Welcome, gentlemen," Axel said. "As you know, we are on a tight schedule here, so I'm going to jump right into it. Please grab provisions for your waist packs; this is what I was able to procure for us. It isn't much, but it should be enough to last us until we return in the morning. We have four short bows as well. Tor, Dans, Tombax, Lester, you four tested as the best shots in your final evaluations; each of you take a bow and a dozen arrows."

Darian and Darnold moved forward with the two other privates to retrieve their bows. It was a far smaller and more compact weapon than Darian was used to, as it needed to be for this type of operation. He briefly tested the pull of the string, then slung the weapon to his back, clipping the small quiver of arrows to the back of his belt.

He retrieved two small skins of water, along with several dried rations to place into his pack. Hopefully they would not need the food, but Axel had said it never hurt to be prepared.

"Have a last drink before you leave, gentlemen," Captain Dunstan said, passing around a large canteen of water. "It's a long march to the Moyie River, and those small skins you have don't hold much. Better to save what's in your own canteens as long as possible."

Darian noted that the other privates' commanding officers had not gone to the trouble of coming to see them off and was grateful for Dunstan. He did not know if the rumors about the man's past were true or not, but he was a captain who genuinely seemed to care for the well-being of the men under his command.

Examining Dunstan when the captain was not looking, Darian took notice of the many lines crisscrossing the man's face, along with several noticeable scars. Dunstan had seen more of war than all of the rest of them combined, and Darian hoped he would have a chance to learn more from the stoic captain. *First things first: survive tonight. Then you can get to know your captain.*

"I know you are eager to be off, Sergeant Stark, so I will wish you all good fortune. Act with honor and integrity and be worthy of the title of Imperial soldier. Always watch the backs of your brothers, and you will all return safely," Captain Dunstan bade them. "I will be anxiously awaiting your arrival."

"Thank you, Captain Dunstan, sir. We will make the Empire proud tonight, I guarantee it," Axel replied. "Let's get moving, gentlemen."

The group marched due north for several hours under the blazing summer sun. Few words were exchanged; none were necessary. They knew what was expected of them, and there was no need to discuss it. The effort they would spend on talking was better kept in reserve. The march was mostly downhill, for which Darian was grateful. The summer sun beating down on the hard brown earth was harsh enough without having to climb uphill at the same time. He was briefly thankful he was not wearing his armor before reminding himself he would probably be wishing for it in only a few short hours.

They reached the banks of the Moyie River after three hours of hard marching, and Axel signaled they could take a brief break. Darian drank what remained in his canteen and both of his water bottles, gulping them down eagerly before refilling them from the river. His friends hurried to follow his lead, and Berj splashed the cold river water on top of his head. Darian knew the Moyie River flowed all the way from the North Sea in distant Thornata to the South Sea in Qwitzite, making it one of the longest rivers in the Empire. To his disappointment, there was no northern chill to the water. In fact, it was rather warm and unsatisfying, but he knew he needed to drink as much of it as possible.

"Five more minutes, men, and then we have to get moving again. The sun will be going down in about an hour, and then the clock will really be ticking on us," Axel called out. "At least as it cools, we won't be quite so miserable."

"How are you feeling, Darian?" Darnold asked, coming up beside him.

"I don't know, to be honest. I don't know if I'm excited or scared. I don't know if I'm dreading what's to come or if I just want to get it over with already. I've never felt quite this way before. How about you?"

"I know what you mean. It still seems surreal that we are on this mission. It seems like yesterday Harter Arsch was berating us for being a bunch of incompetent buffoons. Remember that one time he predicted the four of us would be the first to end up as corpses? He was such a charming man, wasn't he? Let's hope he was wrong."

The pair stood awkwardly for a moment longer, Darian not wanting the conversation to end, but neither having anything of value to add to it. They simply stood in silence, both appreciating the other's reassuring presence. Darian thought again about how fortunate he was to have found three good friends in training and even more fortunate to be with them on his first mission. To have such good fortune, along with being under the command of the man he trusted above any other, was a blessing he could never have imagined.

Their five minutes were up before they knew it, and Axel had them marching south and then west along the Moyie River as the sun slipped out of sight to the west. Before long, they were walking in near-total darkness, which became more of a comfort the closer they drew to Muog. They could not see the city, but they could feel it looming nearby. It was as though the pitch-black sky to their east grew even darker as they marched closer to its shadow. It felt odd to Darian, being so close to such a massive structure yet being unable to see it.

They had been marching south for perhaps two hours when Axel brought them to a halt by raising one hand. All speaking had been forbidden for the past two hours, but Axel raised one finger to his ear and then pointed south. Darian listened carefully, and sure enough, he thought he could make out the sound of falling water in the distance. He fought to maintain his calm demeanor; his heart had begun to race once more. How was it possible for time to pass so slowly and yet so quickly at the same time? He clenched his hands into fists and was surprised to find his palms drenched with sweat.

They reached the edge of the cliffs sooner than Darian had expected, only ten minutes after Axel had first caught the sound of the river falling over the edge. The sergeant immediately went to work securing several ropes to stones and tree trunks near the cliff's edge. These would allow five of them to climb down at the same time. Gathering the group together in a tight circle, he whispered his instructions.

"Okay, men, we need to get down there fast. The longer we stand around here, the higher our chances of being discovered. Tor, Dans, Jenson, Preston, and Lester will go first. Once you have found the opening to the tunnel, wait there for the rest of us. Do not proceed farther into the tunnel, and do not make a sound unless you are under attack. We don't know what type of security the dwarves might have inside. Understood?"

Everyone nodded their agreement, and Darian hurried to tie one of the long ropes around his waist. Axel inspected the knot after he had finished and silently clasped his shoulder in encouragement before moving on to check Preston's. Once he had reviewed all of their knots, Axel nodded for them to proceed.

Darian moved to the edge of the cliff, the waterfall now roaring directly beside him. Berj stood on one side of him, and the young private named Lester stood on the other. Taking one last deep breath, he turned, planted his feet firmly against the cliff, and began to make his way down.

The cool mist emanating from the nearby waterfall was refreshing after the long hot march, but it quickly moistened their hands, making the climb even more perilous. Darian thought back every few seconds to the knot he had tied around his waist, hoping he had made it secure enough to hold his weight if his hands should slip.

Progress was slow but steady. The cliff face adjacent to the waterfall was slick as well, so they needed to take their time, slowly placing one foot after the other. They had been climbing down for nearly ten minutes when Lester, who was closest to the waterfall, hissed in Darian's ear.

"The tunnel entrance is here!"

Darian immediately came to a halt and hissed the same announcement to Berj, who sent it on down the line. Lester went first, moving slowly in an awkward scrambling walk along the cliff and into the waterfall. Darian held his breath for a moment, hoping Lester's rope would hold against the force of the river falling from above. To his relief, it did, and a moment later, Lester's line tumbled back out of the water, indicating that the young man had made it safely into the tunnel. Now it was Darian's turn.

He crouched low against the cliff and began awkwardly shuffling his feet to the right, toward the waterfall. The force of the water caught him somewhat off guard as he entered its flow, but he managed to maintain his grip on the rope. His feet had a hard time gripping the rock, but inch by inch, he made his way through the torrential downpour until he felt a hand close around his foot. Lester helped guide him into the entrance of the tunnel. Darian nodded the young man a wordless thanks as he untied his rope and sent it back out of the cave, signaling for Berj to follow him.

Turning away from the waterfall, Darian squinted through the darkness, searching for some sign of the dwarves, his hand hovering near his dagger. The fact that he was not dead already was encouraging, but for all they knew, there were guards hiding just a few feet away, waiting to ambush them. He took a few steps into the cave, away from the edge of the tunnel, but didn't advance farther. Axel's instructions had been clear: nobody was to advance position until they were all together. Thinking about what might be waiting for them up ahead, Darian was all too happy to comply.

One by one, the soldiers made their way down the cliff and through the waterfall into the tunnel. Darian stood there shivering, for the damp underground air did little to dry his clothes after his climb through the downpour. Axel arrived last, having stood guard for all of his men as they made the dangerous climb down the cliff, just as an Imperial officer should. As soon as his feet hit the tunnel, he cast about, searching for a way to secure his line. He settled on knotting it around a jagged stalagmite as they all silently prayed the knot would hold while they were doing their work in the city. That rope was their only means of escaping the tunnel once their work was finished, assuming they lived that long.

Even if you are lucky enough to survive this, you get to climb back up that slippery cliff afterward, Darian reminded himself.

Once the line was secured, Axel motioned for the men to come closer, drawing several strange objects from the pack at his waist. Showing them as best he could in the dim light, he rubbed the small object in his hands and then pressed it to his clothing. Darian repeated this, noting that the object seemed to be a small sack filled with tiny pebbles. As he pressed it to his clothes, he found that it had an immediate warming effect. It could not dry his clothing completely, but it made him significantly more comfortable, easing his shivering. In the darkness of the cave, he thought he could make out similar expressions of relief on the faces of his comrades.

"We cannot talk at all from this point onward. Stay tight and watch after the man to your left and right. Let's move," Axel said, his voice barely a hushed whisper.

They moved slowly, hardly able to see more than a foot in front of their faces in the pitch-black tunnel, but they dared not light so much as a candle in fear of giving themselves away. They were confident there would be torches lit in the streets of Muog to guide their way to the supplies and back to the tunnel, but they had to operate on touch alone for the time being.

So, onward they shuffled, having no idea how long the tunnel would extend or what would be waiting for them on the other side. Several times, one of them stumbled in the darkness, his comrades the only thing keeping him from crashing to the ground.

To Darian, it felt as if they crept along for hours, though he knew it must have only been a few minutes. The tunnel began to climb steadily, and he knew they were making their way up into the city. Darian kept his hand resting on the hilt of his sword, knowing a surprise encounter with dwarven warriors could happen at any time. He was surprised that after what felt like hours of walking in near-total darkness his eyes had not seemed to adjust at all to the absence of light.

I can't believe they don't have any guards inside this tunnel, Darian thought. They had all assumed they would have to quickly and silently eliminate at least a few sentries to gain entry to Muog. How could they not? Perhaps the dwarves believed they were the only ones who knew about their secret network of tunnels. If so, they had made a costly miscalculation.

When the first hints of torchlight came shimmering into view in the distance, Darian realized just how much his eyes had grown accustomed to the darkness. He blinked furiously against the sudden light, and Axel brought them to a halt to give their eyes a moment to adjust. After a brief pause, he motioned for them to proceed. Darian's eyes were still struggling to adjust, but he knew there was no time to waste. There could not be more than a few hours before the sun would begin to rise, and if they were still within sight of Muog's walls when that happened, it would be the end of them.

They stepped as one out of the tunnel and into what appeared to be a large courtyard. Darian could not help but been amazed at the dwarven craftsmanship as he looked around the square in awe. The stonework was unlike any he had seen anywhere else. To his surprise, the courtyard was adorned with flowers and plants, which hung from every ledge. Axel and Dunstan had told them that dwarves had found a way to grow things in this unforgivable terrain, but he had hardly believed it.

There was no time to sit back and admire the city's beauty. Axel was already motioning for them to follow him into an alleyway.

The thirteen men crept through the alleyway as silently as a cat stalking its prey. Darian could scarcely believe they had made it so far with no resistance. Maybe they had a chance of pulling this off after all.

He was still thinking about how fortunate they were when everything fell apart around them.

They had just emerged from the alleyway into another courtyard when a resounding clatter split the night behind them. Darian spun on the spot, and his heart sunk like a stone as a heavy wooden door slammed shut behind them. Similar crashes sounded out around, and the soldiers frantically cast about in dismay as every passage out of the courtyard was sealed shut one by one. The crashes were followed by a subtle yet far more ominous noise: the sound of bowstrings being drawn.

There were dwarves, dozens of them, positioned on balconies above them, bows leveled straight at them. The Imperials drew their weapons, though they knew there was nothing they could do.

This is it, Darian said to himself, taking a deep breath and hoping the end would come quickly. To his surprise, the terrible pain he braced for did not come; no arrows pierced his body. The dwarves seemed content to sit above them, keeping their bows leveled.

What are they doing? They could kill us all in less than a minute. What are they waiting on?

A heavily armored dwarf stepped out onto one of the balconies above them, smiling down at them in satisfaction.

"That was easier than I thought it would be. I was skeptical that you would be dumb enough to walk right into such an obvious trap. I will make this simple, Imperials. We have no wish to kill you, but we will if that's how you want this to go. Drop your weapons immediately. Any man who refuses to comply will be shot dead on the spot. You have five seconds to decide."

The first three seconds seemed to take an eternity to pass. Darian gripped his sword tightly, wishing the dwarves would have attacked them outright. He would much rather fall in a fair fight than stand here, just waiting on his inevitable execution. But just as the fourth second was passing, Axel cried out, "Drop your weapons! That's an order! We surrender!"

Chapter Thirteen

The darkness was deeply unsettling, and it didn't take long for the doubt to set in. Darian often found himself wondering if he was dead already. The passage of time was impossible to determine; he had no idea how long he had been sitting in the pitch-black hole the dwarves had left him in. It could have been hours or weeks for all he knew. He was not alone; he was sure of that much. He had felt men stir on either side of him, but he had no way to communicate with them. His mouth was gagged, and each of his wrists had been chained to iron bars behind his back. A cord had been wrapped around his neck, securing his head to the bars as well. If he leaned too far forward or to either side, he would slowly begin to strangle himself, a lesson he had learned the hard way while trying to sleep.

The dwarves had taken them into custody immediately after they had dropped their weapons, and they had been none too gentle about it. He had received a vicious punch to the ribs when one of the dwarves felt he was resisting his arrest. They had been blindfolded and shoved through the streets of Muog to the sounds of hisses and jeers that Darian could only assume had come from watching civilians. He had occasionally been struck by heavy objects that he could only assume were thrown by nearby bystanders. They had been brought to this prison, and the dwarves had finally removed the blindfold, though the room was so dark that it did him no good. They had been left here ever since, waiting for the hammer to fall.

Darian was puzzled as to why the dwarves had taken them captive at all. Their feelings toward the Empire and its soldiers were all too clear; why had they not been killed on the spot? He didn't know the answer, but he could not imagine it being a positive thing for them. Perhaps the dwarves planned to torture them for intelligence. Maybe they simply wanted to make them suffer first for the fun of it. Whatever the reasoning was, Darian did not think it was something that should make them feel overly optimistic. They had not been taken alive so the dwarves could host a banquet in their honor.

When the door swung open at last, it was as though the sun had suddenly risen right before their eyes. Darian's eyes immediately filled with tears, obscuring his vision almost as effectively as the darkness had. From the brief glimpse he'd managed to get before his eyes instinctively closed, the source seemed to be a solitary torch in a corridor outside their door. He could hear several heavy sets of footsteps entering the room. He managed to blink against his tears long enough to catch a glimpse of Berj Jenson's face next to his, and then the door was slammed shut once more, plunging them back into darkness.

"Do you enjoy the darkness, Imperial scum? Dwarves can see just as clearly at night as we do during the day. Did you know that? I would guess not. The Imperials have always been rather self-centered, have you not? If you had known, you might have stopped to question why we would have torches lit inside of our city at night when we do not need them. Or you might not have been foolish enough to think we could not spot you from our walls simply because it was dark outside. We could have killed you at any moment of our choosing. Simpleminded fools, you have the nerve to refer to us as savages. Not a single member of your command thought to take the time to learn something so valuable about us. Remove their gags. Do not mistake this as an invitation to speak up. You are not to speak until spoken to, Imperials. If you do, you will be disciplined."

A moment later, the cloth gag was pulled from Darian's mouth. He breathed deeply through his mouth and licked his lips, realizing for the first time how dry they had become from lack of water. They must have been kept in this prison for quite some time. His arms had begun to go numb as well, but unfortunately, the dwarf gave no command to set those free as well.

"I want you to know, Imperials, that I was against the idea of taking you prisoner. I advised Chieftain Odpor that he should have you killed on the spot and hang your bloody corpses from our walls as a message to your brothers. But Odpor's word is the law, and I will obey. Just understand, keeping me happy is your best hope of continuing to draw breath. My name is Krillzoc, and I am your new best friend. Do you know what dwarves say about their best friend? That they have no secrets from them. It will be the same between us, one way or another. Radig, bring their sergeant first," the dwarf ordered, and there was a commotion Darian's left.

He could feel Axel being shoved past him, and then the door opened, the intense light blinding them once more. Darian blinked furiously against the tears that welled up in his eyes and was able to briefly see his friend being forced out of the door. He took a small amount of solace from the fact that Axel was still alive, at least for the time being. The door closed behind him, and they were once again plunged into utter darkness. It took a minute for Darian to realize the dwarves had not bothered to replace their gags.

"Why haven't they just killed us yet? They have to realize we don't know anything of value," came a raspy voice Darian was pretty sure belonged to Max Preston.

"Be careful what you say. They didn't forget our gags by accident. I promise you they are listening in on us right now," came Darnold's scratchy reply.

"So what if they are listening? What do we have to lose at this point?" Berj's voice was right next to Darian. "Every single dwarf in this city can burn as far as I'm concerned, and I hope they heard me say it."

"We all need to shut up," said a voice Darian didn't recognize.

"What do you think they are going to do to Axel?" Darian asked.

"The same thing they're going to do to the rest of us. Stark deserves to go first, leading us into this mess," the unfamiliar voice said.

If Darian had not been shackled to the iron bars, he would have launched himself at the man who had dared to say such a thing. Axel was here with them because he was following orders, and Darian made a silent vow to himself to punch the speaker square in the mouth if he ever had the opportunity. Axel was not to blame for their predicament; the fault lay with the incompetent officers who had thought up this doomed operation. Did this fool really believe it had been Axel's idea?

"Well, it could be worse, right? We're all still breathing. That means there's still hope for us," Berj said.

"Yeah, you tell yourself that," said another stranger. "The only reason we're still alive is because they want to take their sweet time and really enjoy killing us."

"Why so negative? We're Imperial soldiers, and Imperial soldiers don't quit in the face of adversity. Isn't that what Arsch used to bark at us during those sprints he made us do in the burning sun? We can't just give up and accept our fate. Don't be a coward," Berj shot back.

The man had no response.

Not wanting to give anything away to any dwarves who might've been listening in, they sat in relative silence. It did not take long for Darian to lose track of time again; he wished he knew how long Axel had been gone. He hoped his friend was still alive, but he forced himself to accept the very real possibility that he was not. If the dwarves had gotten whatever information they were after out of Axel, there would be little reason to leave him alive. *The same could be said for the rest of us as well.* If Axel was dead, the rest of them were already living on borrowed time.

When the door did finally open again, Darian could hardly contain a cry of relief as two dwarves dragged Axel back into the room. He was prone but still breathing. Once they had refastened his restraints, the two unshackled two of the privates and vanished from the room with them without saying a word. After waiting a minute to ensure their captors were gone, Darian began crying out to Axel.

"Wake up, Axel! What happened? What did they do to you?"

"Our . . . hosts . . . are not . . . fond . . . of Imperial soldiers," Axel forced out, sounding as though each word caused him sheer anguish to produce.

Darian could not see his friend in the blackness, which only made things worse. His mind immediately went to work, imagining up all manner of gruesome injuries that had been inflicted upon Axel. He did not question his friend further, not wanting to put him through the agony of answering. The fact that the dwarves had taken two more men told him they were not satisfied with any answers they might have gotten out of Axel. He was immediately proud of his friend for being able to resist their brutal questioning.

"They're going to ask you questions. You know what's going to happen when you don't answer. Or when you do answer. Or when you take too long to answer. Don't let them break you," Axel murmured before going silent. In the blackness, Darian could only surmise that his friend had blacked out.

After another extended period of blackness and silence, the dwarves returned with their two prisoners, taking two more as they left. This happened several more times until, at last, Darian felt their rough hands unshackling him from the bars and knew it was his turn. He was shoved out of the room and into a bright corridor, light from nearby windows betraying the fact that the sun was up. It must've been the next day, or had they already been prisoners for several days? Time had lost all meaning to him in the blackened room. As his vision finally began to adjust to the newfound light, he recognized that Berj Jenson had been removed from the room along with him. Berj shot him a grim smile; they both understood that whatever happened next, it would not be pleasant for them.

The dwarves did not speak a word to them as they shoved the pair of young men down the corridor and around a corner. Darian stumbled once, his legs numb from atrophy, but his captor gave him no sympathy, only shoving him along even harder. They did not travel far, but the journey was exhausting nonetheless. *It's incredible how quickly our bodies start to go soft on us.*

They stepped into a small room, which was unadorned except for two chairs that sat facing each other in the middle of the room. After forcing Darian and Berj into the chairs, the dwarves shackled their wrists and ankles to the legs of the chairs and then left the room, still never speaking a word.

"I suppose this is where the fun begins," Berj muttered, shooting Darian an entirely unconvincing smile.

Darian's heart was racing. Nobody who had returned after being escorted out by the dwarves had been able to articulate much of what had happened to them. Looking around the room for some sign of hope, Darian's heart sunk even further. There was freshly dried blood on the floor beneath the chairs, confirming his suspicions of what was about to happen to them. The door flew open with a bang, and a large dwarf with a gleeful expression etched across his face entered the room.

"We meet again, Imperials. Do you remember me? We met back in your box. My name is Krillzoc, and I would like to be entrusted with some of the information you carry in your heads. If you cooperate with me, this will go nice and easy for you. If you do not, well, I will still get what I want from you anyway. So, why should there be any unpleasantness between us?"

Darian glanced to Berj, who had not removed his defiant gaze from Krillzoc. Darian admired his friend's courage, but he had a feeling this defiance would only make things worse for Berj later. The dwarf actually smiled at them, his lips splitting wide to reveal a mouth full of broken and misshapen teeth. The smile was confirmation enough of what Darian had already suspected. Krillzoc was a twisted man who would genuinely enjoy what he was about to do.

It's just pain; it will fade in time, he told himself, struggling to control his breathing.

"Let us start with you," Krillzoc said, walking over to stand before Darian. Darian noted Krillzoc was standing slightly to one side, leaving Berj an unobstructed view of what was about to happen. "Answer my questions honestly, and you will be grateful that you did. Fair enough? First question: Can General Sylvester be trusted?"

"I don't know who that is," Darian answered honestly, earning himself a hard backhanded slap across the face.

"We are already getting off on the wrong foot, Imperials. There is no need for this. What about you?" Krillzoc moved over to Berj. "Can General Sylvester be trusted?"

"Who?" Berj spat, provoking Krillzoc to smack him as well.

Krillzoc stepped away from the chairs and began to pace along the far side of the room. Darian's face stung, and he could feel some swelling beginning to form, but if that was the worst Krillzoc had to offer them, it wasn't so bad. However, the smile continuing to stretch across the dwarf's face hinted there was worse yet to come.

"Do you think you are acting brave or noble by protecting your Imperial secrets? Do you think your officers would endure such punishment to protect you if your positions were reversed? Do not be naive."

It was a question designed to make them question their loyalty. It didn't work, but it did make Darian wonder. Would any officer endure the torture they were about to face? He had no evidence to back this up, but he had a feeling that Captain Dunstan would, particularly if it meant protecting his men. Axel had resisted them as well. If he hadn't, Krillzoc would not be bothering with the rest of them. *You don't know that. He seems like a real sadistic ass; maybe this is what he does for fun.*

"My friends, I hope you understand that if you continue to defy me, this is going to escalate. There is no need for that to happen. I care deeply about the safety of my people, just like you. I am not going away. Just answer my question. It is quite simple, is it not? Can General Sylvester be trusted?"

He can ask this question as many times as he would like. It's not going to change the fact that I have no idea who he is talking about, Darian thought exasperatedly. A glance at Berj showed that his companion was just as confused as he was. Whoever this General Sylvester was, the dwarves certainly had a great deal of interest in him.

"Your silence will not serve you well," Krillzoc warned.

"We don't know who you are talking about! Do you think infantry grunts like us have access to generals? Get it through your thick skull!" Berj shouted.

Krillzoc advanced on Berj, his fist clenched. Berj, to his credit, did not flinch, though Darian did at the thought of what was about to happen to his friend. Krillzoc did not strike him; instead, he smiled even wider.

"Very well, we will speed things along. Bring in the cart!"

The door opened once more, and the two guards returned, this time pushing a wheeled cart bearing a number of metal implements. Taking one look at the various metallic objects that rested on the cart, Darian knew Berj had made a terrible mistake by lashing out at Krillzoc.

"Now, Imperials, we will find out exactly what you do or do not know," the dwarf hissed menacingly.

***

Darian was hardly aware of the fact that they were shackling him to the bars. He was back in the dark room, though he couldn't even muster up the strength to care about it. His ears were still ringing, though from his own screams or Berj's, he did not know. He felt as though the metallic taste in his mouth would never go away. The dwarves had not bothered to offer them any water after they had finished with their questioning, and his throat throbbed from the force of the exertion. He could hardly support himself, but every time he slumped forward, the cord around his neck threatened to strangle the life out of him. More than once he was tempted to allow it to happen, just to release himself from the agonizing pain.

His shoulder pained him the most, and having his arms forced behind his back did not help matters. Krillzoc had been particularly happy about that portion of the interrogation. Berj had received it first, and Darian had been forced to watch, knowing all the while that he was next. He did not think he would ever forget the smile on Krillzoc's face. It would be burned into his mind just as the mark was now burned into his flesh.

If I ever have a chance, I will kill that sadistic bastard. I don't care if it's the last thing I ever do. I'll smile into his dying eyes, Darian swore to himself.

Two by two, the soldiers were removed from the dark room and subjected to Krillzoc's cruel brand of questioning. None of them had much of anything to say after they were returned; in fact, a few of them were utterly unable to speak. Darian was finally able to register that all of the men were returned, which gave him a small measure of comfort. Whatever was still ahead for them, at least they were all still alive and together.

"Who the blazes is General Sylvester?" Berj managed to say after what felt like an eternity of silence.

"He's the general in charge of negotiating with the dwarves. They must feel he is not being up-front with them about something," Axel groaned.

Did the dwarves really think men like them would have any real insight into the mind of a general? Or was it merely a matter of Krillzoc looking for an excuse to torture them for his own sadistic pleasure? Still, why had they not been killed at the end of the interrogation? The dwarves were keeping them alive for a reason, and Darian was none too eager to find out what that was.

***

He didn't know how long they had been sitting in blackness when the door swung open once more. More guards were shuffling into the room this time, though his eyes could not see through the blinding light well enough to count them. A waterskin was thrust between his lips, and he drank eagerly, though his throat was so dry that it was a struggle to swallow. Then rough hands were untying the cord from around his neck and unlocking his shackles.

The guard pulled him to his feet, and for a fleeting moment, Darian thought about trying to fight back, to make a break for it. But he knew his body was too weak. The water he had just been given was the only nourishment he had consumed in what felt like days. Any attempt to fight back or escape would likely just result in another round of brutal torture.

Shackles were placed around his ankles, and he realized the dwarves were linking them together. Were they finally going to be killed? The dwarves placed a sack over his head, which gave him a sliver of hope. Wherever they were going, the dwarves did not want them to see. Did this mean they might live long enough to use such information against their enemies? It was a miniscule sliver of hope, but he clung to it.

There was a tug at Darian's ankles, and he knew they were being shuffled along. To his surprise, he managed to keep his feet, though he heard several of his comrades being punished for faltering and holding up the line. He did not know where the dwarves were leading them, but they did seem to be climbing, and at one point there was a long series of stairs. Once the stairs ended, he could feel a breeze like he had not felt since they had been forced into that black cell. For the first time since their capture, he felt a more significant measure of comfort. The wind was familiar; in a way, it even reminded him of his home in Verizia so far away.

It's because the wind is the only familiar thing in this desolate wasteland—the wind and Axel, he reminded himself.

The sack was ripped from his head suddenly, nearly overwhelming his senses. The sun was just beginning to rise on the eastern horizon; they had been captives for at least a full day. As he fought through the tears flooding his eyes, Darian realized they were standing on top of Muog's outer wall. The neutral territory stretched out before them, and at the far end was the Imperial encampment. He would never have suspected that he could look at the camp and feel such a sense of longing. What he wouldn't give to be making his way to the chow hall for another disappointing portion of tasteless rations.

Krillzoc was stalking back and forth in front of them, a scowl etched upon his face.

Well, he would probably be smiling if he were about to kill us, Darian thought.

Another dwarf had just arrived, walking up to Krillzoc and clasping his hand. Darian could tell at once that this dwarf was an important person. All of their guards had immediately snapped to attention at his arrival, and even Krillzoc seemed to be deferring to him. His black armor was similar to that of their guards, though his bore several decorative patterns on the shoulders. He took a long look at the Imperials, his piercing blue eyes boring into each of them before he finally spoke.

"Good morning, Imperial guests. I am Odpor, chieftain of the dwarves and ruler of Qwitzite. I trust your accommodations have been comfortable?" he asked, drawing a laugh from Krillzoc.

"Your hospitality has been quite impressive indeed. It as though we have been housed at a luxurious resort on the coast in Floresta," Berj quipped, drawing a glare from Axel.

Krillzoc advanced on Berj, but Odpor waved him off. He advanced on Berj himself, a bemused smile on his face. He came to a halt no more than a foot from Berj's face.

"You have nerve, Imperial. I like nerve. It is a shame you are on the wrong side of this war; I could make use of a man like you. Now, fear not, my friends. I have not brought you here this morning for any devious purpose. In fact, I am going to order my men to feed you upon your return to your cell this morning. You will probably get more to eat than you have been in your camp these past weeks. Perhaps I will even have a washbasin brought for you. Does that not sound lovely? I hear you have been having trouble with getting supplies in your camp. I apologize for the delay, but you must understand, there was certain information we needed from you. All I need you to do right now is stand there, just as you are. Easy enough, yes?"

Odpor turned away from them and stepped up to a strange implement that had been carved into the wall. When he spoke into it, his voice blasted out with incredible force across the neutral territory. The walls shook with the power of his voice, and Darian had to make a conscious effort not to cringe at the noise, not wanting to give his captors the satisfaction of seeing him quiver.

"Attention, Imperials. I suggest you come out of your tents and see what I have to show you," Odpor called out. He then stepped away from the implement and waited.

Off in the distance, Darian could make out the unmistakable shapes of men filing out of their tents and gathering at the edge of the neutral territory. He was thankful that the distance was great enough that they could not possibly make out his face.

Odpor continued to wait, obviously wanting as large of an audience as he could get. At last, when it seemed as though at least half of the Imperial forces had gathered, he began to speak again, the walls shaking from the force of his voice.

"As you can see, we have captured thirteen of your men. We caught them sneaking into this city with the intent of destroying our stockpiles of food. Shame on you for attempting such an underhanded attack. I thought the emperor considered himself above such devious tactics? Clearly, they were not successful. If you want these men returned safely, the solution is simple: break your siege and march home. You have until dawn tomorrow to begin withdrawing your forces. If you do not do as I ask, one of these men will die tomorrow at dawn. Then, with every passing day, another will die until you have complied or they are all dead. It is your choice, Imperial scum! Your time in Qwitzite is at an end. The dwarves will no longer live under the tyranny of your emperor's rule. I suggest you get moving; you have a great deal of work ahead of you."

Odpor stepped away from the speaking implement and motioned for the guards to take them away. The sacks were placed back over their heads, and they were shoved unceremoniously back to their prison. The promised food was waiting for them—rather meager portions of stale bread and past-ripe fruit, but food nonetheless. Darian wolfed his down and leaned back against the wall. The dwarves had not shackled them to the bars again, for which he was grateful. But now that a deadline had been set, he felt panicked, as though the walls were swiftly closing in around him. He knew the army would never give in to Odpor's demands. There was no chance of it.

In less than one day, one of them would die.

Chapter Fourteen

Nobody seemed to want to stand in the path of Captain Thaddeus Dunstan as he marched determinedly through the Imperial camp. By now, word would have spread throughout the encampment; it was inevitable. Everyone would know that four of his men were among those Odpor had marched out onto the walls of Muog and levied his threats against. He had been summoned to a war council in the tent of Supreme General Cadmus Twilcox, and he was anxious to hear what was being done to free his men.

He was brought to a halt by Twilcox's guards at the tent entrance and was forced to wait impatiently for several minutes while they verified that he was indeed authorized to be there. As soon as he stepped into the tent, he felt a wave of disgust wash over him at the sight that met his eyes.

Cadmus Twilcox had long been known as a hypocrite, though Dunstan had never met the man personally and had never placed much faith in rumors. Stepping into the tent, he found the rumors to be true. He could see that the aging general was not living in the same wretched conditions as the men he had led to this desolate region of the Empire.

If there was a piece of furniture that was not adorned in pure black silk, Dunstan could not spot it. Even the table and chairs that had been gathered for the war council were covered in fine silk cloths, the light provided by elaborate silver candelabras. Dunstan noted fresh fruit and vegetables—luxuries the ordinary soldiers had not enjoyed at all during his time at the front—resting in crystal bowls by every chair.

Supreme General Cadmus Twilcox sat at the head of the table, with several generals and colonels seated around him. All turned as Dunstan entered the tent, and Dunstan snapped a salute to Twilcox.

"Welcome, Captain Dunstan. Please be seated." Twilcox indicated a chair at the far end of the table. "Thank you for joining us. It seemed fitting, considering several of your men are among the prisoners."

Dunstan silently pulled out the assigned chair and took a seat. He noted a few of the colonels giving him disapproving looks. A man of his rank would never typically be invited to such a meeting, but this meant nothing to Dunstan. He also suspected his previous reputation had something to do with several of the glares being sent his way, but again, he could not possibly care less. They could judge him all they wanted. None of these men had been in Thornata. He could sleep soundly at night believing he had done the right thing, regardless of what Imperial High Command thought.

Do any of you pampered fools even remember how it feels to see your blade covered in blood? Or to see one of your men bleed out in front of you?

"Let's begin, gentlemen. I've gathered you here to discuss options. As you know, thanks to that savage Odpor announcing it to the entire encampment, they have thirteen of our soldiers in their custody. Supposedly, they will start killing them tomorrow if we don't signal our intent to end the siege. Thoughts?" Twilcox started.

"They wouldn't dare execute captured Imperial soldiers. It's a bluff to force concessions out of us. I would bet my career on it. Odpor may be a dumb savage, but he realizes we have not even begun to extend ourselves against him yet. Killing those men could provoke the type of assault their defenses cannot hope to withstand," a colonel to Dunstan's right said.

An assault their defenses cannot withstand? Is this delusional fool watching the same war I am? Dunstan wondered. He did not speak, knowing his words would count for nothing at this point in the discussion. He had expected to hear just this type of dismissiveness and had prepared himself for it. If he wanted his voice to count for something, he knew he needed to carefully choose his moment. Speaking up too soon would only sour the opinion against him even further.

"I agree, and besides, we cannot cave in to Odpor's demands under any circumstances. If we show weakness now, they will continue to exploit that until they have won their independence," a general at the far end of the table agreed. "If we negotiate with hostage takers, we will only end up with more of our men taken hostage. We should not show any weakness."

"Obviously, we will not be acquiescing to his demands," Twilcox said. "However, I want to discuss the validity of a rescue operation. While these men are low-ranking and relatively expendable in the grand scheme of things, their execution could damage morale here in the encampment. My concern is less with the lives of these men and more with the larger ramifications their deaths could bring. We need to weigh the potential benefits of such an operation. Even a half-hearted attempt could earn us some goodwill among the men."

It took every ounce of self-control that Thaddeus Dunstan possessed to hold his tongue at that latest statement. He had served in the Imperial Army for decades, many of those years as a commanding officer. In all those years, he had never once viewed a single man under his command as expendable. To hear the man who was in total command of all Imperial forces speak in such a dismissive and cavalier manner made him question if he would have been better off serving his time in the stockade after his misdeeds in Thornata. What had happened to the Imperial Army he had joined as a young man?

"With respect, Supreme General, I just don't see a rescue mission being viable," the first colonel said. "To date, we have only discovered one passageway into Muog, a fact that is obviously not lost on the dwarves. If we send a rescue party after them, the dwarves will simply end up with more hostages to execute. It is distasteful, but I think the best thing we can do at this point is to cut our losses."

"Captain Dunstan, several of these men are under your command, correct?" Twilcox asked, catching the captain off guard.

"Yes, sir, Supreme General, four of them," Dunstan replied.

"I assume you are here to pass on your extensive knowledge of war strategies, Captain Dunstan. You have quite a bit of experience, don't you?" One of the generals snickered, drawing a laugh from several others.

"That will do," Twilcox said softly, though Dunstan noted a smirk flashing across his face as he said it. "What do you think we should do, Captain Dunstan?"

"My understanding of Imperial Army policy says we never leave a fellow soldier behind enemy lines without taking all possible measures to set him free," Dunstan replied.

"You are known for your understanding of Imperial Army policy, aren't you, Captain Dunstan? Remind me, how many men did you get killed in Thornata?" the same general shot at him, no longer smiling.

"With respect, General, I do not believe the Thornatan civil war has any bearing on our present situation," Dunstan said, resisting the urge to walk across the tent and break the man's jaw. He would swing from a noose by nightfall for such a crime, but it would still feel immeasurably satisfying. But he had to maintain his composure. There was nothing he could do for those men if he got himself killed.

Most of the men assembled were in a fit of poorly controlled laughter by this point. Dunstan had known this was coming, but it did not make matters any less frustrating. He would never live down his decision to involve his men in the war in Thornata, and he had made his peace with that long ago. But the men who had been captured by the dwarves had nothing to do with that. He was beginning to suspect he had been summoned to this war council just so these officers could have a cheap laugh at his expense. Their opinions did not matter to him in the least, but he would not allow his men to die at the hands of their captors without advocating on their behalf.

"What do you propose, then, Captain Dunstan?" one of the colonels asked him. "If only that magical little friend of yours were here, he could blast open the gates of Muog with a lightning bolt, couldn't he? Then he could help us fight our way to victory, along with his pet ogre. That was the story you told the disciplinary panel, wasn't it, Dunstan? You come back from Thornata telling your cockamamie tall tales, and you expect us to take you seriously? If only we had magical little boys and obedient ogres to save us. The dwarves would have surrendered months ago."

They were throwing the standard insults at him, and he was almost frustrated by their lack of originality. He did wish Adel were there. The kindhearted young man would never hesitate to step in and help those in need. But he had not seen the young Rawl wielder in five years, and Dunstan had no idea how to get in contact with him. Adel could not help him here. If he was going to save the lives of his men, he had to do so with nothing more than his own ingenuity, and it seemed he would be receiving no help from his fellow soldiers either.

"We could gain entry to Muog with the use of climbing spikes," he suggested, to another round of laughter.

"And I suppose the dwarves will just sit back and let us climb their walls unchallenged?"

"No, I don't expect that they will. That's why we would need to create a diversion. A small company of archers firing on their northern walls would do the trick. The dwarves would move the majority of their defenses to respond to that side of the fortress. The archers could be kept at long range, in relative safety. It would be no more than a feint, but the dwarves would have no way of knowing it. In the confusion, a team of well-trained soldiers could scale the walls, get inside the city, find our men, and set them free."

"Who would lead this mission? And how would they get our men back out of Muog? Once the dwarves realize that the attack is a feint, they will spread their sentries out again. I doubt the team could escape by climbing the walls again. Don't forget, Captain Dunstan, there is an inner wall as well, just as high as the one we see around their outer perimeter," Twilcox said.

"Yes, Supreme General, I realize this. It occurs to me that this would be an ideal opportunity to discover another one of the tunnels that the dwarves are using to harass this camp. I would be happy to lead this expedition myself."

"You think you can just find one of their tunnels out of Muog?" one of the colonels said skeptically.

"Perhaps, but I don't believe we would have time to hunt it down on our own. The dwarves would be after us quickly after we liberate the prisoners. We would need to capture one of the dwarven guards alive and force him to give up the location of one of their tunnels."

They were not bothering to try to contain their laughter anymore. Dunstan realized just as well as they did how improbable such an operation would be, but he refused to leave his men behind without even trying to free them. Those soldiers had willingly put themselves in harm's way for their army, and their commanders seemed perfectly content to disregard that sacrifice as meaningless. Only one man at the table was not laughing, the man directly to Twilcox's right. Dunstan recognized him as General Alexander Sylvester, a man with a reputation for being a cold, calculating commander.

"Alex, you have negotiated directly with Odpor, albeit with rather middling results. What do you make of Captain Dunstan's plan?" Twilcox asked, bringing his laughter under control.

"I respect Captain Dunstan's desire to set our men free, and I find it to be a noble cause. If there were a plausible option for a rescue attempt available, I would be eager to explore it. Unfortunately, I feel his plan has virtually no chance of success and could prove to do more harm than good. A false attack on his city will not fool Odpor. He will realize we want to come after the captives. I do not know if he will follow through on his threat to kill them or not. I have only known him for the span of a single conversation. My instinct tells me he is not bluffing," Sylvester replied.

"With respect, General Sylvester, I still disagree," the first colonel who had spoken up said. "I do not think Odpor will dare harm a hair on those men's heads. We have not yet openly assaulted their fortress, and he will take no chance of provoking such an attack."

"You may be right, Colonel. It's possible that our best move is to do nothing and see what the dwarves elect to do," Sylvester replied. "However, I just want to make it clear what that truly means. We are gambling with the lives of those captured soldiers. We will not know Odpor's true intentions toward them until tomorrow at dawn. Is that a price we are willing to pay? That is not for me to decide."

Dunstan could scarcely believe what he was hearing. He had expected to face resistance, but he had never thought to find such a lack of courage amid so many Imperial officers. Not a single one of them seemed willing to stand with him. Perhaps the men who had risen through the ranks of the Imperial Army had gone soft over the years. Maybe they had always been like that and he had simply forgotten their cowardice. He had always noticed a trend of yes-men being promoted over those who had earned advancement through their courage and deeds.

"I agree with Alex; the best thing we can do at this stage is sit back and wait. It is possible the dwarves will not harm the men at all. Still, I do not want to simply do nothing. Alex, you met with Odpor once. Are you willing to do so again?" Twilcox asked.

"Yes, Supreme General, I will do whatever duty my people require of me," Sylvester replied. "It's quite possible I could free those men through diplomacy. I can depart within the hour if you so desire."

"Good, but wait until tomorrow afternoon. I want Odpor to show his hand first. Let's see what happens, and then you can go and negotiate based on his actions. Take Captain Garrison with you. I don't like the idea of you going into that city alone. The last thing we need is to give the dwarves another hostage."

"As you command, Supreme General," Sylvester replied with a smile that was a little too eager for Dunstan's liking.

"If I may be clear," Dunstan said, drawing every eye back to him. "Our plan is to sit back and wait and see if one or more of our soldiers is executed tomorrow morning?"

A few of the officers looked angry at his nerve, and several opened their mouths for sharp retorts, but Twilcox lifted a hand, restoring silence.

"I understand your frustration, Captain Dunstan, I truly do. Rest assured, I do not take the predicament these men find themselves in lightly. But they understood the risks involved when they enlisted in the Imperial Army. If any man can negotiate their release, it is Alexander Sylvester—of that much I am certain. But we need to see what Odpor elects to do first. Our patience will give the majority of those men their best chance of survival. Thank you, gentlemen. You are dismissed."

Dunstan snapped an irritable salute and left the tent without looking back. Unlike the rest of them, he did not believe for one second that Odpor was bluffing about executing a man at dawn. What had become of the Imperial Army he had joined as an eighteen-year-old man? In those days, it seemed like the fabled organization had stood for things that mattered. He wondered if that had ever truly been the case or if age and experience had merely shown him the truth of things.

He made for his tent, his heart racing with anger at what he had just heard and anticipation of what the following morning would hold. Even if a man was killed in the morning, he doubted anything of substance would be done in response. Those men needed help, and it appeared there was only one man who was willing to do what was necessary.

Chapter Fifteen

When the door opened, Darian Tor already knew what was going to come next. Sure enough, the guards stepped into the cell and set about shackling them together by the ankles, just as they had the last time. Once again, the sacks were placed over their heads, and the dwarves led them out of the room. Darian knew in his heart that the army had not submitted to Odpor's demands. This was not a negotiated release. They were going to be taken back up to the wall. Soon, one of them would be killed to send a message to the Imperial Army.

The march was the same as it had been the day before, a steady uphill climb culminating in a final trek up a long set of stairs. Unlike the previous morning, the journey seemed to go quickly, like death itself was racing to greet them.

I'm going to be the one selected to die first, Darian kept telling himself. He had spent most of the previous day and night reliving his life in his head. When he had signed up to serve in the Imperial Army, he had hoped to live up to the lofty reputations of his father and grandfather. But here he was, doomed to die after less than a month on the front lines. He wouldn't die in battle. He wouldn't be remembered as a man dying in service to the Empire. He would be remembered as the fool who had been captured and executed by the dwarves. His memory would bring shame to his family.

The sudden gusts of wind against his arms told him they had reached the top of the wall. Strangely, he once again enjoyed the feeling of the wind brushing against his skin. If he was doomed to die, he would rather have it happen here, under the morning sun, than in that dark hole they had been kept in since their capture.

The dwarves brought them to a halt and moved down the line, removing the hoods and unshackling their ankles. The sunlight was blinding, but it had never been so beautiful to Darian. If this was to be the last sunrise he ever saw, he was determined to enjoy it as much as he possibly could.

"Gentlemen, I wish I had gathered you all here under more pleasant circumstances." Odpor paced along the wall before them. Krillzoc trailed him, looking as though he considered these to be very pleasant circumstances indeed. "If you will look out across the neutral territory, you will notice that your comrades do not seem to be withdrawing."

"Odpor, these men came here under my command. If you must kill somebody, kill me first," Axel declared. "Give the army the opportunity to negotiate for the lives of my men."

"That is very noble of you, Sergeant Stark. I respect your willingness to accept this punishment on behalf of your men. You are a worthy commander indeed. But a man of your rank is too valuable a prisoner to throw away so soon. I will be selecting the man who will pay the price for your army's foolishness. It will not be you—not today."

Odpor walked over to the same strange implement as the day before, the instrument that allowed him to project his voice all the way to the Imperial Army encampment. Darian had never felt so tense in his entire life, knowing the end could be only minutes away. His heart raced no matter how desperately he tried to urge it to slow.

"Attention, Imperials. If you were planning on accepting my offer, you are running out of time. Or perhaps I should say one of these men is running out of time. Step out and witness the fate that awaits any man who stands in the way of dwarven sovereignty!"

Once again, Odpor gave the Imperials several minutes to file out of their tents and to the edge of the neutral territory. He was about to deliver an important message, and it needed to reach a broad audience.

It wasn't long before what seemed like the entire Imperial encampment had gathered at the edge of the camp. All the while, Krillzoc continued to pace back and forth in front of them, smiling broadly.

When the chieftain was satisfied with his audience's size, he moved back over to the speaking implement.

"Supreme General Cadmus Twilcox, I offered you the opportunity to save these men, yet you did not even bother to send an emissary to negotiate for their lives. What type of message are you sending to the men in your camp, who put their lives at risk every day to serve you? The blood of the man who dies today is on your hands, not mine. So be it." Odpor turned away from the Imperials and nodded to Krillzoc.

With a sharp word from Krillzoc, the guards moved their prisoners into position right at the edge of the wall.

Unable to help himself, Darian stole a glimpse down at the ground and felt immediately ill. How long would it take to fall two hundred feet? Would he die instantly on impact? He hoped so. At least it would not be a long, drawn-out affair. He had worried Odpor would order Krillzoc to slowly torture one of them to death in front of all of their fellow soldiers. *If we weren't so far away, he probably would. He needs a dramatic scene to make sure they feel the impact from so far away.*

Krillzoc began to pace back and forth behind them, clearly waiting for Odpor to make his choice. The dwarven chieftain looked at each of them in turn, his eyes thoughtful. Every time Krillzoc stepped behind him, Darian took a deep breath, waiting for the word to come. Odpor kept them waiting for over a minute, a minute that seemed to go on for several lifetimes.

"Him." The word came suddenly, without warning.

Darian turned to his left just in time to see Krillzoc step up behind the young private named Lester. The dwarf gave the young man a violent shove, sending him toppling from the top of the wall to the ground two hundred feet below. Darian looked straight ahead, not wanting to witness what happened when Lester struck the stone. Krillzoc, on the other hand, had stepped forward into Lester's place in line, leering down eagerly at the scene below.

Darnold Dans was standing beside the dwarf. The crazed look in his eyes revealed that he would've loved nothing more than to send Krillzoc down to join Lester. Darian caught Darnold's eye and shook his head. Such a move would only get the rest of them killed faster.

"Supreme General Twilcox, I hope this serves as a lesson for you," Odpor said into the speaking implement. "Send an emissary to discuss terms of your withdrawal, and I will release this young man's body to you. If we cannot reach an agreement, this same scene will play out once more at dawn tomorrow and every day until you withdraw or all of these young men have joined their departed friend. It is your choice. I hope you do not take too much longer to make it."

Odpor turned back toward his prisoners. Their guards had permitted them to take a few steps back away from the edge of the wall. The guards were making their way down the line, shackling their ankles to prepare them for transport. Darian made no effort to conceal the pure hatred he felt as he met the chieftain's piercing blue eyes, and he doubted any of the others did either.

"You can hate me all you want, Imperials. It is your Supreme General who put you here—make no mistake about that. Your hatred would be better directed toward him. Krillzoc, have them taken back to their cell."

***

General Alexander Sylvester did his best to maintain a somber appearance as the guards led him through the streets of Muog to the home of Odpor, but in reality, he had rarely been so pleased with himself. He had harbored severe doubts about Odpor's capacity to execute the plan properly, but thus far, the chieftain had played his role to perfection.

As he had departed the Imperial encampment, he had already overheard rumblings of frustration. The men were beginning to lose faith in the leadership of Cadmus Twilcox, and it was only a matter of time until that faith crumbled entirely. Now all Sylvester had to do was ensure their belief in him was as strong as ever.

***

Captain Terrence Garrison trailed close behind General Sylvester. Seeing an Imperial soldier tumble to his death from the walls of Muog had been a sickening sight to behold. Even hours later, he still had to fight down the urge to draw his sword and challenge the dwarves who had met them at the main gate. These bloodthirsty savages deserved to be wiped out, and he would be all too pleased to help General Sylvester do just that when the time came.

But that whole display was General Sylvester's idea, wasn't it? That wasn't Odpor's plan; it was Sylvester's, and you know it. And who was it that spoke for Sylvester? It was you. You handed that soldier to Odpor on a silver platter.

It was the dilemma that had waged within his mind ever since the soldier's death that morning. Yes, the dwarves had committed the murder, but had it not all been done at the request of General Sylvester? He himself had been sent to convey that very request. Was he just as guilty as the dwarves? For the briefest of moments, he had even considered going to Cadmus Twilcox and revealing Sylvester's conspiracy with the dwarves. But he knew he could never do that. He owed Alexander Sylvester his entire career, and besides, the general knew what was best, just as he always did. He had to keep his faith in Sylvester.

***

As Odpor's guards led them into the pool room of the chieftain's home, Sylvester allowed himself to smile for the first time, throwing his arms wide to greet the dwarf as an old friend.

"Chieftain Odpor, you outdid yourself this morning. Supreme General Cadmus Twilcox was all too eager to send me here to negotiate with you after that spectacular display. I must extend my deepest admiration."

"I am holding up my end of our bargain, Sylvester, but I fail to see what you have done to hold up yours," Odpor replied curtly, appearing none too pleased to see them.

"I appreciate your patience, my friend, and I ask that you extend it but a little while longer. Within the Imperial encampment, the opinion of Cadmus Twilcox is already beginning to shift. I will be able to usurp his position after only a few more executions; I can sense it," Sylvester said.

"And once you have done that, how much longer will I have to wait for your forces to withdraw? You will still need to convince that bumbling old man who calls himself an emperor to end this war. Every day that I allow these men to continue to draw breath inside my walls while your encampment remains on our land, my people's respect for me wanes a little more. Dwarves care little for these theatrics. They are more interested in seeing results."

"I have found throughout my career that I can be quite persuasive when the occasion calls for it, Chieftain Odpor. It will be the same with the emperor, I assure you. Qwitzite will have its independence in no time at all. Your people may be frustrated now, but think of how they will praise and adore you for gaining Qwitzite's independence without putting their lives in jeopardy."

Did this fool honestly believe such a process would happen overnight? Of course, it would not be happening at all, but Odpor was still none the wiser about that. Dealing with the dwarves was insufferable, but it was a necessary evil. Odpor may have been a simpleminded oaf, but he was still the most efficient means for Sylvester to reach the ends he desired. Soon he would be able to exterminate this stunted, flea-ridden excuse of a people, and the Empire would be better off for it.

"Very well, General Sylvester. I will continue to play your little game. But be warned, the dwarves will never tolerate the likes of you trifling with us. If you do not deliver what you are promising, the attacks on your encampment will escalate to a point you would not like to imagine—I can assure you of it," Odpor warned.

"I would expect nothing less from a leader of your stature, Chieftain Odpor. Now, I have one last favor to request of you."

"I grow weary of your requests, Sylvester. You ask for a lot, and thus far, I cannot see what I have received in return. What is it?"

"I need to visit the men you have in your custody."

Odpor chuckled, and it blossomed into a full-fledged bellowing laugh. His guards joined in within moments, and soon the entire room was laughing at his request. Sylvester forced himself to maintain his smile, though a man of his stature would typically never stand such an insult. *Laugh now, you mindless beasts. We will see who is laughing soon enough*, he told himself. *I'm going to enjoy seeing you all exterminated like the mindless savages you are.*

"Why do you think I would even consider allowing such a thing? How do I know you are not planning to scheme with these men and plot their escape?"

"Chieftain Odpor, I would remind you that I provided you with the information that led to the capture of these men. That seems like an odd strategy. If I simply intended to come help them escape, why would I have helped you capture them in the first place? I need to appear to be a sympathetic general, and they need to know I am advocating on their behalf. Once you release the surviving men, they will return to our camp and tell these tales. This will galvanize my support from the common soldiers. Their support is a powerful tool, one that can be leveraged during my negotiations with the emperor on your behalf."

"Very well, Sylvester. You may have your meeting. But Krillzoc here will be listening to every word you say. I strongly advise that you not try anything foolish. Understood?"

"I would never dream of committing such a crime after you have been so hospitable toward me, Chieftain Odpor."

***

When Darian Tor heard the key shifting in the door's lock, he immediately felt a sense of dread wash over him. It could not possibly have been a full day already, could it? Had Odpor decided to speed up the pace of their executions? Perhaps he had already grown tired of holding them prisoner and had decided to speed up the displays of violence. Maybe he had simply decided to put an end to all of them at once.

Krillzoc stepped into the room, accompanied not by the usual guards but rather by two Imperial officers. Blinking against the blinding light, Darian saw that one of them wore a general's stars. Were they about to be set free? Had this man negotiated their release? For the first time since their capture, he felt a rush of hope.

"Hello, soldiers. For those of you who do not know, my name is General Alexander Sylvester, and this is my comrade Captain Terrence Garrison. We were sent here this afternoon by Supreme General Cadmus Twilcox to attempt to negotiate for your release," the general said.

"We are thankful for your efforts, General Sylvester," Axel said, struggling to his feet and managing a weak salute.

"No need for formalities here, men. I'm sorry to say that I fear that is all the Supreme General sees in these negotiations. I believe he sent me here with the expectation that I would fail. But fear not, I have no intention of accepting defeat so easily."

"And did you fail?" Berj asked bluntly, too exhausted to bother with ceremony, even when speaking to a general.

"I am not giving up on you—rest assured of that. To be honest, the dwarves have not yet agreed to release you. But Chieftain Odpor did agree to allow this meeting, which is progress that once seemed impossible. I have asked him to delay further executions for at least three days to give me more time to broker an agreement. I will also be taking the remains of the unfortunate man who was killed today back to camp for a proper funeral. He was a hero of the Empire, as are all of you."

General Sylvester was saying all of the right things, but Darian could not help but feel skeptical. Odpor would never agree to release them for anything less than the end of the siege—of this much he was certain. After witnessing his ruthlessness that morning, Darian doubted the dwarven chieftain would even consider a temporary pause in the executions. General Sylvester was good at choosing the right words to say, but Odpor would not be an easy man to sway, especially if Supreme General Twilcox was already treating them as a lost cause.

"I have to go now, gentlemen. Your captors only agreed to a brief meeting. Rest assured, I am doing everything within my power to lobby for your release, no matter the cost. Stay strong, and long live the Empire."

"Long live the Empire," came the scattered response from those who were still strong enough to speak.

With that, General Sylvester was gone, and they were left alone in the darkness yet again.

Darian lay down, trying to find a position that did not pain his newly branded shoulder. As he had with every other attempt, he failed and contented himself with the position that proved the smallest amount of discomfort. The other injuries Krillzoc had inflicted upon him in the torture chamber still ached, though they paled in comparison to his shoulder.

"Do you think there's any chance he can get us out of this?" Preston asked, breaking the silence they had lived in for most of the past few days, not wanting to give their captors any information.

"General Sylvester is a well-known and respected negotiator. If anyone has a chance, it is him," Axel replied.

"I just can't imagine what he can offer the dwarves that will convince them to set us free," Darnold said. "The army won't withdraw, and that's all Odpor will accept."

"You may be right, Darnold, but let's not give up hope just yet," Axel replied, trying his best to keep their spirits up.

But despite his friend's best efforts, Darian found his own spirits sinking ever deeper, his hopes slipping further away with each passing second. In his heart, he knew it was no longer a matter of if he would be killed, but when. General Sylvester could say all the pretty words he wanted, but nothing would change that.

Chapter Sixteen

Captain Thaddeus Dunstan had known this argument would be an uphill struggle coming into it, but that had not deterred him; he would not sit back and wait for his men to be executed one by one. General Sylvester had returned to the encampment an hour earlier, bearing the remains of the unfortunate soldier who had been thrown from the walls of Muog. The sight had sparked hope, though it was short-lived. Word had quickly spread that Sylvester had been unable to secure the release of the remaining hostages. There were murmurings of another war council being scheduled, but as of yet, Dunstan had received no invitation, and he assumed none would be forthcoming. He had made his thoughts quite clear the day before, and he doubted anyone was interested in hearing them again. So instead, he had sought out an old friend.

"I'm telling you, Thad, this is a bad idea if I ever heard one," Captain Rolf Reilatt said. "Look, I understand where your mind is; I'd be thinking all sorts of reckless things if those were my men. I'm not judging you, not for one second, but you're already lucky as it is not to be rotting in a stockade for what you did up in Thornata. There won't be any second chances for you this time around. You want to rot away in a cage for the rest of your life?"

The pair had been friends for close to fifteen years. They had met during a conflict in the Elven Isles and had remained close friends ever since. Even though their assignments had mostly kept them far apart, they had continued to correspond, valuing the bond they had formed. Dunstan had been delighted to see his old friend upon arriving in Qwitzite but had never thought that he would be calling on him for this type of favor. It was a lot to ask, even for a friend as old as Rolf.

"To hell with Imperial High Command. The army I joined would never have left those men to die without at least trying to rescue them," Dunstan said. "Rolf, what the hell kind of empire are we fighting for if this is what they allow to happen to the men who are willing to fight and die to defend it?"

"Sylvester went to negotiate with the dwarves; you have to give these things time to play out," Rolf pointed out.

"That's all about optics, and you know that as well as I do. The dwarves won't give up their prisoners unless we offer the type of concessions that you know damn well Twilcox will never give them. Those men were as good as dead the second Twilcox decided to send them on that doomed operation. There was no chance they were going to succeed. They sent those men in there like lambs for the slaughter because he had no other answers for how to respond to all of these attacks. They're paying the price for his shortcomings. It's not right."

Rolf saw things the same way he did—Dunstan was sure of that much—but his old friend was wary of drawing the wrath of Imperial High Command. Having been on the receiving end of that wrath five years prior, Dunstan could not fault him for his trepidations. But some things were more important than your career, and he knew Rolf felt this way just as much as he did. If he could make his old friend see there was a chance for those men, he might be able to convince him to help.

"Okay, Thad, let's look at this logically, shall we? Let's say we do this unauthorized rescue operation you are proposing. Let's say everything goes perfectly according to plan, and we get all of those men out of Muog alive. You and I and anyone else we include on this scheme will still spend the rest of our lives in the stockade for having the nerve to go against orders. That's the absolute best-case scenario we can hope for, but the odds aren't great that we get that. It's far more likely that we end up dead inside that city and all of those men along with us."

He's not wrong, Dunstan admitted to himself, although he would never acknowledge it out loud. What he was asking his friend to commit to was essentially a suicide mission, one that he would be punished for even if he did somehow defy the odds to complete it successfully. He knew perfectly well that if their positions were reversed, he would be every bit as skeptical. But he could not just turn his back on those men, even if it meant he had to go after them alone. Imperial High Command was welcome to do their worst if he returned with his life. If they wanted to punish him for doing the right thing, so be it.

"Now, let's get more realistic about this. Thad, your plan is not going to work. You're stubborn, but you're not stupid. You have no chance of getting up their outer wall without being seen. After that, you would have to get down the other side. Then you have to go up and over their inner wall as well. All of this without being noticed by a single dwarf. Then you have to find these men, and you have no idea where to start. It can't be done. Why do you think Twilcox hasn't attacked them? He can bloviate about how we aren't attacking out of mercy, but you know better than that. You think he gives a damn about civilian casualties, let alone dwarves? He knows attacking those walls is a fool's mission. The only way in and out of that city is through their blasted tunnels. Think we're going to find one of those?"

It was true, but that brought yet another idea to Dunstan's mind. What if he could find one of the tunnels the dwarves had been using to attack them? He could use it to get inside Muog, find the captured soldiers, set them free, and escape through the same tunnel. If he was fast enough, they would be out of Muog before the dwarves knew there had been an intrusion. They could even fabricate a convincing story, making it appear as though the men escaped on their own. Cadmus Twilcox would be none the wiser, and the men would be safe.

"Rolf, what if we used one of those tunnels to get them out? Nobody would even need to know that we helped; the men could say they escaped on their own," Dunstan said. "They would live, and we wouldn't be punished."

"That's a good plan that overlooks two critical flaws. First, assuming we succeed, do you honestly think twelve men are all going to be able to keep quiet about something like that? You were young once. Could you have kept your mouth shut? I sure couldn't, especially after a few drinks. But the more pressing issue is the fact that we have no idea how to get into any of the tunnels. The dwarves have managed to keep them hidden. If our best trackers haven't been able to find them, what chance do we have of doing it tonight? Be realistic, Thad."

"What if I found a tunnel entrance? Let's just assume I can. Would you help me or not?"

"We've been friends for fifteen years, and you know I would never want to see anything bad happen to you. If you find a tunnel and insist on going through with this, I will consider coming with you. But only to make sure you don't get yourself killed," Rolf said exasperatedly.

He doesn't think I can do it. That's the only reason he said yes, Dunstan thought. But he also knew his old friend well enough that he was sure Rolf would at least consider coming along if he did find the tunnel. He hated asking his friend to put himself in such a dangerous situation, but his odds of succeeding without someone to watch his back were minuscule at best. Even with help, they still weren't all that promising.

"Thank you for lending an ear, Rolf. It's good to have a friend like you," Dunstan said, rising from his chair. He meant it. There was no other man he would have trusted to not immediately run off to Imperial High

Command to reveal everything he had just said. Soldiers could be just as cutthroat as anyone else if they thought they had something to gain. He had learned as much a long time ago.

"Anytime, Thad, no matter how much of a bullheaded pain in the rear end you are. Listen, I know this is hard on you, and I feel your pain. Just let Sylvester handle this; he's a cunning negotiator. I think he has a better chance of saving those men than you are giving him credit for," Rolf said.

It was a lie, and Dunstan knew it. Rolf knew as well as he did that Sylvester had no chance of convincing the dwarves to part with their hostages. Those men would be executed one by one, and no negotiation was going to change that. Their only hope was somebody getting inside of Muog and getting them out. Dunstan had hoped the men commanding the Imperial Army would agree with him, but he had been disappointed thus far.

So, he would take matters into his own hands no matter the consequences.

He had barely set foot outside Rolf's tent when he noticed a courier hurrying toward him. Such messengers only served generals, and his curiosity was immediately piqued.

"Captain Dunstan, I have been searching for you. Supreme General Twilcox requests your presence in the war council. You will need to hurry; the council begins in five minutes," the courier said, turning and departing before Dunstan could respond.

Twilcox wanted him in the war council again? He could not imagine what benefit his presence could possibly serve. Perhaps they simply wanted to prod him with insults again. If they valued the prisoners' lives at all, they would have listened to him the first time. Still, he dared not defy an order from Cadmus Twilcox. The last thing he needed was for anyone in Imperial High Command to be paying particularly close attention to him. He broke into a jog, making it to Twilcox's tent just in time.

"Welcome, Captain Dunstan. You are very nearly late," Twilcox said as he entered.

"My apologies, Supreme General. Your courier only found me a few minutes ago," Dunstan replied, taking his seat.

"We are here to discuss strategies, not excuses, Captain Dunstan," the familiar loudmouthed colonel piped up, once again filling Dunstan with the urge to punch him in the mouth.

"Thank you, Colonel, that will be all," Twilcox said. "We are gathered here so that General Sylvester can update us on his negotiations with Odpor. Alex, you have the floor."

General Sylvester climbed to his feet and began pacing the length of the table. Dunstan had never seen the man up close before and noticed for the first time how young he appeared to be for a man of his rank and age.

You would think a man with such a stressful job would show a little more wear and tear, Dunstan thought, knowing all the while how unfair that thought process was. Every man bore the strain of his life in different ways, and he ought not judge Sylvester based on his appearance alone. He had done more to try to secure the release of the hostages than any other officer in this camp.

"I met this afternoon with Odpor. Once again, I found him to be a proud, stubborn man with no love for the Empire in his heart. I attempted to find common ground that could lead to an agreement for freeing the hostages. Once it was clear this was in vain, I pressed hard for at least a three-day halt to the killings, but all to no avail. He says he will continue the executions tomorrow morning unless significant concessions are made."

"Is he still demanding a complete end to the siege?" Twilcox asked, though he hardly seemed interested.

"In the long term, yes, that is his desire. However, he says he would be willing to at least bring the killings to a temporary halt in exchange for a smaller show of faith," Sylvester replied.

"I see. What is it that Odpor wants?" Twilcox asked.

"He requests that the Supreme General of the Imperial Army enter Muog and negotiate with him in person. He says that once you do so, he will grant the remaining hostages a reprieve of at least three days. Furthermore, he is optimistic the two of you can come to an arrangement for them to be set free altogether."

"This is ludicrous," one general cried out. "It is clearly a trap meant to lure Supreme General Twilcox into their fortress. He would be a far more valuable hostage than thirteen infantry grunts!"

Once again, Thaddeus Dunstan found himself utterly repulsed by the total lack of respect these officers showed toward the common soldiers. He knew immediately that these were not the thoughts of one outlier, for every head in the tent was nodding in agreement before the general had even finished speaking. Cadmus Twilcox was trying and failing to appear thoughtful at the head of the table, as though he were seriously considering the proposal. Dunstan knew how the man would reply before he opened his mouth.

"I'm afraid I have to agree. This smells of a trap to me, and a clumsily attempted one at that. I think we all know that Odpor has no intention of negotiating with me in good faith," Twilcox said.

You are nothing but a cowardly rat in a general's uniform, Dunstan thought. *At least General Sylvester has the courage to enter Muog and negotiate with the dwarves. He would be a far more suitable Supreme General than this yellow-bellied swine.*

He did not speak; he understood his words would have no impact other than drawing unnecessary attention to him. He had already concluded that he was going to have to act on his own. It was the only way there was going to be any chance of saving those men.

"I understand your position, Supreme General. I am more than happy to continue to negotiate with Odpor on your behalf," Sylvester replied. "Shall I return to Muog tomorrow?"

"No, let's allow things to stand where they are for the time being," Twilcox said. "Perhaps after a few days, Odpor will realize we are not going to cave in to his demands. He may be more willing to negotiate after he sees he is making no headway."

The thing not being addressed in that statement was that Twilcox was essentially condemning a few more of his soldiers to be thrown from the walls of Muog in the meantime. It was an outrage unlike any other Thaddeus Dunstan had ever experienced. The complete disregard for the lives of men who had willingly put their lives on the line to serve their people was appalling.

The meeting ended shortly afterward, though not soon enough for Dunstan, who had to struggle to hold his tongue. He stepped out into the cool evening air, his mind more resolved than it had been before.

If the Imperial Army would do nothing to help those men, he was going to take matters into his own hands, and there was no time to waste. The dwarves had tunnels from Muog leading into the army encampment, and he needed to find one. He set about his task, alone in the dark, hoping he would not be too late to save at least some of them.

Chapter Seventeen

The memories were almost enough to take Darian's mind away from the impossibly bleak situation in which he found himself. He and Axel sat side by side and had spent the better part of the last few hours reminiscing about their childhood in Verizia. While it could not completely remove him from the despair of their current predicament, it helped to keep his spirits high. Anything to distract them even slightly from the next execution was welcome.

"Do you remember that time we swam out to that island in the middle of Lake Porter? We meant to camp out there for a few nights," Axel said. "We thought we were quite the adventurers, didn't we?"

"Yeah, that was before we found out about all those hornet nests. That wasn't our fault. We did some stupid things in those days, but that wasn't one of them. Nobody could have ever guessed there would be that many hornets on an island," Darian replied with a chuckle. "Seriously, who figures there would be so many damned hornets in the middle of a damn lake? How did they even end up out there in the first place? It didn't even make sense."

"I'm pretty sure I still have scars from a few of those stings. I couldn't believe how bad those hurt."

"Ugh, and remember having to swim back in shame with dozens of those stingers still in us? They just wouldn't stop stinging us until we were back in the water. That was so awful."

"The worst part was how condescending our mothers felt the need to be to us. Our pride was wounded badly enough without them rubbing in how many times they had told us it was a dumb idea," said Axel.

The mood in the cell was not lighthearted, but rather one of quiet acceptance. General Sylvester had departed a few hours earlier, and there had been no word since. They could only assume he had failed in his attempts to have them set free and that another man would die at dawn. Rather than wallow in their sorrow at the inevitability of it all, Axel had convinced the men to take up a casual conversation. It was a noble attempt to keep their spirits as high as possible, and for the most part, it was working.

"At least that wasn't as bad as the time we tried to go down those rapids on a raft we built ourselves," Darian said, sending Axel into a fit of laughter.

"Hey now, don't sell us short on that one. I actually consider that particular adventure to be a success. We made it down the rapids. Just because the raft didn't survive the trip doesn't mean we failed. We got where we intended to go."

"I didn't think we would ever be dry again, but I suppose you're right. All things considered, we should look back on it as a great success."

The memories took Darian back to better days and filled his head with memories of Verizia. It pained him to know he would never see his home or his family again, but he took strength from the memories. They were one small comfort the dwarves could not take away from him. They could torture him and lock him in this cell, but his memories couldn't be touched. He could only hope they would serve as the same sense of comfort when his time came to be pushed from the walls of Muog.

The door of the cell creaked open, and one of their guards appeared, pushing a cart of food. The dwarf closed and locked the cell door immediately behind him, obviously concerned they might get bold ideas of escape. It seemed like a pointless concern to Darian. Even if they did manage to get out of their cell, the odds of them successfully navigating their way out of Muog were slim to none.

The dwarf placed a torch in a bracket on the wall, illuminating the cell. It was the first time any of their guards had done so, revealing just how wretched and filthy their accommodations were.

Darian wordlessly accepted his plate of food, noting the portion was far more generous than any previous meal the dwarves had provided for them. *Maybe Odpor has turned over a new leaf and wants to shower us with kindness.* Once the dwarf had served each of them a plate, he pushed his cart back to the cell door. To Darian's surprise, he did not exit, but rather wedged his cart underneath the door handle and turned around to speak to them.

"We do not have much time, so listen closely. My name is Radig, and you are all running out of time. There will be no reprieve, no delay in the executions. Another one of you is scheduled to die at dawn."

The Imperial soldiers looked at one another skeptically. Why was the dwarf telling them this? They already knew they were doomed. Was this some new form of mental torture Krillzoc had worked up for them?

"We already understand we are dead men walking, Radig. We know that General Sylvester will not be able to persuade your glorious chieftain to release us," Axel said. "Still, do be sure to thank Odpor for his hospitality on our behalf, won't you?"

"No, you do not understand. General Sylvester is not trying to convince Odpor to release you. Your capture was his idea in the first place. He gave Odpor all of the details about your mission so we could capture you. Sylvester is playing intricate games, and you are nothing more than pawns to him."

Once again, Darian wondered if this was some type of mental

torture Krillzoc had thought up for them. According to Axel, General Sylvester had served the Imperial Army for decades as one of their best negotiators. For him to turn against them was inconceivable. This dwarf was playing some sort of game with them. This was too ludicrous to be anything more than another ploy for information from Krillzoc. Darian looked around at his fellow soldiers, and it was clear they were all just as skeptical as he was.

He took a long hard look at Radig for the first time, trying to get a measure of the man. It was hard to determine the age of dwarves, but Darian couldn't imagine he was that much older than most of the soldiers in the cell. His red hair and beard were trimmed close to his face, a choice that seemed uncommon among his people. There was no hint of deception in his eyes, but how could they be sure? They were so unfamiliar with dwarves, how were they supposed to read Radig's intent?

"Okay, Radig, let's say you're telling the truth. Why are you telling us all of this? It seems Odpor would be very unhappy with you," Axel said. "What could you possibly stand to gain?"

"Not all of us want to secede from the Empire. Odpor is taking us down a path that will end in an all-out war with the Empire. Do you think I want to see my friends and family suffer and die for Odpor's stubborn pride? He wants to live like a king, but at what cost to the rest of us? How many thousands of dwarves would die in the name of Odpor? Some of us have formed a resistance to try to fight against and replace Odpor. That is why I am here," Radig said.

"So, you are saying that you want Qwitzite to stay in the Empire? That's nice, but I fail to see what that has to do with us. We can't help you with that, Radig," Axel pointed out. "In case you haven't noticed, our ability to do much of anything is somewhat limited at the moment."

"No, you cannot, not from in this cell. But if twelve high-value prisoners were to escape from right under Odpor's nose, that would look quite bad, do you not agree? Maybe bad enough to make some of his people question his leadership and competence? Even the dwarves who support him are restless at the moment. They think he should have killed you all the second you dared set foot in this city. These games he is playing do not sit well with most dwarves, regardless of their allegiances."

The explanation piqued Darian's interest. He had been extremely skeptical of anything Radig had to say since entering the cell, but any mention of escape would get his attention. Still, he doubted the dwarf could be trusted. Even if he was interested in helping them escape, it was not purely out of the goodness of his heart. He was doing this for his own benefit, not theirs. If he didn't feel their escape would benefit him personally, he would be all too happy to leave them to rot.

"Are you saying that you mean to help us escape, Radig?" Axel asked.

"Why do you think I brought you extra food tonight? Do you think Odpor or Krillzoc care how much you have to eat? You will need your strength if we are going to get you out of here tonight. If you agree to come with me, I will return in a few hours and set you free. I will help you escape Muog via one of the tunnels that runs into the neutral territory near your encampment. The choice is yours, Imperial soldiers, but be warned, General Sylvester has no intention of negotiating your release. If you stay here, you will die one by one."

"Very well, Radig. We will discuss your proposal among ourselves. When you return in a few hours, you will have our answer," Axel said.

Radig looked as though he very much wanted their answer right then and there but decided against arguing the case. Nodding his consent, he opened the door and vanished with his cart, leaving them in silence, the torch he had mounted in the bracket still illuminating the cell. Darian immediately turned his attention to his food. If nothing else, they had gained extra nourishment out of Radig's plea.

They ate in silence for a few minutes; each man was lost in his own thoughts. Once they had all finished, Axel began the discussion.

"Okay, boys, what are we thinking? Can he be trusted?"

"I don't trust him as far as I can throw him, but does that mean we shouldn't take him up on his offer?" Darnold Dans asked. "Any chance at escape is better than sitting here waiting to get thrown off that damned wall."

"For all we know, he is plotting to lead us straight to our deaths," Preston argued.

"What's the point of that, Preston? They already have us at their mercy. They can kill us anytime they choose," Darian said.

"Who knows? Why did that psychopath Krillzoc torture us long after it was obvious we had no information? They're twisted, and they want to see us suffer."

"Unless General Sylvester was able to negotiate our release after all. Maybe Radig is an extremist who doesn't want to see the dwarves let us go," Berj countered, voicing a possibility Darian had not considered. "An escape attempt on the eve of our release could get us all killed."

They bickered back and forth for several minutes. Each man was convinced that his notions of Radig's intentions were correct. Axel allowed them to debate, not inserting his own opinion. He did not speak until it seemed as though the privates had exhausted all possible avenues in their debate.

"Radig may be lying to us. It may all be an elaborate ploy we don't understand. But what do we have to lose? If General Sylvester negotiated our release, why haven't we been released already? Why would the dwarves bother holding us for another night? It's uncertain, and I understand that. But I don't think sitting here and waiting to see if they kill one more of us in the morning is the right move to make. Imperial soldiers are expected to fight to survive at all times. To be clear, I am not making this decision for us. I want us to agree on this. We're all in this mess together."

Darian was inclined to agree with Axel; he would rather take a chance than sit around waiting for death. But it quickly became apparent that not everybody agreed with this line of thinking.

"What if this is just an excuse for Krillzoc to torture us again? I don't know about the rest of you, but one brand is enough for me," one private declared. "How much more pain do you all feel like enduring?"

"Do you really think Krillzoc needs an excuse to torture us? If he felt like doing it, he would come in and do it. Odpor isn't going to stop him; he doesn't care about us," Darnold Dans countered.

"Darnold is right; we would be stupid not to take this chance," Berj said. "I don't want to wait to see what Odpor decides to do to us. Even if it is a setup, I like our chances better out there than in here."

"I still think the smart thing to do is sit back and wait. We should see what happens in the morning," one private said.

"What if you're the one who goes off the wall tomorrow? We can't give them the satisfaction of doing that to any more of us when there is something we can do to stop it," Preston said.

If Darian had not been convinced immediately upon hearing Radig's offer, he was now. They just needed to find a way to convince the rest of the holdouts. He had not participated in the debate much but decided it was time to make his voice heard.

"Listen, I don't want to do anything to draw Krillzoc's wrath either. But we are Imperial soldiers. Are we doing our duty if we don't do everything in our power to escape? We swore an oath, and I mean to hold up my end of the deal. We owe it to the people we serve to get ourselves out of this cell and back to fighting on their behalf. There's another point nobody has brought up. How is this whole ordeal impacting morale back at camp? I can't imagine watching Lester plummet to his death did much for the spirits of the men back there. We can't allow it to continue. Sitting here waiting to die is actually hurting the war effort and our fellow soldiers."

There was no immediate response. Darian saw a few heads nodding in agreement, including those of his friends. There was no rebuttal, which made him hopeful that he had succeeded in convincing those who were uncertain. He locked eyes with Axel, who mouthed a silent thanks. One by one, the men in the cell murmured their agreement.

"I'm glad we are all agreed on this," Axel said. "But I do think we need to plan for the worst-case scenario just in case Radig is manipulating us."

"As soon as he comes for us, we need to demand weapons. At the very least, he needs to give us his. That way he knows that if he double-crosses us, he isn't getting out of it alive," Berj said, and the entire room nodded in agreement.

"I agree, Berj. There's another thing we need to discuss. Radig said General Sylvester betrayed our operation to the dwarves. We still don't know if that's true, though he certainly had the opportunity while negotiating with Odpor. We need to figure out how to handle this. If it's true, he's not going to be pleased to see us back at camp," Axel pointed out.

"I have a hard time believing an Imperial general would do such a thing," a private Darian did not know said.

"So do I, but I think we would be foolish not to prepare for the possibility. If Radig is true to his word and helps us escape, we should assume that he is telling the truth about Sylvester as well," Axel said.

"So, how do we handle a treacherous general?" Darian asked. "It's not like we can just walk up and arrest him. I'm not escaping this hellhole just to end up being hanged for putting hands on a general."

"That's a good point, Darian. It's not like we can walk up and take vengeance on him, no matter how badly we will want to if it turns out he is a traitor," Preston said.

"If it comes to it, I will take this matter up the chain of command to Supreme General Twilcox," Axel said. "We can only hope he will see reason. But we cannot just keep our mouths shut. We would be putting soldiers on future operations in harm's way if we do."

It was decided. They would trust Radig, at least a little, and accept his offer of assistance. It was a gamble every one of them had come to terms with accepting, some more reluctantly than others.

Darian climbed to his feet and began pacing the small cell, trying to restore blood flow to his limbs as much as possible. He did not want to get out of this cell only to be recaptured when his legs failed him.

This ordeal would be over in a matter of hours. Either their escape would succeed, or they would all likely be dead by dawn.

To his surprise, a calmness had set in. The racing heartbeat and cold sweat that had accompanied every opening of the cell door were gone. The agony of wondering if this day would be his last was gone. All that remained was a steady, ice-cold resolve that he would face whatever lay in front of him with courage and that he would fight to survive until his dying breath.

Chapter Eighteen

Hours passed, each minute ticking by more slowly than the one before. The twelve Imperial soldiers had long since exhausted their topics of conversation. All that remained for them to do was wait. They moved restlessly about their cell, continually bumping into one another and not caring. Every man was anxious to see this night done, for better or for worse. Good or bad, they would be free of this cell—as long as Radig was true to his word.

When the sound of the key turning in the lock of the cell door finally split the silence, they turned as one to greet Radig as he stepped inside. Once again, he was pushing the cart used to serve their meals.

"I have brought you all weapons. The selection is not great; I had to bring what I have been able to sneak into this facility unnoticed over the past few days. I hope they will be sufficient," Radig said, pulling back the sheet covering the cart to reveal a small assortment of weapons. "If everything goes according to plan, we will not be needing them."

Darian selected a short sword from the cart and secured it to his belt, which he had been forced to tighten to its last notch during their brief captivity. The blade wasn't the highest of quality, but it was sharp enough to do the job.

He wouldn't be handing out weapons if he meant to betray us, would he? Radig's gesture was a welcome one for Darian, but he silently resolved to continue to keep a close eye on the dwarf. Once they had each selected a weapon, Radig motioned for them to lean in close.

"Once we leave this cell, there can be no talking at all. We are in the Muog prison complex, and there are guards everywhere. There are torches in the corridors, though they are few and far between. As you have discovered, we dwarves do not need much light to see. I will lead you as best I can. It is important that we stay close together. If anybody gets separated, we will not be able to come back for you. I know their patrol routes and can lead us safely through them, but we cannot give ourselves away. If we are attacked, I suggest you fight to kill. If you are recaptured, you will not be treated with kindness and respect, as I am sure you understand."

"How long will it take us to get out of the city?" Axel asked.

"We have quite a journey ahead of us. Once we are out of the prison complex, we will have to make our way nearly a mile through the city. Our route will be winding; it needs to be to avoid detection. It is crucial that everybody keeps up with the group. I know many of you are nursing injuries from Krillzoc's questioning, but you have to keep pace. Once we are out of the prison, patrols will be more unpredictable. If they discover you are missing before you are out of the city, we will have to hunker down and wait for the search efforts to ease. They will immediately lock down all of the tunnels once they discover that you are missing, so the faster we can move, the better our chances of success."

It sounded to Darian as though there were a great many things that could go wrong, along with a great many things that needed to go absolutely perfectly. In spite of this, he couldn't recall feeling so optimistic in recent memory.

We still have a better chance than we would just sitting here waiting for them to kill us one by one, he reminded himself. He locked eyes with Berj Jenson, who was standing next to him. Berj appeared to be entirely in his element, his eyes alight in a way Darian had not seen since their capture. He hoped his friend would keep his head if things got tense. He knew Berj would love nothing more than to get into a fight, to get some payback on those who had imprisoned and tortured them. Darian felt a similar itch, but that was not their objective.

"Is everybody ready?" Radig asked. "We have to get moving."

The dwarf opened the door slowly, motioning for them to stay put while he stepped out into the corridor first. A second later, he motioned for them to join him, and the twelve Imperial soldiers filed silently out of their cell, free at last. Radig led the way down the corridor to the left, pausing every few steps to listen intently before continuing. As he had told them, there were a few torches lining the corridor. It was more than enough for the dwarves, no doubt, but the Imperials had to squint and strain to keep track of one another in the darkness.

When they came to their first crossroads, Radig once again motioned for them to wait while he stepped out into the intersection. Apparently satisfied their way was clear, he gestured for them to continue straight. Darian held his breath as he hurried across the intersecting corridor, expecting a cry to ring out at any moment and give them away. His hand never left the hilt of the short sword Radig had given him. He was filled with a deep resolve that if he was going to die, he would die fighting, taking as many of these bastards with him as he could.

Radig guided them through two more intersecting corridors, taking them left and then right. It soon became apparent to Darian that even if they had managed to get out of their cell without help, they would never have been able to navigate this maze of identical passageways successfully on their own. When they reached a spiral staircase, Radig pointed downward and then held up four fingers, his message clear. They had to travel down four levels. They followed him down the stairs, Darian counting the levels in his head as they went. They were a few steps from the ground level when the dwarf's hand shot up, signaling an immediate halt.

Darian listened carefully, and to his horror, the unmistakable *click-click* of metal boots striking the stone of the hallway below him floated up to his ears.

He lifted his hand, gently easing the sword slightly out of its sheath. He noticed for the first time that Radig carried a heavy mace, and the dwarf had brought it up, just waiting to bring it crashing down upon the skull of his unfortunate fellow guard. Fortunately, that proved unnecessary, as the *click-click* of the metal boots moved in the opposite direction, eventually fading away altogether. Darian allowed the sword to slide fully back into its sheath, breathing a sigh of relief as he did so. *Can we keep getting so lucky?*

Radig motioned for them to wait while he went ahead to check the corridor. Darian glanced at Axel, who smiled encouragingly. He wondered if his childhood friend was suffering the same horrible nerves he was with each and every step they took. He assumed it had to be even worse for Axel, who was, after all, still in command of their small group of soldiers. Axel took that responsibility seriously. Darian knew Lester's death must weigh heavily on Axel's mind. He resolved to sit down and have a long talk with Axel once they were back in the Imperial camp; his friend would need his support. He doubted Imperial High Command would have much sympathy for Axel. They expected results from their soldiers, not excuses.

Radig returned at last, once again gesturing that it was safe to follow him. The Imperials crept down the remainder of the stairs and stepped out into another corridor nearly identical to the one above. Radig led them through a far more complex series of passages this time, turning in every direction. Twice they froze at the sound of footsteps, and twice they breathed a sigh of relief as the sentry moved in another direction. Their guide had not been exaggerating his familiarity with the patterns of the prison guards. He led them through a door in a narrow side passage before bringing them to a halt and motioning for them to lean in close.

"We are nearly out of the prison. I am going to lead you through a side door and then through another side door in the facility's outer wall. There are patrols in the courtyard and guards stationed above. The guards above have an obstructed view of the area we will be crossing, but the patrols are a different matter. Once we are outside, we need to move fast. We will have a window of about a minute between patrols to get across the courtyard," he whispered.

They slinked along the narrow passage until they came to the side door Radig had promised. The dwarf opened the door a sliver, just wide enough for one eye to examine the courtyard beyond. After a few seconds, he threw the door wide and stepped out into the night, the Imperial soldiers rushing to keep up. They cleared the courtyard in twenty seconds, and Radig was already working to unlock the door in the outer wall that would set them free. Darian's eyes repeatedly darted in all directions, his hand clasped tightly around the hilt of his sword. After a few seconds that felt like an eternity, Radig had the door open, and the twelve men spilled through and out into the streets of Muog.

Unlike the night of their capture, no torches were glowing out in the street, a fact that relieved Darian. The only light came from the stars and the narrow sliver of the moon high above. It appeared thus far that Radig was not deceiving them. The dwarf beckoned them off to the left, and they hurried to follow, eager to put as much distance between themselves and the prison as possible. Radig led them into a narrow side street. From what Darian could tell based on the position of the moon, they were traveling north.

They had not been walking long when a horrible noise split the night behind them, the bellowing wail of a horn blowing. The direction it was coming from was unmistakable, and it made Darian's blood run cold.

Radig spun in his tracks, looking back toward the prison, an expression of pure horror etched across his face. Whatever the sound was, it didn't mean anything good for them.

"They have discovered you are gone! Follow me! Run!" the dwarf cried, all attempts at secrecy forgotten.

The group broke into a full run, tearing out of the narrow side street and into a larger thoroughfare. Radig led them down the street, which was thankfully empty, though Darian doubted it would remain that way for very long. Dwarven warriors would soon be searching for them in every nook and cranny of Muog. Radig had told them the dwarves would immediately lock down their tunnels if Odpor's men discovered they were missing. Their hopes of being back at camp that night had evaporated in an instant. Now all they could hope to do was survive until the dwarves had lowered their guard.

Radig turned right into another narrow alleyway, picking up speed all the while. It amazed Darian that a man of such small stature could move so quickly. *He's properly motivated. No matter how bad we will get it if they capture us, it would probably be so many times worse for him*, Darian thought. Krillzoc had taken great pleasure in inflicting pain upon them. The sadistic dwarf would probably be even more gleeful to get his hands on a traitor within his own ranks.

"Radig, what are we going to do?" Axel asked.

"Shut up and follow me; that is what you are going to do. Now stop shouting! You are going to bring Odpor's men down on top of us," Radig snapped back.

The dwarf darted to the left, out of the alleyway, and into an even narrower passage. It was a tight fit for the Imperial soldiers, even in their malnourished states. They struggled through the narrow passageway, pushing and pulling one another through. All the while, they were waiting for a group of dwarven warriors to come upon them at any second.

One by one, they managed to squeeze their way into the square where Radig was waiting for them. Darian's eyes scanned the area, and he realized the dwarf had led them into a dead end. High stone walls stood on all sides, and their only way out was back through the narrow passage.

"What are we doing? There's no way out of here," Darian exclaimed. He reached for the pommel of his sword, certain Radig had led them to their doom.

"Not to your eyes there is not. Now keep quiet; they will hear you," Radig said.

The dwarf moved his hands across the stone wall directly in front of them, his fingers working in fast intricate movements. To the amazement of the Imperial soldiers, the stones of the wall seemed to shift with each touch, forming an opening large enough for Radig to step through comfortably. The rest of them had to duck and scrunch their shoulders, but all were able to squeeze into the gap. Radig nudged his way past them, his fingers working on the stones once more, the doorway closing just as suddenly as it had opened and leaving them in pitch blackness.

"Just give me a moment," Radig said, shoving his way past them once more. "I know you cannot see in here. I will get you some light."

They stood in silence for a few minutes with their hands on their weapons, wondering what would come next. At last, there was a dull flicker of light as Radig lit a torch. The dwarf moved around the room, lighting several more torches until they could see well enough to move about the chamber. They were in a room roughly twice the size of the cell they had shared. A table and chairs sat in the center of the room, and a few hallways led off in different directions, but other than that, the chamber was unremarkable.

"Well, that did not go according to plan. At least you are out of there and we are all still breathing. I think we can consider that much a victory. We can lie low here until the search dies down. If they go long enough without finding you, they will likely assume you got out of the city before they realized you were missing. It might take a few days, but the time will come."

"What is this place, Radig?" Axel asked.

"It is the headquarters of the Resistance. This is where we gather to share intelligence among ourselves and strategize the most effective methods of disrupting Odpor's war effort. I realize it is quite small, but it helps us to remain discreet."

"It appears you are an organization of one," Berj commented, making a show of looking around for more dwarves.

"You are funny, Imperial. Do you think we sit around this room all day and night? Not much would be accomplished, would it? Just because that is how your Imperial officers operate, that does not mean we are the same. We are made up of hundreds of dwarven men and women. We need to live our ordinary lives to keep up appearances. While I daresay my cover has been blown, or will be shortly, Odpor has no idea who most of us are, and we intend to keep it that way."

"You're quite certain Odpor does not know about this place?" Axel asked, his eyes continually darting back to the entryway.

"If he did, it would no longer be standing. Do you think he is not trying to find us? This is the safest place in Muog for you to hide. Muog is a vast city, and it will take time to conduct their search for you. They will not think to look for you in a place like this; you were barely able to fit your bodies through that alleyway. In the meantime, all we can do is wait. Make yourselves at home, as much as you can. I know the accommodations are small for you, but I daresay they are more comfortable than your former quarters. I will bring you something to eat."

Radig disappeared into one of the hallways, and the Imperial soldiers took seats around the large table in the center of the room. It felt strange for Darian to sit in a chair again, albeit one designed for a much smaller person. The last time he had done so was for Krillzoc to interrogate him. They had spent their time in the cell lying on the cold stone floor. It was a small comfort that Darian found meant a lot to him after everything they had been through since their capture.

There was a chill to the room, but the torches were slowly but steadily spreading warm air throughout the chamber. Darian realized for the first time how long it had been since he had felt warmth. The dwarves had never bothered to warm their cell in the prison.

"What do you think, Sergeant Stark? Can we trust him?" Darnold asked Axel.

"I don't know the answer to that question, but I also don't know we have any other options. If we leave and try to find our way out of Muog on our own, we don't stand a chance. They'll find us within the hour. He got us out of that prison just like he said he would. I think sticking with Radig for the time being is going to give us our best shot at getting out of here alive."

Radig returned after a few minutes carrying several plates heaped with bread, dried meats, and even some fresh vegetables. The soldiers eagerly dug into the meal, trusting their host more with each bite. The meal was plain, but Darian had never tasted anything so delicious in his entire life, and he ate until he could stomach no more. Radig did not eat, but rather retreated to a corner, observing his guests. He didn't speak, his eyes moving to each of them in turn as though trying to take a measure of each man.

They had just finished their food when the sound of shifting stone brought every Imperial soldier to his feet. The wall was shifting, becoming a doorway once more. Darian drew his sword, bracing himself for the fight of his life. *We have to kill every single one of them before they can call for help*, he told himself, hoping his skills had not rusted during his time in captivity. His arms felt heavy from the lack of use, but he would fight his best nonetheless.

Six heavily armed and armored dwarves stepped into the room, their eyes taking in the scene around the table. Berj stepped forward, ready to take a leading role in the fight to come.

"Wait, wait, wait!" Radig cried. "Please, my friends, put down your weapons. These are not Odpor's men. These are members of the Resistance. They will do you no harm, I promise."

Darian lowered his sword slightly but did not sheath it. Berj had frozen in his steps but did not back away a single inch, waiting to see what move the dwarves would make next. Radig stepped forward, placing himself between the Imperial soldiers and the new arrivals, his arms spread wide.

"What were you thinking, bringing them here, Radig? This blunder will be the death of the Resistance," a black-bearded dwarf said. "You have killed us all. I hope you realize it!"

"Things did not go according to plan. We had barely gotten outside of the prison walls when the guards discovered they were missing. This is the safest place for them to hide," said Radig.

"They are here now. There is nothing we can do about it," a female dwarf near the back of the group interjected. "Radig acted with his best judgment. We entrusted him with this mission, and we should not second-guess him now."

Darian had never seen a dwarf woman before and was surprised to see one dressed in full battle gear. Women had never been permitted to serve in the Imperial Army, and to his knowledge, most of the Empire's provinces had adopted the same policy. The woman carried a large mace and looked like somebody Darian would not want to anger.

"Thank you, Kalayo. I took the only option available to me, and I did not take it lightly, I can assure you. When the dawn comes and none of these men are tossed from the walls of this city, Odpor's position will be weakened, even among his most ardent supporters. There are loyalists who felt taking these men captive was a mistake, and this will affirm those beliefs. We will get these men out of here and back to their camp as soon as possible."

"This operation was ill-advised from the start. Radig was our most valuable spy, and he was positioned closest to Odpor. If they have not yet figured out his role in this, they will soon enough," the dwarf standing farthest to the right declared. "Now how are we supposed to know what Odpor's doing?"

"A small price to pay," Radig said. "Getting these soldiers out from under Odpor's nose is far more valuable than anything else I could have learned. This is the failure that will begin the process of unseating him from power. It was only a matter of time before Krillzoc sniffed me out anyway. He has long suspected there is a spy close to Odpor."

"Pardon my interruption," Axel cut in, "but can somebody please enlighten us as to what exactly is going on?"

Several of the new arrivals looked as though they did not care to share anything with their guests at all. They may have been opposed to Odpor's war, but it was clear enough to Darian that most of these dwarves still bore no love for Imperials.

We're nothing more than pawns in their game. If it were not for the fact that freeing us would make Odpor look bad, they would have been happy to see us die.

"You are alive, Imperial. Is that not sufficient for you? Be silent and keep your nose out of matters that are of no concern to you," the black-bearded dwarf said.

"Please, my friends, be reasonable. Sergeant Stark has asked a fair question; answering him can do us no harm. Giving these men knowledge about what is going on inside Muog could prove beneficial for us, particularly given what we know about General Sylvester. His partnership with Odpor is dangerous to the Resistance, but these men could help put an end to it once we get them back to their camp," Radig said.

In the tension of their escape from the prison, Radig's comments about General Sylvester had nearly slipped Darian's mind. The dwarf had warned them that the general had betrayed their operation to Odpor, leading to their capture. It was an idea he was still struggling to wrap his mind around, though he could not deny Radig had proven himself trustworthy thus far. Perhaps he did know something about General Sylvester that they did not. If Sylvester was indeed a traitor, they needed to know, and they needed to find a way to raise the alarm.

"You told us General Sylvester arranged our capture with Odpor. How do you know this?" Axel asked.

Radig glanced at his fellow dwarves. Darian followed the dwarf's gaze with his own, trying to measure their feelings. He found dwarves to be unreadable, but apparently, Radig saw something that told him that they did not object to him answering the question.

"I know because I have been present for his meetings with Odpor. I do not normally work in the prison. I am a member of Odpor's personal guard, or at least I was. I imagine I have been stripped of that position or will be soon enough. The first time Sylvester came to negotiate with Odpor, they discussed a partnership. Sylvester intended to aid the dwarven war effort as a means of making your Supreme General Twilcox appear ineffective in the role. He plans to take that role for himself once the Emperor tires of Twilcox's apparent incompetence. As a show of good faith, he gave Odpor details of a supply caravan that was coming to resupply your camp."

"That weasel!" Berj exclaimed. "You mean to tell me that attack was thanks to treachery by one of our own generals?"

"That is precisely what I am telling you. The next time, Sylvester sent his man to negotiate on his behalf. Captain Garrison, I believe, is a rather unremarkable specimen from what I can gather. He seems like a bit of a dimwitted fellow, but he follows orders, perfect for Sylvester's purposes, I suppose. Odpor has a few such men of his own. They are valuable to men like Sylvester and Odpor. Garrison, under orders from Sylvester, told Odpor about your operation to burn our foodstuffs. This included the suggestion to execute you one by one to further weaken Twilcox's grasp on his men. The belief is that your deaths would spark outrage and calls for his dismissal."

Darian sunk back into his chair. He did not want to believe what Radig was telling them, but in his heart, he knew it to be true. It all lined up too perfectly with everything that had happened. It was hard to see how it could be false. He and his friends had often complained during their training about the self-serving nature of Imperial officers, but this was beyond anything any of them could have ever imagined. An Imperial general sacrificing soldiers like lambs for slaughter so he could advance his own career was the most appalling thing Darian could imagine. He felt like throwing up.

"Once they captured you and Odpor executed your first man, Twilcox sent Sylvester to negotiate once more, as you know. He commended Odpor on his performance and reiterated that the executions needed to continue. He then requested a meeting with you to deceive you into thinking he was negotiating on your behalf. The eventual plan was for Odpor to release a few of you to demonstrate Sylvester's capable negotiating skills. You would go back to your camp, heaping praise on Sylvester for freeing you. This would make him appear to be superior to Twilcox among your peers, you see."

A stunned silence fell over the room. Had Radig not just helped them escape from under Odpor's nose, none of them would have believed a word of his tale. But all of the pieces fit together too perfectly for this to be a deception. The caravan attack, the dwarves knowing exactly when and where their operation would take place—it had all gone too smoothly for the dwarves.

Darian felt as though he had been punched in the stomach.

"Now what, Radig?" Axel asked. "We need to get back to our camp and expose Sylvester as the traitor he is."

"Yes, but that will take time. As I said, any tunnel leading out of Muog will be locked down while they search the city for you. It could be up to a week before the search is called off. I no longer have any way to be certain. For now, the best thing we can do is wait and keep our heads down."

"What are we going to do when we get back to camp?" Darnold asked. "Accusing a general of treason is going to be met with a healthy dose of skepticism. Let's be honest—if anyone else came in with this kind of story, we wouldn't be quick to believe it."

"That's what we are going to spend this time figuring out, gentlemen," Axel said. "We will be patient, and we won't make a move until the time is right. Our escape just became much bigger than us. The entire Imperial Army is depending on us to get back to camp and set this right. They just don't realize it yet."

Chapter Nineteen

General Alexander Sylvester woke shortly before dawn, his spirits already high. Another one of the captured soldiers would tumble from the walls of Muog within the hour, and the perception of Supreme General Cadmus Twilcox would plummet along with him. At the same time, the opinion of Sylvester would only continue to grow; he was the only general courageous enough to step into the enemy stronghold to try to save the lives of those unfortunate men. The whispers around the camp, reported back to him by Terrence Garrison, were already beginning to speak more favorably of him than Twilcox. The men saw his efforts as being hindered by Twilcox's reluctance to make meaningful concessions. They felt Twilcox's plot to authorize the mission in the first place had been foolhardy. Sylvester's plan was proceeding precisely as he had hoped.

Garrison reported that he had overheard multiple conversations expressing anger toward Twilcox over the past day. The soldiers felt the old fool was sending Sylvester to negotiate but not giving him the necessary authority to act in the captured soldiers' best interests. Even in his most optimistic moments, he had never dared to dream that his plan would unfold in such a smooth manner. He had anticipated numerous possible complications, none of which had arisen as of yet.

Sometimes I impress even myself, he thought as he stepped outside into the chilly predawn air.

A glance to the east told him the sun would rise in roughly twenty minutes. He assumed Odpor would call out to the camp around the same time as the previous two days; the chieftain had proven to be nothing but punctual thus far. There were far more soldiers milling about the camp at this hour than there usually would be, making Sylvester all the more pleased. Common foot soldiers almost never rose earlier than required by duty. He could only presume they were up and about wanting to see what would happen at dawn. That suited his purposes perfectly well. The larger the audience for the next execution, the better. Tales of their fellow soldier's death were all well and good, but actually seeing it take place would produce a more visceral reaction.

Captain Terrence Garrison arrived within minutes, delivering Sylvester's breakfast as he did every morning. Sylvester did not know how Garrison was always so attuned to his needs, but the captain never left him waiting more than a few minutes for his morning meal, no matter what hour he woke. At times, he suspected Garrison woke hours before dawn and watched his tent, keeping an eye out for the first signs of life.

"Good morning, General Sylvester. Would you like your breakfast at the table this morning, sir?" Garrison asked.

"Yes, Captain Garrison, that will be acceptable. Thank you for your promptness. I would like to be done eating by dawn for obvious reasons."

They stepped into the general's tent, and Garrison placed the tray of food down on the table. Sylvester took his seat and dug in, eager to finish his meal quickly. Garrison stood off to one side, not speaking. Sylvester had always appreciated the other man's ability to know when he was needed and when it was better to remain silent. It was a trait most servants could never perfect, but it seemed to come naturally to Garrison.

I will need to promote him once I am Supreme General. He will know far too many of my secrets, and another promotion should ensure his silence.

Sylvester finished his breakfast within minutes and motioned to Garrison that he was ready to dress. The captain hurried forward, helping Sylvester into his armor and bringing him his sword. Most soldiers would not be fully uniformed at this hour, but Sylvester preferred to convey a professional image, particularly at such a critical time. His plans to overthrow Cadmus Twilcox would come to a head in the coming days. He needed the soldiers of the Imperial Army to associate him with safety and stability. Throughout his career, he had found appearances to be every bit as important as substance. Men trusted what their eyes could see above all else.

"Let's head toward the edge of the neutral territory, Captain Garrison. I daresay our friend Odpor will be making an announcement for us shortly. We wouldn't want to miss it."

"Yes, sir."

The pair stepped back outside, this time finding the encampment more alive than ever before.

Excellent. At this rate, every single soldier in this camp might witness the next death, Sylvester thought, full of glee while maintaining a somber outward expression. As they made their way toward the edge of the camp, soldiers stopped to salute him as he passed. This was not an uncommon occurrence for a man of his rank, but it seemed to Sylvester that the men were looking at him with more reverence than usual. They knew, after all, that he was doing everything in his power to set their comrades free. If only his negotiations weren't being hindered by the overly stubborn Cadmus Twilcox, who had once against declined to show his face. At one point, a shout even called out stating as much, forcing Sylvester to conceal a grin.

Sylvester and Garrison arrived at the edge of the neutral territory just as the sun was coming fully into view. Hundreds of Imperial soldiers had already gathered, anxious to see what would happen.

The general looked out across the barren plain at the walls of

Muog. The city was distant, but to his surprise, he could not make out the forms of dwarves at the top of the walls. The day before, he had been able to see the soldiers being led out onto the wall for Odpor's speech, but now there was nothing. *Perhaps he plans to make us wait just a while longer to build suspense. Perhaps he has more of a taste for theatrics than I suspected.*

But as the minutes continued to pass with no sign of activity atop the walls of Muog, Sylvester's concern began to grow. Had the dwarves allowed the soldiers to escape? There had been no word of them returning to the encampment, so that did not make sense. Even if they had escaped and been killed in their attempt the flee the city, Odpor should at least announce as much. What was going on?

The more time went by, the more soldiers began to file away from the edge of the camp, setting out to perform their daily duties. The overall mood had made a turn from somber and anxious to jovial and relieved. A few soldiers even stopped to thank him for his work negotiating with the dwarves, heaping him with praise. He forced himself to smile back, ever the master of outward appearances, while inside, he seethed. Garrison was looking at him for guidance but trying to be discreet about it.

This is what happens when you place your trust in simpleminded dwarves. He cursed himself repeatedly in his mind. He had handed Odpor everything he needed on a silver platter, yet the oaf had somehow managed to mess it all up.

"Let's return to my tent, Captain Garrison. It appears there will be nothing to see today," he said quietly, turning and stalking away, eager to put the city of Muog out of his sight.

***

The mood inside the home of Odpor was no more cheerful. The chieftain had been in a foul mood ever since receiving the news of the escape the night before, and every hour that passed only made matters worse. Even Krillzoc, the ice-blooded interrogator, the man always called upon to perform the most unpleasant of jobs, was wary of Odpor's wrath.

He entered the room knowing perfectly well that his chieftain would not be pleased with the information he had to share.

"What do you have for me, Krillzoc? I need something of value. Have you found the Imperials?" Odpor asked.

"Chieftain, I have interrogated all of the dwarves who were on guard duty last night with the exception of one," Krillzoc said.

"Why have you not spoken with all of them?" Odpor demanded. Patience had never been a virtue the chieftain possessed in abundance, and it was no surprise to find him short of it now. "What have you been doing all this time?"

"The lone exception was Radig. I did not interrogate him because I was unable to locate him. After questioning the remaining guards, I now believe Radig was involved with helping the Imperial soldiers escape."

Krillzoc had seen Odpor in fits of rage plenty of times before, but never had his chieftain appeared as enraged as he was at that moment. If there was one thing that was guaranteed to set Odpor off, it was the betrayal of somebody he had placed his trust in. Radig had been a member of Odpor's personal guard for years; he had placed his life and well-being into the hands of a traitor. The chieftain would see this as the ultimate betrayal. Krillzoc did not envy Radig if Odpor ever managed to get his hands on him.

"Why would Radig do this?" Odpor asked, surprising Krillzoc with the calmness of his voice.

"I do not believe he could have accomplished this on his own, nor do I think he would have any reason to try. I am sorry to say that I believe Radig may be working with the Resistance."

Odpor rose from his chair and began to pace the length of the room. The Resistance had been a minor thorn in his side to this point, but such a bold move was one none of them had ever suspected the rebellious group of being able to pull off. Odpor had not come down hard on the group, knowing such a move could alienate him in the eyes of some dwarves. When dwarves fought dwarves, there was no benefit for any of them. But this move would force his hand, leaving him in a precarious position. The opinions of the populace would no longer matter. The Resistance had overstepped and would now need to be eliminated.

"It is my own fault. We should have stamped them out the moment they first saw fit to oppose me. Krillzoc, you have identified several members of this organization here in Muog, have you not?"

"I have, Chieftain Odpor."

"And these dwarves have no idea that you are wise to their little secret?"

"They remain quite ignorant, Chieftain Odpor."

"Very well. You know what I need you to do. Bring these dwarves in for questioning. Interrogate them by any means necessary to get the information you need. If they do not know where the soldiers are, they should still know where the Resistance is headquartered. Get the information out of them, and we will raid the location tonight. Once you have extracted all useful information, kill them. We cannot have them slipping away and warning their fellows of what is coming."

"Yes, Chieftain Odpor."

Krillzoc bowed before turning to leave the room. Odpor's orders did not surprise him; they were the same that he would have given if he were in the chieftain's position. There were four known members of the Resistance he needed to round up. He motioned for a few men to join him; they would need to capture all four before he could question them. If one Resistance member suddenly went missing, the others might be spooked and go into hiding. Once he had them, he would extract every last piece of useful information from every single one of them, just as he always did.

***

Alexander Sylvester poured himself a fourth glass of whiskey as he waited impatiently for Terrence Garrison to return. It was well past noon, and still no word had come from the city of Muog. He had placed his trust in the wrong people, and now he was paying for it. What had he been thinking, believing those subhuman scum could execute such an elaborate plan? They were barely fit to scrub the mud from rocks! The day he could purge the dwarves from the Empire couldn't come soon enough.

He was well into his sixth glass by the time Terrence Garrison stepped back into the tent. The captain glanced at the nearly empty bottle of whiskey but wisely chose not to address it. He stood in silence as Sylvester finished his glass.

Sylvester looked up at Garrison, appearing as though he was barely able to make out the captain's face in his drunken haze.

"What are they saying, Captain Garrison?"

"Sir, the spirits throughout the camp are high. The men are optimistic the captured soldiers may be set free soon," Garrison replied.

"And what else are they saying?"

"The general attitude seems to be that the men believe that Supreme General Twilcox is the reason that no man was killed today. They believe he likely made some small concessions to Odpor and managed to keep them quiet," Garrison said, clearly knowing as the words left his mouth how Sylvester would react.

Sylvester snatched the bottle of whiskey from the table and hurled it to the ground, sending shards of broken glass hurtling across the tent. Garrison flinched away as the liquid showered him. Sylvester staggered back into his chair, seething all the while.

"So, you are telling me that thanks to a rabble of incompetent dwarves, that bloated old fool Twilcox is receiving credit for being a savior of the hostages?"

"I'm afraid so, sir," Garrison replied, not meeting his eyes. "You are still being talked about in high regard, but most of the men seem to believe Twilcox authorized you to make a deal with Odpor to spare their lives."

"All of my hard work ruined by that oaf Odpor. Has there been any word of the soldiers? Have they been released?"

"No, sir. They have not returned to this encampment, nor have we had any word from them."

"Well then, I need to get back to Muog and find out what is going on." Sylvester climbed back to his feet but stumbled and fell back to the floor, his stomach churning.

Garrison hurried over to help Sylvester, who shoved him away violently. Garrison stumbled backward, almost losing his footing.

"I don't need your damn help. I don't need anything from anyone. I am Alexander Sylvester, and I am the rightful Supreme General of the Imperial Army. Do you understand that, Garrison?" His voice grew louder with each word, and Garrison's eyes darted repeatedly to the tent opening. If anybody had heard that last comment, there would be trouble.

"I understand, General Sylvester. You do not want to see all of your hard work undone. Neither do I. But we have to be careful," he whispered.

***

The sight before his eyes was a disturbing one to Terrence Garrison. He had never seen General Sylvester in such a state, and it was a sight Garrison did not care for one bit. Once again, his doubts about Sylvester's motives flashed through his mind. Was the once-great general still acting in the best interests of the Imperial Army? Or had he become overcome with vain ambition, his lust for more power? Should he address his concerns with another general? But looking down at the distraught general on the floor, the man to whom he owed his entire career, he knew he could not do it. Alexander Sylvester may have had his faults, but he was a good man at heart, a man who had given Garrison opportunities he would never have received from any other general.

"Listen to me, General Sylvester. You will figure this out. I know you will. You are the most brilliant man I have ever known. You are the greatest general this force has ever seen. Whatever has gone wrong, you will find a way to overcome it. You are the leader this army needs; you will not fail. The Empire is depending on you. You have worked too hard and come too far to give up now."

Sylvester looked up, his eyes locking on Garrison's. For the first time since Garrison had entered the tent, he felt that Sylvester was fully cognizant. The general had understood him, and his mind was going to work, the wheels already turning in his brain. Had the motivational speech been what was needed to get Sylvester back into the right state of mind?

"You are right, Garrison. I am acting like a fool. I can still make this work. I must succeed; failure is not an option. The future of the Empire demands my success. Now, help me to my chair, my old friend, and let's get back to work."

Chapter Twenty

Darian Tor sat propped up against a wall in the headquarters of the Resistance, the thoughts racing through his mind not allowing him to sleep. A full day had passed since Radig had brought them here, and he was still trying to fully process everything that had happened since he had arrived at the front lines.

The last few weeks of his life had been a whirlwind, and he could not foresee matters calming down anytime soon. He had known the life of a soldier was a hard one, but he could never have imagined anything like this. In all his conversations with his father about his time in the Imperial Army, there had been no hint of such chaos.

He was so lost in thought that he hardly noticed Axel Stark walking over and taking a seat beside him.

"It's been an interesting few days, to say the least. I don't know about you, but they haven't been what I had in mind when I enlisted," Axel said.

"That would be a fairly accurate assessment," Darian replied with a gentle laugh.

"What do you think would have happened if we had stayed in Verizia? It's something I've been thinking about ever since we were captured.

Used to be that I couldn't wait to get out of there. I longed for times like this, the thrill of true excitement. Lately, all I've wanted is to go back. You remember those sweet rolls my mother used to make for us? I would give anything to get my hands on one of those right now."

"I'm sure we would have found different ways to get ourselves into trouble, though I doubt our circumstances would be quite as dire as they are now. Oh, and screw you for mentioning those sweet rolls. That sounds so good right about now," Darian said, eliciting a laugh.

It was a question he had not given much thought. He had thought a great deal about his family and his home, but very little on the path not chosen. He and Axel had always been close friends. At one point during their childhood, they had talked about buying a shipping barge and delivering goods throughout the Empire, but they had forgotten that dream long ago. After all, such a life couldn't possibly provide enough adventure for them. The Imperial Army had been the only path either of them saw fit to provide the thrills they craved so desperately.

"I always wondered if we would have succeeded at owning a shipping barge. Remember how we used to talk about it?" Darian asked.

"Where's your faith? We would have succeeded for at least a few days. Eventually we would have ended up smashing the thing to bits like we did with all those boats and rafts we tried building, but it would've been a good time while it lasted."

Darian let out a snort of laughter. Indeed, they had experienced a good deal of bad luck with watercraft in their younger days, and the barge probably wouldn't have ended any differently. *No, but you weren't likely to end up imprisoned and tortured had you chosen that path*, he reminded himself.

Axel sighed. "I don't suppose these types of thoughts do us much good, but it's not like there's much else for us to do at the moment, is there? It's better than living in the moment. Isn't that what your mother used to say to us? That we should always live in the moment? Bet if she was in this particular moment with us, she would change her mind on that."

"Well, I'm not one to defy my mother. Have you had any more thoughts about what we are going to do about General Sylvester?"

"Lots of them, but no definitive answers. Accusing a general of treason will not end well for us if we don't think it out carefully—or if we do think it out carefully for that matter. Unfortunately, the word of twelve grunts isn't worth much to anyone in Imperial High Command. They're more likely to discipline us for failing our mission than believe us about Sylvester's treachery."

"I've been thinking about it myself. I think we should start by going to my commanding officer, Captain Dunstan."

"Dunstan? I don't know him very well. He doesn't have the best reputation among Imperial officers. I've heard rumors about him, but who can say how many of those are fact? Of course, Sylvester has a brilliant reputation, so that shows us how much stock we can put in such things. Why do you think we can trust Dunstan?"

"He seems like a good man, and he seems to genuinely care about his men. He was the only one who bothered to come see us off on this suicide mission, wasn't he? I think if we can convince him of the truth, he will help us, or at least try," Darian said. "At the very least, I don't think he will turn around and sell us out. After all, as you said, he's had his own issues with Imperial High Command."

"Do you think this Captain Dunstan will believe you when you reveal your intelligence comes from a dwarf?" a rough voice cut in. The pair turned to find Radig walking past with a smirk on his face.

"Don't make assumptions, Radig. Dunstan isn't like most Imperial officers," Darian replied, remembering the captain's statements about the dwarves in the past. He felt that if there was a single officer in the Imperial Army who would believe their story, it was Thaddeus Dunstan. "You would be right to be doubtful about most officers, it's true, but Dunstan is different. He will believe us."

Radig grunted noncommittedly and kept walking. He had saved their lives, but they still knew next to nothing about the tight-lipped dwarf. Neither he nor any of the dwarves who had come and gone from their headquarters over the past day had shared any more useful information. It felt as though the Imperial soldiers were a burden most of their hosts couldn't wait to have gone. The Resistance fighters were still a mystery to Darian, but he could not help but feel a certain respect for their courage. After seeing firsthand the type of brutality Odpor was capable of, conspiring against him was admirable, despite their poor attitudes toward the Imperials.

"Well, I suppose we will see what Dunstan has to say if you're sure we can trust him," Axel said.

"I'm not sure if I can trust anyone anymore, other than you, Berj, Darnold, and Preston. This business with Sylvester has shaken my faith in the Imperial Army. But we need to go to somebody, and I think he is our best bet."

"Well, you've always had good judgment as far I'm concerned, Darian. You always seemed to find better fishing spots than I did. That has to count for something, right?"

"You could never catch anything if your life depended on it, so I'm not sure how confident that makes me." Darian laughed, shoving his friend's shoulder.

"Hey, I caught that massive sturgeon from the Tyms River, don't you remember?"

"The one that drifted up onshore, already dead? How many times do I have to tell you that that doesn't count?"

As Axel chuckled, Darian looked around the room, appreciating for the first time how fortunate they all were to still be alive. Berj and Preston were sitting at the table, eating the last few bites of their supper. The rest of the soldiers were spread about the chamber, some of them napping. There were a few dwarves as well, including Radig and the woman named

Kalayo. He realized that he did not see Darnold Dans. His eyes swept the chamber, at last finding the young man standing near the wall where they had first entered the headquarters. His face was intent, as though he was listening carefully, trying to hear something. A split second later, all the color left his face, and he turned toward the rest of them, his sword coming out of its sheath as he did.

"We have a problem!" he cried, drawing every eye toward him instantly.

Radig and Kalayo sprung to their feet and hurried over to join Darnold near the wall. Radig put his ear to the wall, pulling it away a second later. Darian listened carefully as well and thought he could make out the faint sound of something striking the stone on the other side.

"They have found us! Draw your weapons; this is going to be a fight!" Radig cried, retrieving his mace and tossing another to Kalayo.

Darian and Axel leaped to their feet, drawing their swords in unison. The sounds of impacts on the stone outside were getting louder; they must've been close to breaking through the door. Darian moved toward the center of the room to stand alongside his friends from training. Axel took a position in front of all of them, the first line of their defense.

"Imperials, you know what's coming for us. Fight as if your life depends on it, because I guarantee you it does! We've seen what these bastards are capable of. Let's show them how Imperial soldiers respond to getting punched in the mouth!" Axel cried, raising his sword above his head.

"Yes, sir!" the eleven privates shouted in harmony, coming together in the center of the room.

The first visible cracks appeared in the wall a few seconds later. Within moments, a sizeable hole was forming. Darian wished he had a bow so he could fire on their attackers before they came through the wall. It appeared as though the dwarves outside were using massive hammers to bludgeon their way through the stone. Before long, a hole large enough to admit a dwarf had been cleaved in the rock. A second later, their attackers began to pour into the chamber.

Axel met them head-on, his sword cutting down the first dwarf who ran at him and then the second in two fluid motions. Then there were more dwarves pouring through the hole, and everything erupted into pure chaos.

A dwarf raced toward Darian with a spear in his hand. Darian braced himself to meet the attack, but his attacker never got close, hacked down from the side by a crazed Berj Jenson while he was still several feet away.

Darian was surrounded by mayhem; the sound of steel weapons colliding rang in his ears while the stench of blood and death filled his nostrils. He spotted a dwarf about to drive an axe into Max Preston's back and lunged forward, his sword hacking into the dwarf's shoulder before he could strike. He fell with a scream, but there was no time to finish him off, for another attacker had already stepped forward to take his place. The scene was so chaotic that Darian could scarcely tell how many had come to attack them or distinguish between friend and foe.

He did not know if they were winning or losing; there was no break in the action long enough for him to determine that. He knew he had spotted at least a few black Imperial uniforms lying on the ground along with the attacking dwarves, but there was no opportunity to stop and count. He could only hope they were wounded, not dead. All he knew was that some of them were still alive and fighting, and that would have to be enough. He did not know how long the battle raged on before a cry split the chamber.

"Enough, break off the attack. Enough, I say!"

The voice made Darian's blood run cold. He would recognize the hated voice of Krillzoc anywhere. The dwarf attackers slowly fell back, retreating toward the shattered wall through which they had entered. Krillzoc stepped to their forefront, his wickedly sharp sword covered in blood. It was the first opportunity Darian had to examine the extent of the damage that the battle had done to them.

Axel Stark was still on his feet, still standing at the front of their group in a defensive position, though Darian could see a rapidly growing puddle of blood pooling near his feet. Berj Jenson was just behind him in a kneeling position, a smaller but still significant pool of blood forming beneath him as well. Darnold Dans stood just to Darian's left, and he appeared unharmed. Max Preston was slightly behind them, one arm supporting a clearly wounded Kalayo. To Darian's dismay, the rest of the Imperial soldiers lay upon the ground. The fortunate men were already dead. Those who weren't writhed in agony, their wounds obviously too severe for there to be any hope for them. There was no sign of Radig, but he could only assume their rescuer was somewhere in the heap of dead dwarves. Among those, Darian couldn't discern friend from foe.

More dwarves filed into the chamber behind Krillzoc. They outnumbered the defenders at least threefold.

We escaped that prison only to die here in this dark room. It isn't fair, Darian thought angrily. He tightened his grip on his sword. They might kill him, but he would take as many of them with him as he could. If he could manage to thrust the blade through Krillzoc's evil face before they cut him down, he could at least die a happy man.

"Drop your weapons, Sergeant Stark. Or do you want to see more of your men die? You do not have many of them left to spare," Krillzoc said. "I doubt any of the men on the ground will live to see the dawn from the look of them. Why keep this going when you have no hope of victory?"

"You'll just kill us all anyway," said Axel. "Do you think we are going to let you throw us from that wall for your amusement? Eat rocks, Krillzoc."

Berj Jenson had forced himself back to his feet, though he looked as though he might collapse at any second. Kalayo and Preston had staggered forward to stand beside him. All three looked unsteady but determined.

None of them would give in. Krillzoc's gaze locked on the dwarf woman, and he smirked.

"General Sylvester wants some of you back alive to prove his competence. I assume that traitor Radig told you about that? If you surrender, some of you may still survive. I cannot guarantee it, but it is the best chance you have to keep breathing for more than the next few minutes. Think of your men, Sergeant Stark. What is their best chance of survival?"

Axel made no move to attack or surrender. Darian watched his friend carefully, not envying the choice he had to make. Axel didn't trust Krillzoc any more than he did; Darian was sure of that much. But was there any truth to what the dwarf interrogator was telling them? There was the possibility that they could still survive as pawns in Sylvester's treasonous game. More dwarves were still coming into the chamber, and they had no hope of winning a battle against such great odds. Still, none of them wanted to die like Private Lester, tossed from the wall as a message to the Imperial encampment.

Axel turned to face his men, locking eyes with each of them in turn as if trying to gauge their feelings silently. He met Darian's eyes last, and Darian knew at that moment that they were thinking the same thing. While they would both rather die fighting than by being executed by Odpor, the more cowardly act would be to give in to the inevitability of their demise. As long as there was hope, no matter how slim their odds, an Imperial soldier should have the courage to embrace it.

"Very well, Krillzoc. We surrender," Axel said, turning back toward the dwarf and dropping his sword at his feet. His men followed suit, as well as Kalayo, though the dwarf woman did not appear the least bit pleased with the turn of events.

"You have made a wise decision, Sergeant Stark. I know you needed to swallow a great deal of pride to do so, and you have my respect," Krillzoc said, stepping forward. As he reached Axel, he stooped to pick up the soldier's fallen sword, then paused for a moment, seemingly deep in thought.

Darian realized what was about to happen a split second before it did, just as a cruel smile split Krillzoc's face. "But as I said, I could not promise that all of you would be spared."

Krillzoc straightened his back and plunged his sword into Axel's chest, running him through completely, the blood-soaked tip of the blade emerging from the sergeant's back. He twisted the blade before wrenching it free, leaving Axel to slump lifelessly to the stone floor.

"Take the rest of them into custody. Chieftain Odpor wants to hang them from the city walls first thing in the morning for their Imperial friends to see."

Darian never stopped to think about what he did next. It was an out-of-body experience for him as he bent and snatched his sword back up from the floor. He was vaguely aware of his friends shouting at him, but he could not make out their words over the blood pounding in his skull. He went straight for Krillzoc, determined to hack the life from the twisted, murderous psychopath.

You're going to die for that, you piece of scum. I don't care what they do to me afterward.

Two of Krillzoc's men stepped in front of their leader with their weapons raised defensively. Darian swung with such force that he tore the first dwarf's axe from his hands, a second swing splitting the man's skull a moment later. The second dwarf landed a strike on Darian's leg, the tip of his sword opening a deep gash below his knee, but Darian paid the wound no mind. His sword slashed out twice more with vicious intent, leaving the dwarf bleeding to death on the ground.

Once again, Krillzoc was right in front of him, the twisted smile sneering at him. Krillzoc held out his sword, the blade still dripping wet with Axel's blood, and beckoned for Darian to come forward.

He was all too happy to oblige, bringing his sword down toward Krillzoc's head with all of the force he could muster, hoping to cleave it in two. The dwarf parried the blow with apparent ease. To Darian's amazement, Krillzoc was far stronger than the two comrades who had sought to defend him.

Krillzoc struck back, his sword racing for Darian's chest. Darian sidestepped the attack, but Krillzoc was already launching his next attack, a slash directed at Darian's right side. Darian brought his sword around to parry the blow, but the impact shook his entire body. He knew he was slowing down, that the blood loss from the wound in his leg was starting to impact his ability to fight. He had to finish Krillzoc immediately.

No sooner had the thought crossed his mind than the dwarf's sword found its mark, opening a second far deeper wound in Darian's other leg. Darian struck one last time, a final desperate slash directed toward Krillzoc's face, a primal scream forcing its way through his lips as he did so. Krillzoc easily deflected the blow, knocking Darian's sword from his hand in the process. All the while, the sneering smile never left Krillzoc's face.

"Not bad for an Imperial weasel, but you are no match for me, boy," Krillzoc taunted, the tip of his sword hovering inches from Darian's eyes as he slumped to his knees. Darian's eyes snapped upward. "Step back, or I will start taking pieces off of him, and I promise you I will make his death last for hours!"

Darnold Dans had stepped forward to come to Darian's defense but withdrew at Krillzoc's threat.

I'm so sorry, Axel, Darian wept in his mind. The body of his oldest friend lay beside him, his eyes staring into Darian's, empty and lifeless. *I tried to give you justice, but I failed.* He locked eyes with Krillzoc once more, waiting for the end to come.

The dwarf shot him another of his cruel smiles before he struck, not with the blade of his sword this time, but the pommel. He brought the hard metal down onto Darian's head with brutal force, and instantly, Darian's world went dark.

If you enjoyed my dad's book, please consider leaving a review! All of the book money goes to my chew toys and treats! Thank you! ~ Teddy

Acknowledgements

It's really hard to put into words how good it feels to release this book. Letting all of 2023 pass me by with no new releases was not a part of my plan, but life had other ideas in mind! I do hope you found *The Soldier's Burden* to be worth the wait! I don't expect you will have a long wait for the second book of this trilogy! This book would not have been possible without the many amazing people I am fortunate to have in my life. I want to take moment to acknowledge some of those people here.

My editor, Natalia Leigh of Enchanted Ink Publishing. The only editor I have ever had, and the only editor I ever want! Thank you for your never-ending patience with my habit of repeating myself! Thank you for always spotting my rambling sentences and my drifts into the wrong POV! Thank you for pointing out every time I tend to overuse the same word. Thank you for always ensuring I'm not repeating myself! You see what i did there?

My cover artist and one of my oldest and closest friends, Joseph Gruber. He also helped me fully lock in my title this time, because I have to tell you, naming these books is never easy! Joe, somehow you always manage to give me my favorite cover yet! I can't wait to see what comes next, and i hope to have your beautiful work on the cover of every book I ever write!

As always, my wife, Mercedes. My rock in this world. What would I do without your love and support? Probably nothing noteworthy! Thank you, my love.

Last of all, thank you to every last reader who has supported my career! *The Thrawll Saga* continues! There will be two more books in this trilogy and then more books to follow. There will be more stories as well, hopefully a lot of them. My sincere hope is that 2023 was the last year that will pass without a new book from me for a very long time! With that in mind, I had better get back to work! Until next time!

~Pete Biehl

About the Author

Pete Biehl is a lifelong lover of stories who always felt the pull to create his own. When not sitting in a room by himself and making things up, he enjoys traveling, gaming, and searching for his next read. He is currently hard at work on the next installment of his epic fantasy series *The Thrawll Saga*. He lives in Idaho with his wife, dog, and so many rescued/spoiled cats.

Milton Keynes UK
Ingram Content Group UK Ltd.
UKHW010639030624
443529UK00010B/89/J